Gagarin and

GAGARIN AND I

Stephen Blanchard

Chatto & Windus
LONDON

First published in Great Britain 1995

1 3 5 7 9 10 8 6 4 2

Copyright © Stephen Blanchard 1995

Stephen Blanchard has asserted his right under the Copyright,
Designs and Patents Act, 1988, to be identified as the author
of this work

Published in 1995 by
Chatto & Windus Limited
Random House, 20 Vauxhall Bridge Road,
London SW1V 2SA

Random House Australia (Pty) Limited
20 Alfred Street, Milsons Point, Sydney
New South Wales 2061, Australia

Random House New Zealand Limited
18 Poland Road, Glenfield
Auckland 10, New Zealand

Random House South Africa (Pty) Limited
PO Box 337, Bergvlei, South Africa

Random House UK Limited Reg. No. 954009

All rights reserved. No part of this publication may be
reproduced, stored in a retrieval system, or transmitted
in any form, or by any means, electronic, mechanical,
photocopying, recording or otherwise, without the prior
permission of the publisher.

A CIP catalogue record for this book
is available from the British Library

ISBN 0 7011 6298 8

Designed and typeset by
SX Composing Ltd, Rayleigh, Essex
Printed in Great Britain by
Clays Ltd, St Ives Plc

When the influence of gravitation began to disappear I felt excellent. Suddenly everything became lighter, in general I had a sensation of unusual lightness. You know this is a very unusual feeling. My arms and legs and my own body felt as if they did not belong to me. They had no weight at all. You yourself do not sit, do not lie, but as it were hang suspended in the cabin. All unattached objects also hover in the air. At this time I wrote something down, only it was necessary to hold the pad with my hand or it would have sailed away.

Yuri Gagarin

One

My aunt and mother in the kitchen — a wet mid-week morning, the radio playing and steam lifting from the washing on the line above their heads. Fat spits from the sausages in the pan. My aunt stamps about in her housewife's boots. She feels like a wasp in a steamy jam-jar.

'Can't they do something about this weather?'

Her thigh jars the table and a cup slops tea into its saucer. My mother turns on her angrily, holding an egg which slips awkwardly egg-shaped between damp fingers and falls to the worn linoleum of the floor.

'Your fault!'

'Not mine!'

Calamity! They watch without breath as it spills from its broken shell. Before they can take thought or intervene the parts begin to separate, the white calmly distancing from the yellow solar yolk, turning round and silvery . . .

If the Yanks got there first I knew my heart would break.

'Part of his intestines had to be replaced by twenty feet of plastic tubing!'

'Twenty feet! Surely a man's intestines can't be as long as that!'

'A man's intestines can be up to forty-five feet in length,' Aunt Irene said.

My mother made herself shudder. 'I'm sure you must mean inches.'

The sisters were tall and dark — big-featured, large-nosed women with quick hands and aggressive elbows. There was less than two years between them and people asked if they were twins.

'You would think so!'

In fact people said you couldn't distinguish. Aunt Irene was the older sister and the big house was in her name, the house of my birth. The women rented the place from a landlord and let rooms. They complained that it was always a struggle to make it pay. The house was narrow-fronted but tall and deep, with a shady hall and stairs. It had attics and cellars, a deep coal-hole, a long back garden with bushes and woody vines, paths of herringbone brickwork, a hen-coop with a wire run, a rockery.

The house was demolished in the future and the women were rehoused in a maisonette filled with the heavy old-fashioned furniture they had decided to keep. By this time they had quarrelled over some small thing and fallen out permanently. They had sworn a vow of mutual silence and now lived mostly in their separate bedrooms, carefully ignoring one another in the shared parts. In the lounge or the kitchen for instance. As far as I know they never spoke to one another again, but then maybe they did not have to. They were called Eileen and Irene and people often made mistakes. Maybe in the end they became confused themselves and thought they were the same person.

In the past, this time I am talking about, new people moved into the two rooms upstairs, at the back of the house, connecting rooms which made a flat. They were a couple but the man was much older than the woman. They both worked in my mother's hospital and she had put them forward although my aunt made the final decision. The rooms had been empty for almost a month.

'A porter,' my mother said. 'They're a slovenly lot but he isn't like that. Takes a pride in his appearance: his collars are always spotless. He was a Barnado boy and brought up strict.'

'An *orphan*,' my aunt said. 'What was his name again?'

'He calls himself Norris.'

My aunt laughed. 'Then we shall have to call him that!'

I sat at a cleared space on the living-room table, working my way through a text-book of mathematics. I was absent from school because of my illness. I had to follow my own studies. The TV was on but with the sound turned down.

'It is *she* who concerns me,' my aunt said.

She smoothed the tips of her nails with an emery-board, making them into perfect arcs.

'Who's *she*?' my mother asked. She answered herself. 'The cat's mother.'

'I'd be surprised if she's eighteen,' Aunt Irene said. She blew away the fine dust of her work and held her fingers up to her eyes.

'She swore to me she's twenty-one.'

'She was lying, mebbe. These lasses look older with make-up. She looks too young for him, anyway.'

My mother did not reply. The women were preparing themselves for an evening out, sitting on the upholstered log-boxes on each side of the fender. The dog Jeff sat between them, tucked into a corner close to the grate, its right side singeing, the left side cold.

I cleared my throat.

'We are disturbing Leonard,' Aunt Irene said.

My mother took the poker from the coals and spat at its tip to test its hotness. If the iron was too hot then the hair would singe. The black hair of the sisters was wavy but not naturally curly. The dog shifted its position, groaning to itself. I turned the page to another set of exercises. My mother wound a strand of hair around the tip of the poker. There was a dry smell, like a taste at the back of the throat.

Twice or three times a week the sisters spent an evening in the Albemarle, a two-sided pub on a corner opposite the buildings of the steam-dairy. Its sign showed a ship in full sail tilted on a stormy sea. Inside was a lounge and a public, and then a small snug bar. The connecting doors were caught back with brass hooks so that tobacco smoke circulated from one room to another. My aunt and my mother sat always at a particular table between the door and the piano, their handbags between them on the bench, their backs to the wall. Mrs Goffrey would sometimes be there, or Mr and Mrs Flowers. Dolly Greenbanks went round with the raffle tickets, jingling her silver in a pint-pot. Mrs Guisewood played the upright with heavy-handed skill. The customers took turns to sing at the microphone over the talk and the crack of dominoes.

'The thing is that they are regular payers,' my aunt said. 'I don't want this thing of them owing weeks on end.'

My mother shook her head. 'You needn't fear that, Irene: he works all the hours God gives, you see. He's a bugger for the overtime.'

She laughed to herself and tested the spring of another curl, waiting for the poker to heat.

'Well, mebbe he wants to save and get on,' my aunt said, frowning. 'There's nothing wrong with that.'

'Only life is short!' my mother said.

'Only it can be long as well.'

When I was smaller I grew quickly and thoughtlessly. I freely put on weight and height. My body gathered its long molecules from nowhere, from sandwiches and potato crisps, meals with a book before the plate, the TV scratching and glowing. If you drew a graph of this, plotting weight against age, you would see a steeply tilted curve. But then when I was twelve or a little older my growth began to lose its way. I reached eight stone six or so, my weight stabilised for a few months and then started to fall. That's to say, its curve flattened and then declined, heading down the other side of the diagram. With its upward and downward slopes it began to follow the outline of a bell. You'll see that if you continued this curve then you would again approach zero.

One day after this had happened, after the curve had flattened and already begun to fall, one day when I was between fourteen and fifteen I came back from walking the dog and saw Captain Oram lying on the pavement in front of the house, just outside the barrier of the thin privet hedge. He lay on his front so that I could not see his face. There was a long skid of tomato close to his heel and I knew that he must have slipped on this and fallen.

I left him and ran up the front steps. I pushed my hand through the letter-box and found the key on its string. The hall was dark after the street but I ran its length and then through the empty living room. Jeff ran before me, excited and barking. My aunt was smoking a cigarette at the kitchen table. She pressed it into the glass ashtray when she saw my face. She and my mother were giving up and allowed themselves only five a day.

4

'The old fellah,' I said. 'He's fallen!'

I ran to Mrs Goffrey's. She kept two lodging houses on the other side of the street, mostly for transport. They were called the Hotel Belle Vista. Lorries were parked along the kerb outside and on the muddy wasteground at the corner of the street. I squeezed between two of them. The doors of the houses were close together and I knocked on one and then the other, letting the iron knockers fall with a crack. While I was standing at the second she opened the first. She was a small woman who wore shoes which made her look taller. Her hair was pressed into shiny waves with red tinges. She cleared her throat.

'Who's fallen?' she asked.

'The old fellah! He's slipped and split his head!'

She stepped out of her doorway to see but our view was blocked by the back of a lorry.

'He's *unconscious*!' I said.

Mrs Goffrey touched a curl at the side of her face. 'Then I'd better call the ambulance.'

I ran across the street again. A man on a moped blew his horn. One of the dairy workers in his white overalls had stopped and was leaning over Captain Oram. Ralph Sneddon from the attic rooms stood beside my aunt holding a glass of water. Someone had taken off the captain's hat and laid it brim-up on the pavement. I could see the band of pale smooth leather inside it. The old man's bare head and the back of his neck looked shiny and yellowish against the knobbly tweed of his collar. The hand that was in sight was squeezing and un-squeezing.

The dairyman looked up at my aunt. 'He'd been *drinking*, I think.' He pushed a newspaper deeper into his pocket and smiled.

My aunt did not smile back. 'It's the day he gets his pension. A fellah of his age is entitled to a drink,' she said.

The old fellah received a monthly cheque from a shipping line.

I pointed to the squashed tomato near his foot. 'He must have slipped on that and fallen over.'

No one seemed to take any notice. I felt it was an important detail that was being overlooked.

5

My aunt frowned. Ralph handed her the useless glass of water and then lowered himself awkwardly until he was kneeling on the pavement. He was a thin man with thin cheeks and half-grey hair combed to the side and barbered to the level of the tops of his ears. He had big hands and a false foot because of an accident at work. The whites of his eyes were yellow. 'Is the ambulance coming?' he asked.

'Mrs Goffrey's ringing for it,' I told him.

He nodded and laid the tips of two fingers on the back of the old man's neck.

'You're feeling for a pulse, mister?' the other man said. 'You can see that he's still breathing.'

Ralph stared at the other man but did not reply. A boy came up the road on a push-bike. As he went by he turned his head to stare at us, keeping us in view until it seemed impossible that he could twist his head so far around.

'There's nothing so interesting as another's misfortune,' Aunt Irene said.

She nodded across the road. Already a couple of front doors were open. A long lorry had parked on the wasteground opposite and the driver was leaning against the side of the cab, his arms folded, watching us.

'We'll take him inside,' my aunt said. 'Away from prying eyes.'

Slowly the two men rolled the captain on to his back and then tried to lift him from the ground, their hands under his back and arms. The old man was solidly built and the dairyman started to look doubtful. 'Sometimes it's best not to move them,' he said. 'He's what you call a dead weight, you see.'

'A man isn't a dog,' Aunt Irene said.

They began to lift again. The back of the old man's heels dragged against the pavement. His head lolled backwards and I saw a crescent shape of blood where it had struck the ground.

'He's injured himself,' the dairyman said. 'Maybe he has concussion.'

My aunt rubbed her hands together. She still wore her apron and I knew she hated appearing like that on the street.

'Are you a doctor then?' Ralph Sneddon asked. 'Only you seem to be an expert.'

The man pursed his lips. 'More of an engineer.'

They started to move towards the door. Ralph seemed to lose his balance for a second but then recovered with a jerk.

'He's a heavy old fellah,' the dairyman said. 'Mebbe as well the youngster could help.'

I went closer but my aunt caught my arm above the elbow and then let go of it. 'Only he's not been well,' she said.

I could smell the sweetness on Captain Oram's breath. I tugged at his coat while Ralph and the other man lifted. Ralph held the old man's legs, swearing under his breath as he fought with their sliding weight. The captain's head sagged and Aunt Irene came forward to support it. His mouth was open and I saw the sliding crockery of his false teeth.

'Be careful he doesn't swallow them,' Ralph said. He pushed his fingers into the old man's mouth and suddenly the dentures were out and shining wetly on his palm.

'Oh, don't show me them!' my aunt said, turning away her face.

Ralph pushed the dentures into the old man's coat pocket. I tried to circle my arms around the captain's middle but couldn't clasp hands because of the thick folds of his coat. Mr Sneddon grunted and coughed and the mechanic winked again, bent under the weight of the captain's shoulders. Moving crab-fashion we carried him up the steps and into the hall. We squeezed past the hall-stand with its coat-hooks and narrow mirror. My aunt freed an arm and opened the door of the front room.

'Lie him down in here, please!'

We manoeuvred through the doorway. Inside, the light came white and even through net curtains. Ralph and the dairyman began to make towards the couch but Aunt Irene stopped them. 'No, lie him down on the floor!'

'On the floor?' Ralph asked.

My aunt looked uncomfortable. 'Maybe he's broken something and needs to be *flat*, you see.'

Captain Oram made a long sigh as he was lowered on to the rug. I saw that the inside of one ear was dark with blood. My aunt took a gold embroidered cushion from one of the easy chairs and placed it under his head.

'There's still his hat outside,' the dairyman said. He went outside and came back with it. With a smirk he laid it brim-down on top of the piano.

'You've been very helpful,' my aunt said.

'Glad to be of help, missis.'

We watched the old man in silence for a minute. His eyelids twitched and showed a white line of eye.

'There was something hard in his pocket,' the dairyman said.

My Aunt Irene felt into one coat pocket and then the other. She drew out a flat quarter-bottle of whisky and handed it to Ralph Sneddon. It was Johnnie Walker. Ralph stood it on the piano beside the old man's black hat.

The dairyman wiped his palms in the front of his white over-alls. 'Lucky he didn't fall on it! Favoured his other side, like.'

'You've been ever so kind, mister,' my Aunt Irene said.

He nodded, smiling. 'I'll go then, missis. You've got two big men with you anyway.'

'The lad should be at school,' my aunt said. 'Only he's sick.'

'How old is he?'

'He's fourteen.'

The dairyman grinned across at me. 'He's tall then!'

'Tall, but too thin,' my aunt said.

She sighed. The dairyman still did not move towards the door. He rubbed his hands together and looked down at Captain Oram. 'A skinful, you see.'

'I beg you pardon?' my aunt said.

The man laughed and turned to Mr Sneddon. 'Out celebrating mebbe, I was only saying.'

'He only slipped,' my aunt said. 'He's a merchant seaman and can hold his drink.'

The dairyman nodded at the bottle of whisky, smiling. Suddenly Ralph took it from the top of the piano and pushed it towards him. It was about a third full of sloping liquor.

'Here, have this. That's for your time.'

The man looked uneasily at my aunt and then slipped the bottle into his hip pocket.

'I could see him looking at it,' Ralph said. 'That sort always expects payment.'

Aunt Irene looked down at the old fellah. 'I'm glad he's gone, to tell the truth. He was too familiar. Insolent, if you like.'

'*Insolent*,' Ralph repeated.

The captain made a gurgling sound as if he were breathing through some sort of broth. My aunt knelt beside him and touched his forehead with her fingertips.

'Where is this ambulance?' she asked. 'Bring me a damp flannel, Leonard. Hold it under the cold tap and then wring it well out. For his head.'

I went into the hall. Mrs Rinse from the room on the landing was standing on the stairs and looking over.

'Is something up, Leonard?'

'The old fellah,' I said. 'He slipped and fell over.'

She raised her hands. She leaned further over the banister, her eye on the open door of the front room. 'Was he tipsy, Leonard?'

'No,' I said. 'He slipped on a tomato.'

She nodded. 'He was sometimes unsteady on his feet. People are less able to take it as they get older.'

I fidgeted below her. I did not know how to escape. Her dark red lipstick made her mouth look big and shiny. She wore a blue dressing gown and a plaid scarf wrapped closely around her throat. Through the banisters I saw that her feet were bare, the toes crabbed against the ball of her foot. She lived with her husband Wilf, a french-polisher, in the middle room upstairs.

'I won't come down,' she said. 'I know I'd only get upset.'

I went through the living room and into the kitchen. My aunt's cigarette was still alight but turned to a collapsing tube of ash. I turned on the cold tap above the sink and soaked one of the flannels. As I went back into the front room I heard the bell of the ambulance, already quite close. It grew louder, went past the house and then died away.

Two

'People fall,' my aunt said. 'You come to expect it of them.'

With foamy water smelling of disinfectant she swilled the front steps, the path, the pavement outside the house. The wet flagstones looked glossy and brown as if they'd been varnished. She looked at the sky. It was already heavy and threatening rain.

She sighed. 'Only I needn't have bothered,' she said.

She smoked a cigarette in the living room, her feet on the leather pouffe, flicking ash into a glass ashtray she would later clean carefully. She blew out smoke.

'My nerves are all in pieces, Leonard!'

After the launch of the first Sputnik the weather over the town became jammed in a changeable and untrustworthy March. Winds blew from the north-east, across the Arctic Circle, over Scandinavia, picked up their freight of water from the North Sea and then funnelled towards us along the estuary. On rare days the sky unwrapped its bandages to show a chilly blue, the sun fizzing like Aspro. Then the clouds uncurled from their pits below the sea – fat anacondas or battleships in formation, landscapes standing one above the other. This went on for nearly nine years.

I went upstairs, past the back room with its new lodgers, past the door of the Rinses and the scratch of their radio behind. I climbed quietly the last two flights to the top of the house. I had a special purpose.

Ralph lived in the two attic rooms which opened off the top landing. They were not connected, so that you had to leave one and cross the corner of the landing to enter the other. His bedroom looked out through a small attic window along the length of the back garden. The other room, his sitting room, had only a hinged skylight set into the slope of the ceiling. I had never seen this window open. There was a pulley and ratchet but the cord had long since disappeared and the frame was welded shut by layers of old paint. The glass was frost-patterned and mottled with dirt, letting through a soiled light.

The sitting room was furnished with scruffy wicker chairs and a couch with a froth of stuffing showing through its arms. He sat reading on the couch, lounging against its side with one leg stretched out ending in a foot-shape of glossy black leather. The room smelt of aircraft-adhesive and stagnant water. As soon as I went inside I could feel the heat from the big glass tanks standing on frames one above the other against the front wall. The fish floated in the brown water like spindles of sweet-wrapping.

'I must be going deaf,' Ralph said. 'Because I didn't hear you knock.'

In the middle of the room was a folding table of the sort used for cards. Its top was protected by sheets of newspaper stretched tight and taped to the edges. An anglepoise lamp shed an oval of electric light. The plane he'd been working on was already painted in camouflage colours. It was complete except for the transfers, its undercarriage extended.

'A Messerschmitt,' I said. I went closer to look at the detailing. I could see the lines of rivets and the painted pilot under the clear plastic of the cockpit cover. I reached out with my fingertip.

'Don't touch! The paint's still tacky!'

'I wasn't going to!'

'As you're here you can sit down,' Ralph said. 'Only don't fidget with your feet.'

'I never fidget.'

'You don't know when you do: it's what they call an involuntary action.'

I lowered myself into one of the noisy chairs. The cushions were stiff and had a feel of damp. Ralph closed his magazine and threw it on to the rug between us. 'Patience is a sign of the mature mind,' he told me. 'A product of inner calm.'

I looked at the cover of the magazine. A man was pulling a

11

struggling woman into an white open-topped car. The woman's skirt had lifted and you could see the top of her stockings. One of her red high-heeled shoes was about to fall off. The man was laughing around the stub of a cigarette.

'Have a read,' Ralph said. 'Educate yourself.'

I picked it up and turned the pages. I looked at adverts for body-building and ju-jitsu, memory-training and hypnotism, binoculars which looked like a pair of ordinary spectacles. *As used by scientists. Brings objects so close you feel you could touch.*

'Is there any news?' Ralph asked.

'About what?'

'Why, about the old fellah! What did you think I meant?'

'Mam rang the hospital from work. She says he's still unconscious.'

'That's the worst sign possible,' Ralph said. 'It means that life is almost extinct.'

He'd been smoking his pipe and trapped smoke still hung below the ceiling. I leafed through more articles. *My Korean Hell. Goering's Spanish Child-Bride.*

'He'll die, you know!' Ralph said.

'You don't know that! How can you tell?'

'I was in the army, remember. You learn to recognise death when you see it.'

I looked through another article. Thousands of fanatical Japanese still lived in dug-out cities in the deep jungles of the Philippines. After a while I got up and walked to where the aircraft hung by threads from the slope of the ceiling. They were painted mostly in matt camouflage colours with the undersides of the wings and fuselages an invisible-making pale blue. Ralph had brushes with just one hair for applying the finer details. Curling cigarette cards were pinned to the wall at the back of the display giving details on the types of aircraft. I pushed a Mosquito bomber so that it swung on its thread.

'Those aren't toys,' Ralph said.

'What are they then?'

He sent me a sad look. 'They're scale models.'

I left the Mosquito to swing and went over to the twin tanks. This was Ralph's other hobby. The fish were small and nondescript when I compared them to the spectacular creatures I

12

sometimes watched in Webster's pet-shop. They swam in a cloudy soup between stones and scraps of floating weed. My mother complained that the weight of the water was too much for the floor to bear, that one day there would be an accident. A small pump on the floor near the skirting forced tiny bubbles through a plastic pipe. In the quiet nights I listened to its soft beat from my bed below.

'I need a candle, Ralph,' I said.

He lifted his hands, pretending to be surprised. 'You must eat those things!'

I shook my head. 'The last was a fortnight ago and it's down to a stub.'

'To light your *hero*,' he said.

'Not just mine. He was awarded the Order of Lenin.'

Ralph laughed. 'They'll award anyone: they give that to tractor-drivers!'

A cupboard with beaded glass doors hung in the corner of the room above the enamel sink. Behind the glass Ralph's packets and tins stood on two oilcloth-covered shelves. The candles were in a box in the corner. I opened one of the doors.

'Help yourself,' Ralph said sarcastically.

He turned his face towards the sweet-wrapping fish. A spider tracked across the wall at the back of the cupboard. I took a new candle out of the box and slipped it under my sweater into the breast pocket of my grey school shirt.

Gagarin and his wife sat in the through-lounge of their small home in Star City. They listened to the hum and grind of traffic along the new arterial road. A hiss sounded from the fuel plant as vaporising carbon monoxide was released into the dry summer air. Gagarin flicked through the pages of a technical journal. His wife stared through the polished panes of the patio doors into their tiny garden with its rockery and electric-powered fountain. There had been silence between them for days: she knew he was withholding something. Suddenly Gagarin threw down his reading and began to pace the room, from one end to the other and back again. He slid back the door of their cramped diner-kitchenette, meaning to fill the kettle for coffee, but then closed it, slamming it against its rubber stop. He turned to his wife who continued to stare into the garden.

'Please put a clean shirt in my bag,' he told her. 'I'm going on a trip to outer space!'

The sky above the garden was covered with cloud broken by dark moving spaces. The moon was invisible behind the roofs opposite. Somewhere over my head Voskhod II orbited the Earth carrying the cosmonauts Pavel Belyayev and Alexei Leonov. I sat on the metal-framed chair set against the back wall of the house. Its foam seat was damp. There was a light in the room above me, shining into the dark. In a deep, clear voice a man sang from behind the curtains.

A sentimental song. Very slowly the dark spaces moved over the sky and uncovered Aldebaran and Sirius. Sirius, the Dog Star.

I could read the page of my notebook by the light overhead. I wrote, *Observed Sirius*, and added the time and the date. That night Colonel Leonov would astound the world by stepping out of his capsule and floating at the end of a tether for ten minutes. I put down my pencil and searched the sky again, though I knew that even without the clouds the Soviet spacecraft would be invisible to the naked eye. It might just be seen through a pair of good binoculars, shining by the light of the sun on its polished body.

I had no binoculars, not even ones that looked like ordinary spectacles.

'I'm so glad in my heart that she's not you,' Norris sang above me.

Between the old man's dying and his funeral I had an appointment at the hospital. There were no seats together on the bus and Aunt Irene and I had to sit on opposite sides of the aisle. My aunt sat closer to the front. At almost every stop she turned in her seat to smile at me. Towards the end of the ride I pretended to be interested in what was passing by the window.

At the last stop but one she stood up and pointed towards the door.

'It's miles yet,' I complained.

She stood alongside my seat, bracing herself against the jolting of the bus. She reached over the other passenger and put her hand on my shoulder. 'Well, let's just make sure!'

She rang the bell and the bus stopped. We had about a ten-minute walk before we saw the big building set back from the road. There was the new wing with the old wing behind it. My aunt opened her bag and began to search through it, holding it up close to her face.

'I haven't got the card!'

'I saw you with it!'

She looked again. She held up a pad of coloured paper, a man's handkerchief, a small purse. A shilling fell and rolled along the pavement. I stamped it flat and then picked it up for her.

'We don't need the card,' I told her. 'I know where to go.'

She tugged small things from her bag and then returned them to their corners.

'It's on the ninth floor,' I said, becoming impatient. 'Dr Munro.'

We crossed the car park and went through the glass doors into the entrance hall. The air smelt of stewed tea and antiseptic. There was a queue before the reception hatch.

'We could go straight there,' I said.

She shook her head. 'You have to let them know as soon as you enter the building, just in case.'

'In case of what?'

'If there's a fire, say.'

We waited for the lift. The hospital had twelve floors with a basement and sub-basement. It was not the one in which my mother worked. That was a different type. My mother worked her long shifts in the canteen of a mental hospital.

'We're early,' Aunt Irene said.

'I knew we would be.'

'But there's nothing wrong with waiting. Don't you want to be well, Leonard?'

'Yes,' I said.

'Then you'd think you'd show more *enthusiasm*.'

The glass numbers changed above the door. Green lights

15

shone through them from behind. When the lift came most of the space inside was taken up by an empty bed on wheels. A nurse and a porter stood beside it.

'Room for one more and a little 'un,' the porter said, winking at me.

It was only when we stepped into the lift that I saw a very old lady lying in the bed. Her face and hands were so white that they had been invisible against the pillows and sheets. The nurse held a plastic bottle. A tube filled with clear liquid ran from its inverted neck into the bedclothes. Bubbles rose up the curve of the tube and then through the liquid into the empty space above it.

'Which floor?' the porter asked.

'Ninth,' I said.

'Ninth floor,' my aunt repeated.

The porter pressed the button, winking at me again and then at my aunt. Then he winked at nothing, smiling to himself. I realised then that there was something wrong with his eye. The lift doors closed and we bumped upwards.

The nurse smiled at us and cleared her throat.

'Leonard here's very interested in science,' my aunt told her.

'Is he so?' She looked down at the watch clipped to her uniform.

'He wants to become an astronomer,' my aunt said.

I looked down at the old woman. She opened pale eyes suddenly and made a small noise like the noise a kitten makes.

We reached our floor and got out. The nurse and her patient climbed to the top floors. 'That woman was *Irish*,' my aunt said. 'A lot of them are nurses. The women are saints and the men are buggers.'

We pushed through sloping double doors made of rubber with clear plastic windows. When we reached Dr Munro's office we found about six younger kids sitting with their mothers on the long bench outside. The last pair shuffled to the end of the bench and we sat down.

'We might have to wait for a while,' my aunt said. 'You could have brought a book if we'd known.'

The kids fidgeted and gave bored looks and the women did not speak to one another but looked straight ahead. I took off

16

my raincoat and put it on the seat beside me. A big woman with a small girl came out of the doctor's room and walked back towards the lift. The woman clasped the thin hand of the girl in her big fist with the fingers bunched together. Then the doctor pushed out his head and stared down the row of seats.

'*Next*, please!'

We waited for another half-hour before we were called. Dr Munro smiled at us and beckoned. My aunt sighed and picked up her bag.

'Don't forget your coat, Leonard!'

'No.'

The surgery was a small square room with a single square window. The doctor smiled again, first at my aunt and then at me. He pointed to the chair before his desk.

'Sit down, Leonard,' my aunt said.

Dr Munro glanced up from the file on his desk. 'I meant the chair for you, Mrs Chope. The young man can stand for two minutes, surely!'

'Only I'm not Mrs Chope,' my aunt said. 'I'm his aunt, and anyway the lad is ill.'

'I feel okay,' I said. 'I'll stand.'

I walked towards the window. There was a row of plants with dry transparent leaves on the sill. My aunt sat down with her handbag in her lap. Despite the stuffiness of the room she did not unfasten her coat. I looked at a poster on the wall. A man's lungs were filling with red smoke.

'So, Leonard!' the doctor said. His voice came from his chest and seemed to have bouncing springs inside it. He turned to my aunt. 'His mother was unable to attend?'

Aunt Irene frowned. 'Unfortunately she has to work, you see. But I'm his next-of-kin after that.'

There was a circle of baldness in the doctor's dark hair and I noticed that his left hand was covered by a flesh-coloured rubber glove. Then he looked up at me suddenly.

'He still looks a little anaemic.'

'He's always been what you call pale-skinned,' my aunt said.

'You must be anxious to see him back at school.'

'He was doing very well. Whenever he applied himself.'

Dr Munro glanced at his watch and then pressed himself up

17

from the desk. 'So! If you can remove your footwear, Leonard.'

I unlaced my shoes. This was the part to which it all led. A set of tall white-bodied scales stood in the corner of the room close to the window.

'My socks as well?'

He shook his head. 'Don't bother with those.'

He waited, breathing quietly. I stepped on to the rubber mat of the platform. The arm of the scales swung and rattled against its stop and Dr Munro slid the silvery weights about until it had stopped moving.

'Thank you, Leonard. You can step down now.'

I put my shoes back on and laced them. The doctor made a purring sound as he wrote in my file. On the desk beside his elbow was a paperweight made from a cube of clear glass which held its own angles reflected inside it. I stared at it. I had always been fascinated by the qualities of glass, its ability to reflect and refract, to bring far objects close and extract colours from white light.

'You see, he has lost almost a kilogram since his last visit,' the doctor said. 'Which was in . . .'

'Only a month back,' my aunt said.

'A month ago. And at this stage in his life he should be growing rapidly.'

'He's still tall for his age,' Aunt Irene said.

The doctor nodded. 'Oh, it isn't so unusual. The growth of youngsters is often irregular and contradictory.'

'*Contrary*,' my aunt said, to rhyme with Mary.

'But if left to go on it will obviously affect his future health.' He smiled without showing his teeth. 'I'll make a further appointment. Perhaps it's better he stays just for a night in the hospital.'

My aunt held her bag on her lap. The clasp clicked as she squeezed the top tight. 'He has to go into hospital then?'

'As a convenience only. I'd like to do a series of tests, and staff and equipment are not always at hand, you see.'

'He's never spent a night away from us,' my aunt said. 'Not even on holiday.'

The doctor smiled at her and played with his glass cube. His

18

hand was reflected on the inside of it, the fingers coming from nowhere to make pale prints on the surface.

'How much did you say?' my aunt asked. 'That he's lost?'

I looked at the conversion tables on the back of a school exercise-book. 'One kilogram is two pounds three ounces.'

'That's nearly three pounds,' my mother said.

'He said *almost* a kilo. That means less than two pounds three ounces and not more.'

My mother slid her eyes over my face and on to Aunt Irene's. 'And they want him to stay inside?'

My aunt sat at the living-room table, filling in the rent-books, checking them against a picture calendar. She ringed the payment days in red biro. 'Only for a night, he said.'

'It's always only for a night, and then it's two nights.'

'For *observation*,' I said.

'I know them with their observations!'

My mother had just returned from work and still wore her pale blue apron beneath her coat. She walked into the kitchen and then back again. Her square heels made a solid sound against the floor. She stopped in front of the fire and stared down at the dog. 'Once they decide there's something wrong with you then you can never get away from those places.'

'*Three pounds*,' Aunt Irene moaned. 'That's nearly half a stone he's lost!'

'More like two pounds,' I said.

My mother took a cigarette from the shell-topped box on the mantel-piece. She closed the lid on *Lara's Theme*. The dog sighed from its corner with a dog's-breath smell.

'I don't trust that doctor.'

'He's supposed to be a specialist,' Aunt Irene said.

'There's something inhuman about him. He looks at you from the corner of his eyes.'

My aunt sighed over the ruled pages. 'You have to be grateful for the help they give you, Eileen.'

Three

This was in the wartime: the slam of great weights, shudders stepping from the docks like thousand-ton boots. The window shivered like a nervous dog. A crack made a slow difficult path across the pane from top to bottom. My aunt ran up the street, one shoe off and one shoe on. She dipped her stockinged toe in an oily puddle and struggled with her clothes as a hot wind rushed past her. The roof of the typewriter factory was opened like a can. The big building siphoned smoke and clouds, sucking air into its belly of melted glass and red-hot iron. Cars and lorries exploded in the factory yard. Women ran through the red emergency doors with their shellacked hair on fire.

My room was more than half filled by its narrow bed. There was a chair and a folding table and then behind the door a narrow wardrobe with a mirrored front. I listened to the passage of a car on the main road with, below it, the slight hum of the town, the constant sound of the electricity moving through its wires. If I listened very carefully I could isolate these sounds and then hear the faint shiftings of the house itself.

I took out a match and dragged it along the side of its box. It caught for a second but then went out. I tried with another. The flame held and lengthened. I lit the candle and turned out the overhead light.

Above the table were pictures cut from magazines and newspapers, carefully pasted to the wall. All were of the moon – the full disc or else details of certain features. I dripped molten wax into a saucer and stood the base of the candle in the congealing pool. The flame leaned and then burned straight, breaking at its tip into a line of smoke. It penetrated the depths of the craters. The Lunar Apennines ran alongside their shadows like a crack striking across the lunar disc. The rays of

Copernicus wound like glaciers over their surrounding plains. There was a black pool near the line separating night from day and then a balancing light as some peak caught the sun. I heard Ralph moving above me, the scuff of his leather heel against the rug. He made a noise in his dry pipe-smoker's throat. I leaned close to the dividing wall and put my ear to the embossed pattern of trellis and climbing-rose. I listen for a while to the synchronised breaths of the sisters.

The picture was above my bed in its thin gilt frame. I took up the candle, holding the flame to the side so that it would not be reflected in the glass. The cosmonaut looked into the flash of the camera with his narrow spaceman's stare.

My mother did not go to work on the day of the old fellah's funeral. The service was at two o'clock and she decided to pass time in the morning by cleaning the stove on the middle landing. We carried hot water up the stairs in two enamel pails.

The stove stood just opposite the Rinses' door. It had a sour smell of old fat. An old pickle jar stood on the shelf above it with a tangle of spent matches inside like a spiny creature.

'It will take our mind off things,' my mother said. She used a blunt table-knife to pare a curl of dark grease from the ironwork of the range. 'Look, Leonard: it's inches deep.' She lowered her voice. 'She's *slack*, you see.'

I pictured a length of perished elastic. She meant Muriel Rinse. The Rinses' room had no cooking facilities and Mrs Rinse used the stove most often.

'It's early for her and she'll still be asleep,' my mother whispered. 'He sneaks out in the morning so as not to disturb her. He's like a mouse going down those stairs!' She lowered her voice still more. 'He calls her *pet* all the time. *Pet* this and *pet* that. When you hear it it's enough to make you sick.'

The Rinses had lived in the same room for years, so that I couldn't remember a time before them. Mr Rinse was a dark, excitable man – small and quick-gestured, narrow-framed so that his clothes always looked too big for him, his jacket slipping off his shoulders, his trousers rucked in at the waist by a broad leather belt. He was a french-polisher and his nails carried a dark rind of polish. His wife was small but softer, slow-moving and slow-speeched. She had problems with her chest.

'She won't be attending the funeral,' my mother said. 'But she'll turn up for the drinks afterwards.' She began to dismantle the top of the stove, taking up the halves of the hob and then lifting the heavy gas-rings. She pulled a face. 'Irene hates anything like this. Anything to do with dirt, you see. She's got a good heart but she's squeamish.'

Aunt Irene was out buying sliced ham and potted meat for the sandwiches and cold-cuts they would offer after the funeral. My mother handed me the various parts of the range so that I could dip them in the hot water.

'Mind your clothes, Leonard. Just leave things to soak for now.'

She opened the oven door and sniffed.

'It's not so bad in here. She likes everything *fried*, you see, and hardly uses it . . .' She took another glance towards the Rinses' room. 'Shall I tell you something, Leonard?'

She beckoned me and spoke close to my ear. 'They're already after his room: the old fellah's. He's not in his grave yet and they've already asked Irene about it. Muriel said that her health was bad and it was getting hard for her to manage the stairs.'

My mother closed her eyes to keep out the contamination of the lie. When she opened them the whites had turned bluish. She slid the shelves from the oven and began to wipe inside, angling her head and pulling faces as she reached into the far corners. She rinsed the dirty cloth in one of the pails, her knuckles flashing white as she wrung out the water. Then she stood up and rubbed at the small of her back.

I watched her clean the oven door and then the sides of the stove and the shelves above it. The shelves were covered with strips of oilcloth and their iron brackets were shiny with grease. She removed the pots and pans from them and stood them under the cooker, pulling a face.

'I don't see why we should wash these for her!'

I tried to pick up one of the buckets, the one in which the gas-rings stood soaking. The weight of it seemed to lengthen my arm.

22

She took it from me. 'You can carry *this*, Leonard. We'll come back for the rest.'

She handed me the pickle jar. Its sides were sticky between my palms and the spent matches had a sweetish woody smell. She lifted the bucket and winked at me. 'She has a cat in there, you know!'

'A *cat*?'

'Irene says it's my imagination but I can hear it sometimes. They can never let it out, poor thing.'

She nudged me towards the door. Still holding the pickle jar I stepped over and laid my ear against the panel. For a second I could hear nothing but then made out a faint repeated whistle.

My mother had put her head beside mine. 'That's *her* still asleep. She's another who breathes through her nose.'

The noise of Mrs Rinse's breath was like a sad, thin plant sprouting in the darkened room.

'I can't hear the cat,' I said.

'Next time you might.'

We laid the pieces of the range in the kitchen sink. She poured a kettle of boiling water over them and the grease melted like grey ice. The metal came up black and shiny, with a bluish tint when you held it to the light. She handed the parts to me and I dried them one at a time with a cloth.

'Your grandmother was particular about her stove, Leonard. The stove was the first thing with her. Old people don't eat much and she would clean it more often than she used it . . . It had become a habit with her, you see.'

There was a knock at the living-room door. She looked at me with serious sideways eyes.

'You go and see.'

I dried my hands on the towel and went to the door. Norris was standing outside in his narrow dark suit. He had a sharp-boned face and wore thick, dark-framed spectacles. He held a bunch of flowers in a cone of cellophane and paper. He gave me a long-toothed smile.

'Missis in?'

'My mother is,' I said. Missis usually meant my Aunt Irene, although she was not married.

He laughed. 'Well, either one will do.'

23

My mother came from the kitchen, peeling off her rubber gloves. She took the flowers and laid them in the crook of her arm. She smiled over them. The light made coloured reflections on her face.

'*Lovely*,' she said. She closed her eyes for a second to appreciate the scent. 'And ferns as well. I'll put them in water.'

Norris wore a slim silver tie set with a jewelled pin. His black pointed shoes made a dancer's shuffle on the mat and his throat jerked as he swallowed. He caught hold of the door-frame, slanting himself across the opening. His sleeve had four round fabric-covered buttons in a row like black peas.

'I'm sorry we can't be there today, missis. Susan is ever so upset.'

My mother nipped away a brown leaf. 'You both have to work, Norris. And young people shouldn't be bothered with funerals. Or only immediate family.'

'He'd been drinking. I could never drink during the daytime, Leonard. God divided the day into light and dark.'

'He works at night!'

'Then he has to take his pleasure when he can, granted. And when I said young people I was referring just to her but he was pleased, I could tell. Men are vain, you see, although they won't show it.'

She carefully separated the flowers from their wrapping and then filled a glass vase and stood them in water on the kitchen table. Bubbles gathered densely along the magnified stalks.

'Lilies are attractive but don't last,' she said. 'Always buy dahlias and chrysanthemums for a funeral; they don't look so much on the actual day but afterwards they are better value.'

There'd been some rain the night before and the ground was damp. When you lifted your foot you could see water oozing from below. At first there was only the man from the Society of Mariners.

'He's come to make sure everything's done as it should be,' my aunt whispered as we waited on the grass.

'It's only right as they're paying for it,' my mother said. 'Cheap as may be. He must go to a lot of these affairs because he's got the face for it.'

24

My aunt tucked in her chin. 'You can't expect the poor fellah to laugh and joke! His name is Mr Harbut. He's very pleasant when you talk to him.'

The coffin was now being slid from the back of the hearse. Mr Harbut took up position near the doors. My mother and aunt half turned so that they could watch without seeming too curious. They wore their dark suits and stood with hands limply clasped as if they expected to be asked to pray at any moment. My aunt's suit was a dark grey and she wore a matching hat with a curled-up brim. My mother's suit was navy blue.

'This suit's too *bright*.'

'It's a very *dark* navy, Eileen.'

'The reason is I can't stand black. And you can't buy an outfit just for the odd occasion.'

My aunt glanced at her sideways. 'You would look nice in black. Because you're what they call high-coloured.'

'I'm exactly the same colour as you.'

My aunt shook her head. 'No, Eileen. You're more what they call ruddy.'

The coffin was carried over the uneven lawn. Mr Harbut was at the back and had to stoop slightly because he was taller than the rest. One of the bearers was as old as the captain had been but more slightly built. He stumbled once so that the other men had to shift their positions quickly.

'He'll give himself a heart attack!' Aunt Irene said.

'He might be an old ship-mate. We could invite him back when it's over.'

They peered over at the struggling group. You could see the splashes of water when they put down their feet.

'He was a heavy-built old fellah,' my aunt said.

My mother made a sigh. 'If it wasn't for that fall he'd have gone on for years ... What about the man from the Society, then? Should we invite him?'

Mr Harbut had taken off his hat. His hair was thick and dark behind his ears but missing from the top of his head, as if it could not quite reach. His shiny scalp caught a reflection of the sky.

'This'll only be part of his job,' my aunt said. 'I expect he has to be back at work afterwards.'

My mother lightly touched my arm. 'See those two men standing over there, Leonard? Well, they're the men who dig the graves. You're supposed to tip them afterwards because they don't get much money for it.'

'You don't have to but it's the custom,' Aunt Irene said.

The coffin was now being lowered on to broad bands laid across the turf at the head of the grave. The ex-seaman put his hand to his side and said something in joke to one of the men beside him. My aunt stared across at them, raising her chin. She had a dry smell of powder and scent.

'It looks as if the others are all from the undertakers, Eileen. Four of them in two cars, you see. However cheap this is it must be costing them something.'

My mother looked dissatisfied. 'They'll get special rates, I suppose . . . And is that society paying for a stone?'

'He said a dignified memorial.'

'*Plain*, that means. I suppose we could buy something ourselves. An urn, say.'

'You might be surprised at the price of urns, Eileen!'

The vicar began to say some words, lifting his arms slightly. I noticed that he was standing on a small square of rubber to keep his shoes dry.

'They're lovely words,' my aunt said. 'From the Bible.'

'Funerals used to make me weep,' my mother said. 'Then I decided to toughen up . . . Now watch this, Leonard: it's very clever the way they do it.'

'His feet will be soaked standing on this grass,' Aunt Irene said. 'It's nearly done now and maybe he should go home.'

'I'd like to stay,' I said. 'Just for this part.'

The men stood three to each side. They picked up the end of a band each and pulled until the coffin rose an inch or so from the ground. Then they began to shuffle sideways, inching the coffin forward until it was over the hole.

'That's the way the pyramids were built,' my mother said. 'They had no tools, you see.'

Then the men slowly let the bands pass through their hands so that, slightly head-first, the coffin began to disappear into the grave. My aunt made a noise and started to cry. She unclipped her bag and tugged out a handkerchief. A shiny golden tube of lipstick fell down on to the grass and I bent and picked it up to give it to her. Instead of taking it she caught my head between her hands and pressed my face into her side. I breathed in the slightly moth-bally smell of her dark suit.

'He's just a lad, Irene!' my mother whispered urgently. 'He doesn't understand death.'

My aunt still sobbed. Some of the men around the grave looked over at us. When she let go of my head I could feel my hair standing up at the side. My mother sighed and pushed some coins into my hand. She waved me away. 'You go now, Leonard. You know the buses, don't you? Me and Irene have to stay and talk to a few people.'

You crossed a road and then the old part of the cemetery started. It was no longer used and its perimeter walls were broken in places so that the fallen blocks lay among the weeds and brambles. Shrubs and young sycamores made a band of wavery shade along the pavement. The trees and weeds were dark and well-nourished. Among them you could sometimes see a leaning memorial or the tall shape of a stone angel.

I was waiting by myself at the bus stop when someone put his arm around my neck from behind.

'Your bus fare!' he called into my ear. 'Or I'll snap your spine!'

He pushed his knee into the small of my back. I struggled round to face him. The woollen rub of his sleeve chafed my neck. He was a couple of inches shorter than me, fat-bodied with a heavy round head. His dark hair hung over his face and he flicked it back with his free hand.

'Your money or death!' he said, laughing.

I could feel cold spit on my neck where his mouth had come close. A smaller boy stood behind him looking at us with his arms folded, face on one side. He was thin, with a shrunken-looking face. He wore a long tubular sweater of blue wool. A damp inch of cigarette pushed out from between his lips.

'I knew it was you!' I said.

I knew only the fat one. He was in my year at school but in another class. He grinned and relaxed his arm without re-leasing me. I was twisted sideways in a way which made it difficult to keep my feet.

'I bet you were pissing yourself!' Fat Derek said.

The other boy looked down the road with narrow old-man's eyes. He looked bored and dissatisfied. He flicked a drooping piece of ash from the end of his cigarette. A bus was coming but I could see that it wasn't mine.

'You're still skiving then?' Fat Derek asked.

'I'm not skiving! I get notes from the doctor.'

He started to twist my head again so that I was almost pulled off my feet. '*Liar*! You're a skiving get!'

I didn't answer but coughed to show that he was choking me. The other kid took the cigarette from his mouth. He cleared his throat and spat a big grey gob through the air. It landed in the road. I was impressed despite my fear.

'Let's *go*!' he said. 'Let's just *fuck-off* now!'

'No! I want to interrogate him.'

Derek put his head close and stared into my face. His breath smelt of caramel. Then he leaned his weight on me as if he were trying to bear me down to the ground.

'Where are you off to all dressed up?'

I couldn't answer because of his arm across my throat. I looked down at the pavement and saw a brown beetle heading for the shade, picking itself a path between leaves and fallen bits of twig. Derek started to pull on my neck again. The other boy had walked around in front of us. He stared at me. His cigarette was just a soaked twist of paper between his lips. He took the last drag from it, his face puckering. Then he hooked it from his mouth and threw it back-handed into the bushes.

'That'll start a fire,' Derek said.

'Sod fires!' He squinted down at my dark shoes. 'Don't you ever have to go to school?' he asked softly.

'They don't allow skeletons,' Derek said.

He laughed at his joke. I felt the trembling of his belly against me. The smaller boy nodded and then lifted the side of his sweater. From somewhere around his waist he took out a small flat box. It had gold lettering on a blue label. He turned it so that this caught the light.

'So tell us where you've been!' Fat Derek demanded.

I managed to push my hand between his arm and my throat and suck in a breath. I tried to speak but there was phlegm in my throat.

28

'*What?*' Derek asked. He pushed his knee into my back again.

'A *funeral.*'

He started to smile. 'A funeral then? Your mother's?'

'No.'

'Your dad's then?'

I swallowed. 'Just this old fellah . . . He lived in our house.'

Derek looked away as if this was of no interest. He flexed his arm so that I felt its pressure against my throat again. The smaller kid stepped forward and held the blue box up close to my eyes. He opened the hinged top for a second. I saw a silver flash like the side of a fish.

'It's a mouth-organ!' Fat Derek said.

The other kid looked disgusted. 'A *harmonica.*'

Fat Derek looked down proudly into my face. 'We nicked it! From Cornelli's.'

His friend turned on him. 'It was me that nicked it! You were just fucking about!'

'A harmonica,' Derek said in a softer voice.

A woman in a hat was standing at the bus stop now. She looked over at us and then away. Her lips went tight and creased. A lorry went by and then some cars.

'I'm not musical,' I managed to say.

The small kid shrugged. Derek twisted my head again, forcing his forearm under my chin. For a while I couldn't breathe.

'Let's just go,' the other kid said.

'No! We have to fine him for telling us bollocks!'

I could feel the hot blood in my face. I took hold of his fat wrist with both hands and started to twist the skin in opposite directions. I was doubled over now with my head forced around so that I could see the woman at the stop still staring down the road, carefully ignoring us. I twisted Fat Derek's skin and heard him hiss with pain.

'He's got fingers like bones!' he shouted. He kneed me hard in the side until I let go. I heard his breath close against my ear.

'Get his money, Alec!'

'Who needs his money?' the other kid asked.

'Get it, will yeh! Feel in his pockets!'

The other kid stared into the bushes for a while. His old-man's face wrinkled and then he shrugged and slipped behind us. When I felt him tugging at my clothes I struck at him with my heel.

'*Fucker*!' he said.

The woman at the stop made tutting noises. Someone caught my foot and pulled it backwards. My shoe came off. I felt cold air against my sock and at the same time my head was squeezed out of Fat Derek's grip like a cork out of a bottle. I pushed against him and rolled on to the ground. The other boy shouted and spun on his heel. His arm made an arc. Then they were already running, laughing and whooping into the distance. I looked up into the sky and saw my shoe sailing through it, flying like a black aircraft above the tree-tops of the cemetery.

'There's some thieves about!' the woman said. 'Here's my bus now.'

I balanced on one leg. My sock was trailing from my foot and I tugged it back on. The 63 was slowing down towards the stop.

'You come to pay your respects and you have to deal with hooligans,' she said. 'You tend the grave of the departed and they hide in bushes and shout all sorts at you!'

The bus squealed and stopped. Its front rattled with the movements of the engine. The woman sniffed and got on as soon as the doors folded back. The conductor waited for me for a second and then rang his bell. There was a line of snot on my upper lip and I wiped it away with the back of my fist. The sun had slipped down and the shadows of the bushes reached almost to the kerb. I started to walk in the direction of home. The pavement was covered with small seeds and fallen bits of bark which stuck to the underside of my sock. After a while I took it off and stuck it into my jacket pocket. The flagstones felt cool under my sole. A man in an overcoat walked by but did not notice that I had one bare foot.

After a minute I came to one of the iron side-gates. It was locked by a chain and a rusty lock but the top hinge had snapped so that it leaned at an angle between its stone posts. I went closer. Through the gap I saw a narrow path through the bushes but with sky above it from the time when it had been larger.

I looked down the road. Another bus was coming but there was no one at the stop. The shadows of the trees moved over its windscreen. Before it came level I was squeezing through the opening. My jacket caught on one of the rusty curls and I heard the rip of a seam.

I stood on the other side, among bushes and the close-packed stems of young trees. The branches carried cuckoo-spit and the striped shells of small snails. The path was made of soft earth and gravel. I felt the sharpness against my foot and then the cold ooze of mud like a soothing ointment. There was a smell of dust and sap.

I pictured the black trajectory of my shoe. I knew that I would have to retrace my steps until I was again opposite the bus stop. I knew it could not be far from the road but my heart sank when I looked at the tangle of stems. Sprouts of sycamore pushed up through the mud with new leaves uncrinkling like fans. Sometimes you heard the traffic from the main road but in between things went quiet with just the odd warble of a bird. Some of the graves were visible in the green light – a pillar on the slant, a cross with a stone circle.

I started to walk. After a few yards I came to a wider path crossing the first. It was more open to the sky and the graves lining it were larger and better kept. I passed a miniature church with windows pierced through the stone and a steeple topped by a cross, and then another like a small square house with a peaked roof. My bare foot was becoming tender from the stones. A bird or something went plummeting through the bushes to my left and made me stop. My heart went thump but then the juddering stop of a bus calmed me. I looked towards the road, and through the branches I could see yellow sunshine on the windows of the top deck.

I bent down to pick a stone from between my toes and heard a noise or not quite a noise behind me, as if someone had almost spoken but then decided not to. I turned. A narrow gravel walk passed under the trees and at the end of this, in the centre of a clear space, an angel read from a scroll.

I stared at him. It was my first angel. He was turned half from the path so that I could see only the line of the stone cheek and the leaning forehead. The top of one wing was missing but the other curved above the head and then returned to sweep along the creature's back in parallel feathers.

There were already colours in the sky and I knew that it was getting late. The birds had gone quiet. I had to step over a fallen tree trunk and then another grave like a long brown box. There was a low fence of stone posts topped with what looked like stone pineapples. Chains with links carved of the same pale stone hung between them. Some of the chains had been broken and their ends hung to the ground. The area inside the fence was covered with white gravel, large rough-edged pieces with patches of ground showing below. The angel read with its head inclined to the scroll, the stump of its snapped-off wing now turned towards me.

I stepped into the enclosure where the chain was broken. I wanted to read what the angel read. It stood on a carved base like rocks set with fronds of stone fern. I think it was more than life-size and its big toes peeped out through the straps of carved sandals. One of its feet was set higher than the other and the leg revealed by the folds of the robe was well-muscled although the face of the figure was smooth and small-chinned and could have been a woman's. I gripped the base where the rocks made a handhold and managed to pull myself from the ground. The stone was slippery in places with some kind of brown scum and I felt myself sliding. I threw up my hand and caught at the arm of the angel where the elbow was bent. I pulled myself higher, holding on but off-balance. For a second I had stretched high enough to see the face of the scroll. Then I dropped down, falling, landing on my knees.

My hands were stinging, patterned by the press of the gravel. For a second the angel seemed to rock, as if it was going to fall. I closed my eyes and saw the wordless surface of the scroll. As I stepped back my bare foot found something smooth among the gravel. I turned and picked it up. It left a pierced oval in the mud.

It was a separated link of the perimeter chain, made from a kind of white marble with a pinkish tinge. I rubbed off some dirt and saw that it was threaded with rust-coloured veins. I weighed it in my hand, feeling it grow warm against my palm. A bird twittered and stopped. The sun was below the tops of the trees now and the sky had turned pale and transparent. I lifted my bare foot to massage it between my hands. For the first time I noticed that the moon had risen.

Four

I was twelve years old when Gagarin toured the North. He sat in his colonel's uniform in the back of an open-topped Zil. A small man in a big car. He did not feel the cold after his experience of absolute zero.

'They'll wine him and dine him, you see. Then he'll have to listen to their speeches.'

'No pleasure without pain!'

The Zil was a black limousine with bulging shining chromework. It smoothly circled the public toilets with their stepped monument of pigeon-shat Victoria. The crowd stood behind a white ribbon guarded by police horses. Helium balloons like silver snub-nosed rockets floated on string above their heads. The mayor and corporation waited below bunting on the steps of the town hall.

'But he mightn't know a word of English!'

'He'll have his own interpreter.'

The dog pulled, gasping against the tug of its collar. It was powerful and young, without abscesses and internal problems. Its eyesight was okay. I wound the lead tighter around my hand. The black car continued its circling. The cosmonaut Gagarin might have been asleep below his peaked cap.

'He doesn't want to get out, Eileen!'

My mother winked. 'He thinks he's still in orbit!'

Then after another circuit the Zil unpeeled from its path around the monument. A police horse stamped its foot and the crowd fell silent. Gravel snapped under the white-walled tyres. The car turned again before the steps and halted, its bodywork shuddering for a second as the engine stopped. The official driver stepped out and swiftly opened the black wing of the passenger door. The mayor waited with his hands clasped, smiling and shiny-faced. After a pause to compose himself

34

Gagarin alighted in his uniform with its top-heavy gold-braided cap.

'He's just a short-arse then,' my mother said.

My aunt nudged her elbow. 'They pick 'em small, Eileen! Like jockeys.'

The crowd behind the horses arranged itself tighter. The silver balloons ducked and spun. Bird-mired Victoria stared towards the east holding a full-rigged ship in her lap.

'All those medals: you'd think he'd overbalance! Does he wear them to bed?'

The mayor adjusted the height of his microphone and a squeal came from the trumpet mouths of the loudspeakers. Parti-coloured pigeons deserted the monument.

'The mayor'll make a speech.'

'You couldn't stop him.'

'They'll give him the freedom of the city, you see.'

'He's welcome to the hole!'

Gagarin, a small man in a large cap, smartly climbed the shallow steps between rows of councillors and officials.

'I wouldn't trust them with a penny. Fingers in every pie.'

'A lamb among wolves, Irene!'

The mayor and the spaceman shook hands and held the pose for the flash of the official camera. They were both about the same height. Then Gagarin stepped forward impetuously and caught hold of the mayor's shoulders. The chain of office chimed against the cosmonaut's medals as they embraced.

'It's the way they say hello over there. Like rubbing noses.'

The crowd began to cheer and whistle. A balloon was released and then another. They headed into the white sky above the square, catching the light as they turned, becoming small quickly.

'You're quiet, Leonard!'

My view was blocked by a horse's rear. The crowd made another cheer and pushed. The dog growled. Setting its paws square it began to bark. The sharp sound rebounded from the public buildings, fracturing into two dogs, three, ten. Gagarin's smile was lopsided. He had taken off his cap. His hair was wheat-coloured and shiny with oil, combed smartly to the side but a lock of it escaping to his forehead. He turned to the monument and raised his arms. The crowd cheered and the police

35

horses stamped, raising sparks from the paving. At the cosmonaut's signal the rest of the balloons were released in formation. They rose with their hanging tails of string, leaving the shadow of the square, all of them catching the light at the same moment. Gagarin waved his glittering cap.

I ducked below the ribbon. Another boy was already dashing into the open space before the steps, running with his head down. The police horse reared and I saw its blotched belly and sex. Jeff the dog barked hysterically, dragging me forward. I ran, head-down, half falling. There was already a scrum before him: children, men and women holding out torn envelopes, rent-books, betting slips. Gagarin lifted his arms, signalling that they should be calm. His driver was shadow-like beside him, handing the cosmonaut a pen and a grey official folder. Gagarin slid out a wad of glossy photographs and began to sign his name quickly and expertly across their lower corners. Smiling, he passed them one after the other into the crowd.

An undertaker's car was parked outside the house, dried splashes of mud up its black sides. One of the funeral men was sleeping in the passenger seat with a newspaper over his face. The door of the house was open a few inches and I heard music seeping down the long hallway from the living room.

'Well, here's the wanderer . . . !' Aunt Irene said.

She wore the driver's peaked cap at an angle on her head. The driver and the old man who had helped with the coffin sat in chairs drawn up to the table. A decanter of port and dark bottles of Guinness were set out on paper serviettes. The trays of food were already empty, leaving a few waxy sausages and a crumbly wedge of cake. Mrs Rinse sat shiny-lipped on the low couch next to Mr Harbut. Mr Harbut seemed to be dozing but then lifted his head and looked at me with sleepy narrow eyes.

My mother rushed in from the kitchen, a cigarette in her hand. At once she spotted my bare foot. 'Where's your shoe?' she asked. 'Leonard?'

'His shoe!' my aunt repeated, slower on the uptake.

I did not know how to answer. I looked down at my foot against the pattern of the carpet. The dried mud had turned pale and dusty. There was mud on my remaining shoe and on the hems of my trousers.

'I *lost* it,' I said quietly.

'The lad lost it!' my aunt said.

My mother stared at me. She picked up a half-glass of Guinness. Her cheeks were rosy and her forehead moist. It was true that sometimes she had a higher colour than Aunt Irene. 'But how can he lose a shoe?' she asked.

'I'm like that with gloves myself,' my aunt said. 'Some things beg to be lost.'

'Grief takes people in different ways,' the driver put in. 'I've seen a woman take off everything at the graveside.'

The retired seaman laughed over his glass. My aunt giggled and pulled at the peak of the cap. 'How do you mean, *everything*?'

The driver gave a nod. 'I mean she stripped right off until she was starkers.'

My mother let her eyes slide from me and sat down at the table. 'I can't believe that for a second,' she said. 'You're pulling our legs there.'

Frank Ifield sang from the record player. The sisters both liked those big-chested ballads. The man from the Mariners' Society sat forward suddenly in the armchair and pointed to me with a shaky finger. 'Give that fellah a drink!'

'He can't drink when he's just a bloody kid!' my mother told him angrily. 'And I want to get to the bottom of this shoe business.'

My aunt reached out and tapped her arm. 'No, the gentleman's right, Eileen. He needs to drink the health of the departed. Part of the occasion, you see.'

My mother narrowed her lips and took a small gilt-rimmed glass from a row on one of the doilies. She half filled it with port wine from the decanter and handed it to me with a look. I sat down at the table and lowered my upper lip into the glass while the others watched. The wine was sweet and rich and I felt the blood beginning to migrate to the surface of my skin.

'That's the lad!' Mr Harbut said. He tried to sit up straighter, twisting himself on the couch so that the springs rocked and Mrs Rinse almost spilled her drink. 'Steady now,' she complained.

I took another long sip and then lowered the glass. There

was still a dark slip of wine in the bottom but my mother moved it out of my reach.

'Did you lose your sock as well?' she asked.

I felt in my jacket pocket. The pierced stone was there, heavy and smooth, warmed by my thigh. I pulled out the sock and showed it to her.

'He went barefoot sooner than wear it out,' Aunt Irene said.

My mother took hold of it, lifting it between her fingers.

'It's a sock all right,' the retired seaman said.

'It's all mud and bits,' my mother complained, 'and his foot looks as if he's been walking across fields.'

My aunt sighed from under the peaked cap. 'Lads will be lads, Eileen. All the socks in the world can't change that! Let's leave it for now. We have to do justice to Captain Oram.'

'I only want the facts,' my mother said.

'The facts can wait until tomorrow, surely!'

'Where's Ralph?' I asked, hoping to leave the subject behind. My mother gave me her wide-eyed stare of warning. She went over to the record player and turned over the record.

'Ralph's leg is poorly,' Aunt Irene said. 'Of course, it always is but it's better on some days than others.'

'He didn't see fit to attend,' my mother said.

Aunt Irene shook her head. She listened as the tune lifted from the record player with an introduction of strings and horns. 'It's not that Mario Lanza, is it?'

'And what if it is?'

'He doesn't sing but only bellows, if you ask me.'

My mother closed the lid on the turning record. 'He shows some feeling at least!'

'They get too emotional,' Mrs Rinse said from the couch, 'all those people in warm climates.'

The retired seaman nodded. 'They get worked up over the simplest things, missis, and need careful handling on occasion. Between the tropics, you see. The moon's as big as a melon and casts its spell.'

'Help yourself to another drink, mister,' my aunt said. 'Don't wait to be prompted.'

I still had the rich taste of the port at the back of my throat. 'Can I have another?' I asked.

The funeral driver laughed and raised his glass to me. My mother lifted her hands. 'See, you've started him already! He shouldn't drink until he's sixteen at least: his system is immature, you see.'

Mr Harbut twisted on the couch again. His eyes looked bleary and yellow. His shirt was open at the throat and I noticed the shiny dark silk of his tie folded into the breast pocket of his jacket. 'Go on, give him another,' he said. 'One for the journey back!'

'He's going nowhere,' my mother said.

Mrs Rinse laughed. She sat uncomfortably beside the Mariners' Society man, her arms folded. 'It might do him good. He's already got some colour in his face.'

My aunt peered at me. 'He's just blushing, mebbe. He can be shy sometimes.'

'Sometimes he is,' my mother said. 'Sometimes he can be forward.'

The seaman winked at me. He took the small glass between finger and thumb and filled it from the decanter.

'That's far too much!' my mother complained.

He laughed. 'I can't pour it back now, missis: the neck's too thin.'

He slid the glass over the table. My aunt looked at him with shiny eyes. 'I'll bet you'll miss him,' she said. 'The captain.'

There were nods and sighs around the table. The old man sat more upright in his chair, pursing his lips. 'He was a first-class seaman, though he never reached the ranks he should. Wouldn't push himself forward, you see. He had too much self-respect.'

'But you have to sometimes,' my mother said. 'Or you'll be left behind.'

The old man nodded. 'True, missis. There's a line you have to tread.'

My aunt topped up her glass from a bottle. The foam rose on top of the black drink. 'He kept his room spotless and himself as well. I'd stand outside his door sometimes and hear him brushing his shoes. Whenever you saw him you could catch your reflection in them.'

The old man looked proud and excited. He rolled the sides

39

of his glass between his palms. 'Oh, you need to be smart in the Merchant Marine! It's part of the calling. Wherever you go you represent the flag, you see, and the habit gets ingrained. And half the time you're in drink in those places.'

I sipped the port. Blood gathered at the tip of my nose. I slipped my hand into my trousers pocket and with my fingers touched the smooth 0 of the stone.

My mother was sharp-eyed. 'What've you got there, Leonard?'

'Nothing,' I said.

I pulled out my empty hand. Mr Harbut leaned forward in his seat and was sick over his lap.

'I knew it!' my aunt said. 'He'd turned a colour.'

'Can't stomach his drink,' the driver said. 'He's famous for it in the trade.'

'Then he shouldn't have partaken!' my aunt said sternly. She still wore the driver's cap turned at an angle. She stood up and pushed Mr Harbut back in his seat. His face was like paper with red flushed spots on the cheeks. Muriel Rinse leant away from him into her corner of the couch, her mouth screwed tight.

'And you shouldn't have encouraged him,' my aunt added.

The driver smiled up at her. 'Some people are gluttons for it, missis.'

'It's a sad sight in a young fellah,' the seaman said. 'He's more refined than some and that's been his downfall.'

The driver pushed back his chair. He stood up, brushing crumbs from his uniform. 'He wouldn't be much use in a force nine, Captain!'

'*Engineer*,' the old man said. 'I only take what's due to me.'

'Very right too! Now, if I can have my cap back, missis.'

My aunt looked surprised. 'You're not going to leave us with him, surely!'

'I can't have him in the cab like that! It's not as if it's my own vehicle.'

'You can lay him in the back part,' my mother suggested. 'We'll wipe him down for you.'

The driver leaned over the table to pluck his cap from my aunt's head. Instead of putting it on he folded the crown

40

around the peak and pushed it into his pocket. My mother brought a cloth from the kitchen.

'It hasn't gone on the carpet, has it?' my aunt asked.

'Only a little.' My mother averted her face as she wiped Mr Harbut's dark jacket. She turned the cloth carefully and handed it to the retired seaman. 'Maybe you could do the rest, mister.'

The old man wiped Mr Harbut's lap with a controlled, delicate look on his face. 'He's lost his dinner all right!'

'I'll throw that thing away now,' my mother said.

The record had ended. You could hear the needle skittering over the blank part. The driver and the old fellah lifted Mr Harbut from his seat and supported him between them. Mr Harbut opened his eyes to watery slits.

'You could show us the door then,' the driver told my aunt with a wink.

Aunt Irene sipped from her glass, sitting back in her seat. There was a ridge in her hair where the cap had been. 'When you've got a navigator with you?'

The retired seaman laughed.

'Dead people: I've no time for them!' Ralph said. 'I had enough of that during the war. When you see a dead person face to face then you see that they're nothing!'

He sat at his table before the twin tanks, round-shouldered under the angled lamp, breathing fiercely down his nose. The bar of the electric fire glowed and the radio sent out talk from behind its grille. Threads of dust rose, turning in the hooded light. Dust was the curse of aero-modelling.

'They're just empty clothes,' Ralph said.

He nodded to himself and began to apply a transfer, taking it to the side of the model on the end of a fine camel-hair brush. His hand had a tremble because of the fineness of the operation. He did not breathe until the transfer floated from the bristles on a fine film of water and attached itself to the camouflaged plastic. Then he leaned back.

'That's *adhesion* for you, Leonard! The mightiest force known to man. The temples of the Incas were built using no cement at all. They cut the blocks to a thousandth of an inch

41

and then polished the faces like gems. If an atom bomb dropped they'd be the only things left standing. Where does that leave your Russkies now?'

'*Soviets*,' I said. I knew that he liked to tease me. I looked at the transfer. The black cross soon lost its shine and turned matt. It clung to the curve of the fuselage, moulding itself to every line and rivet-head.

'I heard the goings-on downstairs,' Ralph said. 'Someone was incapable.'

'The man from the Mariners' Society made himself sick. They had to carry him out in the end.'

Ralph smiled with the side of his mouth. 'Oh, there's nothing much escapes my notice. I heard the cars start up. You came in with one shoe on, one off.'

'I lost it.'

'One shoe off, one shoe on,' Ralph repeated. 'How did you manage that?'

I ignored the question. 'He was *paralytic*, Ralph! He was nearly sick on Mrs Rinse.'

He gave a little laugh and raised one shoulder. 'If that's the style of person they want to encourage . . .'

The loose transfers floated in a saucer of luke-warm water. When you soaked them from the backing papers they turned to thin, coloured films. They were so light they could not exist on their own. They sought contact again, anything would do – the brush, your finger.

'Don't touch!'

'I was only looking!'

'Eyes in your fingertips! Where's Mrs Rinse now?'

'She went to bed with a headache.'

He laughed again, enjoying himself. 'They want that room, you see!'

'Mrs Rinse?'

'Him and her. Her mostly, though he'll follow. She says the stairs are too much for her.' He shook his head, smiling. It was a point of pride to him that he lived at the top of the house despite his injured leg.

'Aunt Irene'll give it to them,' I told him. 'She said so.'

Ralph shook his head again. He glanced towards the fish in their tanks, as though their movements were a source of divination. 'She only intends to, Leonard. They count their chickens but the greatest virtue is patience. Everything comes round again, you see. As the Earth turns.'

Five

I went to bed early and slept late. With a death in the house I had some licence. When I got out of bed the women were already busy downstairs, cleaning out the old man's room. I gathered my clothes from where I had thrown them, felt the stone in my pocket and put it on the table below the moon pictures. When I went downstairs the door of the middle room was open on a smell of soap and disinfectant.

'The lad is alive,' my aunt said.

The old fellah's bed had been stripped and the sheets tied in a bundle. The carpet had been rolled back and my mother stood in the centre of the floor cleaning the lino with a mop. 'Who is he?' she asked. 'He's a man of mystery!'

My aunt laughed. 'You shouldn't torment him!'

'I'll torment him until we find the truth.'

'He's your lad,' Aunt Irene said softly.

My mother nodded, closing her eyes. She squeezed out the mop in its bucket.

'We shouldn't interfere with each other,' Aunt Irene said. 'When there's some things we need for dinner.'

She peeled off her pair of rubber gloves and left them in a ball on the mantelpiece.

'I'm tired of pork luncheon meat,' my mother said. 'It's coming out of my ears.'

Aunt Irene sighed. 'Then I wouldn't dream of buying it. Only it's good value.'

We waited in silence until she had gone. My mother took up the mop again.

'A man on his own is never really clean, Leonard. They only *hide* their dirt from the world. Their secret. They might wipe things now and again, and dust, but they never *scrub* and in that way the dirt becomes ingrained.'

44

Habits and dirt became ingrained. It was a word which explained many things. I stood close to the old fellah's bed. There was a sweetish smell of whisky about it as if the vapours had soaked into the covers and sheets. A corner of paper was falling from the ceiling in a curl. My mother went over to the cupboard beside the gas stove and opened one door. She turned away her face quickly.

'There's food gone off in here, Leonard! Don't you touch anything yourself: I'm wearing rubber gloves.'

She knelt and began to take tins and packets from the shelves and stack them in a washing-up bowl. I heard my aunt go out and the key dropped back through the letter-box, chiming against the door as it swung on its twine.

'Shoes are expensive,' my mother said. 'And one's no good without the other. You could keep it all your life and not find a partner. You were fighting yesterday, weren't you?'

'They wanted my bus money. They caught hold of me from behind.'

'They were thieves then. Did you know them?' She nodded to herself. 'If you hadn't have known them first then they wouldn't have touched you.' She stared into the cupboard, angling her head. 'All this lot can be chucked out. Some of it's still fresh but I wouldn't like to use it. No.'

I took the food to the dustbins in the yard. It was all stuff in tins and packets – corned beef, instant custard, sardines. When I got back she was wiping the shelves with Dettol and warm water.

'Were they from your school?' she said.

'No,' I said.

'I'll bet they were. You have to learn more to stand up for yourself.'

'There was two of them!'

She nodded. 'Then you'll have to wait your time, Leonard. Always carry what happened in the back of your mind: never forgive or forget.'

She began to wipe the shelves and the front of the cupboard. I looked around the room at the photographs in their shiny black frames. The pictures were faded by sunlight but in some of them you could make out grey water and trees. Above the fireplace on one side was a photograph of black people standing outside a white-walled building. Some of them were dressed but others weren't. Because of the fading you could not see the details.

'I have what they call an unforgiving nature,' my mother said.

She laughed and stood up to ease her back. I was looking at a picture of a steamship on the wall above the bed. It was low in the water and carried two leaning funnels and a dark triangular sail at the back of the cabins. The sea on which it floated looked like grey jelly.

'He wasn't really a captain, you know,' my mother said. 'It was his bit of make-believe and you couldn't deny him that. I think he was a first mate or something. That's still a responsible job.'

I finished looking at the pictures and sat down on the edge of the bed.

'Don't do that, Leonard! Not on his bed.'

The bed sprung back as I stood up. We heard Mrs Rinse calling from the landing. '*Helloooo*!' she called, her voice going high.

We waited until she called again.

'We can't just ignore her, Leonard. She's what you call human as well.'

The Rinses' room always had a smell of paraffin. A heater with a chromed reflector stood under the window and I heard the liquid tick as fuel dripped into the reservoir. The curtains were still closed against the daylight. They stirred slightly in the warm air. Sometimes I'd see Mr Rinse carrying a five-gallon container up the stairs. The blue liquid would slop against the clouded plastic. He'd pause at the small landing to catch his breath and wipe his forehead with the cuff of his jacket. They slept together in a big bed with an embroidered counterpane which reached the floor. The rest of the room was almost taken up by a square table with thick turned legs. Mrs Rinse filled two mugs from an aluminium pot. The stream of tea was pale and transparent.

'The water of life,' Mrs Rinse said. 'Only that's whisky.'

46

She winked at me. There was no air in the room, only the vapours of the paraffin and a smell of cat. I glanced at the space below the sink and saw a saucer with a rind of dried food around its rim.

'I think of your mother whenever I use the stove,' Mrs Rinse said. 'I'm sure we couldn't exist without her.'

'No,' I said.

She stirred the teas, smiling. 'You shouldn't be so reserved with me, Leonard! I've known you since a baby. I saw you when you were first home from the hospital. You were only as long as that cushion.'

She held the door open for me as I carried out the mugs, her other hand on the collar of her dressing gown. She wore slippers with pom-poms but her feet were as big as a man's. I was relieved to step out into the cooler air of the landing.

'Thank you, Mrs Rinse!' I said.

She put her head on one side and gave me a dimpled smile. 'Oh, there's no need to use that word with me, Leonard!'

My mother emptied the tea into the old fellah's sink. She ran the cold tap to rinse it away.

'You might think this is spiteful, Leonard, but really it's only hygiene. There are differences between people, different standards of cleanliness. Was there any sign of that cat?'

'No,' I said.

'That's because she keeps it hidden.'

She reached into the bottom of the wardrobe and took out a pair of brown brogues with wooden stretchers. The leather was glossy and finely creased.

'See how he looked after his shoes! These are better than new because the leather turns supple with polishing.'

She turned them over to show me the soles. I saw the polished heads of brass sprigs and two oval patches where the thin layers of leather had worn.

'These are good quality: made on a last, you see . . .' She pointed to a patch of leather finely sewn into the uppers near the heel. 'That's where he's had them repaired. He could have been buried in these only they're brown.'

She tucked the shoes neat and parallel under the base of the

47

wardrobe and then tugged open the deep drawer and took out a pair of ox-blood loafers, then tins of wax and a pair of meshed brushes. She reached into the far corner and took out a flat parcel wrapped in grey linen tied crosswise with yellow twine.

'So what's this?'

She picked at the twine for a minute and then handed the parcel to me.

'Your fingers are smaller than mine.'

Something very light stiffened the linen. I turned the bundle about until I found a knot. I teased at it for a while with my fingernails and managed to unpick a loop. Then the knot slipped easily apart.

She held out her hand. 'Give me it, Leonard!'

My mother turned the parcel over on itself, letting the linen unfold until there was more than a yard of it. A faint smell of lavender was released. Inside all that material there was just a square of yellowed card which she opened up like a book.

'Maybe it's of the old fellah,' I said. 'When he was younger.'

She bent over the photograph. 'No, the eyes are different. And he was never good-looking. You can tell.'

The photograph was mounted by its corners to one side of the card. A dried sprig of lavender had stained the margin so that you could see its curled shape. The man had a pale long face and a visored cap. He half smiled in half profile away from the camera. The two halves of the mount gave out a feeling of secrecy as if they had made an airtight seal between them. Already the photograph seemed to be darkening and when my mother tried to close the mount the stiff card split along its hinge.

The sisters sat on the couch, a space between them, smoking their allotted cigarettes and speaking to one another in the short silences left by the TV.

'They think that it's settled!' Aunt Irene said.

My mother lifted her chin. 'You've told them that? I might have my own ideas.'

'What ideas are those?'

'I mean only that he isn't cold yet: they shouldn't *rush in*.'

Cold in his grave, she meant. I pictured the old fellah shivering without his tweed overcoat.

'They've always wanted that room,' my aunt said. 'It was as good as promised to them years ago. Because of her chest, you see.'

My mother rubbed the palms of her hands together. The dry skin made a noise like paper. 'Her chest is no worse than mine! And if they move I'll have to scrub that place as well.' She lifted her eyes.

Aunt Irene frowned. 'Only it's understood between us. I can't disappoint them at this late stage.'

'Leonard will tell you how I've worked today! There was years of dirt just under that carpet.'

I felt their eyes on my back as I sat at the table. I read a library book already a week overdue. Although insignificant in terms of the solar system the moon was unusually large and massive relative to its primary (Earth). It shone only because of the light it reflected from the sun, i.e. it had no radiance of its own. The points or horns of the moon were known as *cusps*.

'I'm surprised at that,' Aunt Irene said. 'He was a clean old fellah.'

'I'm not claiming that he wasn't, Irene. Only that things look clean but when you examine them you'll find dirt ... That one upstairs has his dirt!'

'And who's that?' my aunt asked. 'Does he have a name?'

'Fish are dirty creatures!' my mother said. 'And he never changes their water. I'm certain I can smell them from the landing downstairs.'

My aunt laughed. 'It's your imagination, Eileen! They're his hobby: to take his mind off. You can't begrudge the fellah a few fish!'

They left for an evening of dominoes and song. Above the garden the sky stretched from roof to roof, lifting above the back gardens towards the invisible railway. I could feel its tightness in my throat. Hidden things were going on under cover of the last of the light. Out of the corners of my eyes I caught the shimmer as stars trembled into visibility.

I sat down on the chair against the wall to wait, half turned so that I faced towards the east and the roofs opposite. The hens made soft noises and gave off their smell of fermentation. The casement above my head was hinged out into the air with the room dark behind it.

I closed my eyes to prepare myself and let my vision adjust. After a minute I felt the slow creep of gravity and when I turned back to the sky again the moon was already at the edges of the houses, full and unlikely, its bright edges punched sharp so that they seemed to go right through the sky as if light from somewhere far behind were streaming through a hole.

The light of the moon was the reflection of the sun. It sailed above the roofs. The hens clucked and fidgeted. I could make out the dark areas of the lunar seas and the rays of the big craters like luminous cracks. For a long time I did not take my eyes from the satellite. Its rays conducted silvery power. I braced my feet against the ground and my hands against my knees but still did not lower my eyes.

Above me a door opened, slamming back against its wall. The shock of it passed down my spine. I tilted back my head and saw the girl lean from the open window and throw something black into the air above the garden. It fell into space. Her white face looked down at me, mouth open.

We stared at one another.

'Who's that?' she asked, between angry and afraid. 'Who's there?'

I stood up and stepped back from the wall.

'It's me.'

'Who's *me*?'

'Leonard,' I said.

'*Leonard* . . . ? Oh! Were you taking a walk?'

'No.'

She lowered her voice. 'I dropped something . . . Did you see where it went?'

I stood in the middle of the scruffy lawn holding a man's black shoe. It was thin and pointed, so shiny that when I turned it in my hands it gave back small crackles of light. I felt more than saw that the back was low and the heel compact and tapering with a short arch between it and the sole. The tips of my fingers found perforations in the leather and slick rows of

50

parallel stitching. The light was on in their room now and I saw her shape against the window with Norris standing close behind her, his hand on her shoulder. His glossed-back hair shone with a highlight.

'We were larking,' he said.

Susan jerked her chin. 'It's the moon!' She pointed to it. 'It's a lovely night but chilly. Is that what you were looking at?'

She leaned out again. I saw the slight shine of her smile. Norris lifted his head and began to howl like a wolf. He gripped her narrow waist. She laughed and struggled back against him. 'You'll have me over in a second!'

'The truth is, she threw it,' Norris said. 'She was practising her shoe-throwing.'

'Or else I'd have broken something, Leonard. Do you know what I mean?'

'Yes,' I said.

'You see, Leonard understands!' She still leaned over the sill. The softness of her belly was pressed against the frame of the window. 'The moon . . . ! Do you think there could be people on it?'

'No, it hasn't got an atmosphere.'

'No atmosphere, you see,' Norris said, butting in. He made a joke of it I did not understand. He stood beside her, pushing against her with his hip, and gave me a cunning smile, pointing past her shoulder. 'They could mebbe live under glass bowls!'

I passed the flimsy shoe from one hand to the other. 'Meteors would break them and the air would leak out.'

Susan laughed and he leaned forward, pressing the side of his face against hers. He kissed her hair with a faint smack of lips.

'You'll never beat him, Norris,' Susan said. 'He's got the facts at his fingertips.' She clapped her hands once and held them apart. 'Chuck it to us then!'

I thought for a second that she meant the moon.

'That's an expensive shoe,' Norris said. 'You be careful with it!'

'He can *throw*!'

In fact I was nervous of throwing. I was clumsy and cack-handed at any game involving a ball. I went closer to the wall

51

and lobbed the shoe underarm so that it went almost straight up. I did not want to miss and break the window. Susan made a grab for it but it fell between her arms. I rushed forward and managed to catch it.

Norris groaned. 'Again!' Susan said. 'Throw like you mean it!'

This time my nervousness made me overshoot and I think it might have hit her in the face if his arm hadn't snaked out. He caught it one-handed. '*Ole!*' he called.

'You're too clever sometimes!' Susan said. 'You make a person sick.'

He looked surprised, pressing his spectacles back against his face. 'It's only co-ordination – hand-and-eye like.'

She peered down at me. 'What can I do about this fellah?' She gave her lunar-lit smile and turned away.

Norris stayed leaning against the frame, cuddling his shoe. He nodded towards the moon. It was higher now, swinging away from the line of roofs into the full sky. 'I still say there's people on it! Something like that must have its own population. Next time I meet one I'll introduce you.'

'Thanks,' I said.

He turned the shoe about, inspecting it for signs of damage.

'It's tricky to throw,' I said. 'Light.'

'They're for *dancing*, you see, not digging ditches. Do you go dancing, Leonard?'

'No.'

He nodded at me sorrowfully. 'Is your mother in tonight?'

'They've gone out.'

'Ah! Maybe I'll see them later; I had something to ask.'

He looked at the shoe thoughtfully and then stood it by its narrow toe on the palm of his hand, balancing it there. It dipped and trembled for a second and then stood upright as if it were anchored by a plumb-line. I watched from below, standing close to my shadow on the wall. The moon was behind me with its light on my back. In my mind's eye I saw the flicker as he snatched back his hand. The shoe fell like a knife towards me.

Six

A man in a small blue van called for the old fellah's clothes and bedding. My mother scraped at the brittle old linoleum with a blunt table-knife, lifting it piece by piece. The boards underneath were covered with a layer of sticky black sediment. She scrubbed them with boiling soapy water spiked with powerful disinfectant, working with the french windows open to let out the fumes.

The cosmonauts Leonov and Belyakev landed by parachute in a field of wheat. After a medical check they chatted briefly to Soviet newsmen.

'They send them up and then they come down again. Where's the sense in that?' my aunt asked.

She sat in the low armchair, trimming her toenails over a sheet of newspaper. The dog sighed to itself, shifting its angle to the heat of the fire. We heard the noise of the door.

'That is her,' Aunt Irene said quietly.

My mother was home from work. She put down her bag and unbuttoned her coat. 'I can't speak,' she said. 'I'm that tired! So don't quiz me.'

She took off her low-heeled shoes and crossed the living room in her stockinged feet. For a while she sat by herself in the kitchen, sipping tea, putting the cup back on the saucer with a small chime of noise. Sometimes she had a delicate and silent way of drinking.

My aunt worked on, pursing her lips at the toughness of her nails. The parings jumped into the paper like translucent fleas.

'Only you'd think you might be curious,' my mother said from the other room.

Aunt Irene did not stop her work. 'Only curious as to what you might mean.'

'I mean that I've spoken to someone.'

'Why, what about?' My aunt looked surprised, holding the small scissors.

'About what we were talking about. Surely you've some memory of it?'

Aunt Irene sighed. She folded the paper to gather up the clippings. 'I can't think, Eileen. Can you mean about the room?'

'At last we've got there!'

My mother rinsed and dried her cup and came back to join us.

'Then who did you speak to?' Aunt Irene asked.

'Those who I mentioned! Or it's them who spoke to me . . .'

My aunt replaced one of her slippers. 'Well, was anything decided?'

'Wait for a second, Irene. I'm saying that they spoke to me. And then they went away. To think. Half an hour later they were back! You see, I'd told them there was already an interest shown.'

'Only in a way,' Aunt Irene said. 'And we can't pretend the room is anything special.'

'And what's the use in selling ourselves short? They said tomorrow they'll give me a deposit. *Key-money* you could call it.'

My aunt sucked her cheek to make a hollow. 'We have all the keys they'd want, Eileen. And we've never asked for deposits before.'

My mother began to sound impatient. 'I didn't ask but they suggested. People expect it now. It makes them feel safer. And they're not short of money: there's overtime galore in those kitchens.'

'*Galore*,' Aunt Irene repeated. 'And they're Poles you said?'

I looked up at this. I drew a mental map on the blank screen of the television. I knew that Poland was a communist country, part of the Warsaw Pact and an ally of the Soviet Union.

'A Pole is only like you or me,' my mother said. 'Just that the life is better for them here.'

Aunt Irene looked surprised. 'You'd think that it was hard enough! And these Poles drink, you know!'

'People drink in every walk of life. The Queen drinks if you could see her.'

'I'm only saying that *some* of them drink, Eileen,' my aunt said defensively. 'Granted others of them will be moderate. And they will be Catholics?'

'There's nothing wrong if a person is religious. Norris knows them and he says they're respectable.'

'Only he's not so much himself, mebbe ... And two of them! How will they sleep?'

'One works days and the other nights,' my mother said. 'It's as easy as that. They take all the work that's going and they're never short of money.'

My aunt threw the ball of newspaper underarm into the back of the fire. 'So long as they're punctual with their payments ... But foreigners though: it makes me shiver at the thought. And what about Mr and Mrs?'

She meant the Rinses.

'They can stay upstairs until this place collapses!' my mother said.

My aunt laughed. 'You are so dramatic, Eileen! And you've never liked them. You can't pretend.'

'I'm only indifferent.'

'You know she'll be upset.'

'Mrs Rinse will never rinse a cup,' my mother said.

'You shouldn't speak ill of people!'

'Only not of the dead.'

The dog pointed himself at trails of urine, sniffing, turning his limbs rigid when I tried to pull him away. His blunt nails scraped against the pavement. Away from the dark corners of the house you could see that the rash on his back was getting worse. He crooned and lifted his head. When I looked into his eyes I could see two fine white circles around the dark discs of the pupils.

'Jeff!' I said, pulling him away from the corner.

I pushed my free hand into my pocket and touched the stone for luck. I carried it about with me now, slipping it into a pocket in whatever clothes I wore, transferring it at night to the small table below the lunar pictures. Sometimes in a quiet spot I'd take it out to look at its glossy off-whiteness and the dark embedded veins. I felt uneasy without it, in the way that

someone would feel without their watch or wallet. Its smoothness seemed to mould to my grip and my thumb fitted into its
pierced centre.

'You have something there!' Mr Webster said.

I took my hand out of my pocket. 'No.'

The narrow back of the shop was a kind of menagerie of
unusual pets – tailless lizards, flop-eared rabbits, a toad with a
horny back. The tanks and small cages lined both walls. The
air smelled of drying shit.

'And how is the animal?' he asked.

'He's okay.'

He winked at me. 'When they reach a certain age, you see.
There's no such thing as their old-age pension . . .'

The dog swivelled his eyes, nervous at so much strangeness.
It made a kind of bleat in its throat.

'What's his name again?' Mr Webster asked.

'Jeff.'

He nodded. 'Jeff. I didn't forget. Or only for a minute.'

His assistant laughed to herself behind the counter.

'And what's so amusing, Trudy?'

Trudy gave him a look and then closed her eyes on him.
'*Nothing*!'

Mr Webster stared at a tank of terrapin. There was a fine
sweat on his forehead. 'This young man will want his worming
tablets.'

The dog returned to its space near the fire. The space fitted the
dog exactly and was empty without it, as if a part of the room
had been mislaid. I walked through to the back of the house.
Peas were soaking in a bowl on top of the table. In the back
garden a pool of water lay in the hollow seat of the chair. I
went back into the house. The dog stared at me, swivelling its
eye to follow as I crossed the room.

The door of the old fellah's room was open. The mirror of
his wardrobe showed my own face and the African pictures
leaned in a stack against the wall, torn paper backings towards
me. I went upstairs. The Rinses and their captive cat were
silent as I crossed the landing. In the master bedroom the
sisters' beds were arranged at right angles so that their heads

faced away. My aunt's bed was the nearest. The curtains of both windows were closed and a shaded lamp was lit on a small table between them. In a glass ashtray I saw a spent match and half-a-dozen hair-grips placed parallel. The ashtray under the lamp seemed to be the source of the house's silence. I closed the door and climbed towards Ralph's rooms, first one flight and then the other.

'*Shhh*,' said my mother.

She made the sign against her lips. She sat on a step halfway to the top landing, turned towards me but leaning forward against the step before her. She wore her outdoor clothes but she had taken off her shoes so that I could see her stockinged heels under her skirt. She signalled to me again. I knew I had not to talk but to listen.

She rested her chin on her hand. She was all attention but I could at first hear nothing. Both of Ralph's doors were closed and apparently locked, but then through the side door, the door to his bedroom, came a thin slide of sound which could have been just a breath only it lasted much longer.

I knew this was the sound of the thing which went on between a man and a woman, this breath that went on too long.

The sisters argued. The snap and grumble of it came through the wall. I followed the pattern of rose-and-trellis, tracking them through the room. There were places in the wall where the voices were cloudy and set off a dull echo, then others where they were thin and clear, like a small dog's bark.

'It's only for comfort sometimes!'

'For what a man can provide!' my mother said with a sharp laugh. 'Being short in the leg department . . .'

'You mock the afflicted, Eileen! The child is to go to hospital again and you would turn him against me.'

'Don't mention the lad in the same breath!'

'You'd poison his mind towards me!'

My aunt began to gasp and hiccup.

'You've had your pleasure,' my mother said. She walked about, barefoot. The pressure of her heels left small impressions in the rug.

'It wasn't what you'd call pleasure, Eileen. You won't understand, I think.'

'It'll be a feather in his cap,' my mother said. 'You won't hold him now: he has his advantage.'

My aunt made a rattling sigh. 'I think I'll sleep now, Eileen.'

She turned out the bedside lamp. My mother drew back one set of curtains to leave a narrow opening. The light of the street lamp would slant up into the room. They would look at the shape it made, thinking.

In sleep the breath of the sisters synchronised like pendulums in a closed room. It made the slow deep vibration which was the heartbeat of the house. I listened for it in the dark, my cheek resting against the embossed wallpaper. When the time came I lit the candle, shielding it with my hand against the draught from below the door.

Gagarin's transparent visor was hinged back, his face tilted upwards slightly, eyes narrowed against the camera lights. His thrust-out chin was hidden by the heavy flange of the helmet. It was a studio portrait but dramatically lit and with a feeling of movement and liveliness.

C   C   C   P

The widely spaced letters followed the curve of the helmet. I studied the picture, bending closer until it was threatened by my shadow. *Hero First-Class and Pilot Cosmonaut of the Soviet Union*. I puzzled over his smile, the divergent angle of his eyes. A moped went past in the street, its racket stretching and then fading through gear changes. It turned the corner into the main road. My room was silent again except for the fizz of the flame.

People were troubled by gravity that year. They were prone to it. It reached a certain point and they could not resist it. They tripped, slipped, collapsed, went weak at the knees. It was an epidemic and you could not guard against it.

Twice a month a man from the education board called to check my progress. He leaned his heavy-framed cycle against the kerb and passed a chain through both its wheels. He sealed the chain with a small brass padlock and then removed the enamel cycle clips from the hems of his trousers, pressed them

58

one inside the other and slipped them into his jacket pocket. Last of all he took the cigarette from his mouth and carefully put it out on his heel.

'Mr Dorman is here,' my aunt announced. 'You'll have to organise yourself!'

Mr Dorman was compact and shiny-faced. His short curving fingers were orange with nicotine. Aunt Irene showed him into the front room, fussing, opening the door and then stepping aside to let him enter. She was nervous and deferential because he was a professional man.

'And how is Leonard?'

'Oh, he's been applying himself.'

My aunt touched the back of my neck with her fingertips so that I squirmed slightly. She smiled shyly at Mr Dorman. I sat on the piano bench with my back to the locked keyboard, my exercise books on my lap. I felt more at ease like this than sitting in one of the deep leather armchairs.

'I'll bring you some tea and biscuits,' my aunt said.

Mr Dorman spread his hands. 'There's no need, really. Especially not the biscuits.'

'Nevertheless!' Aunt Irene said.

She went towards the kitchen, leaving the door slightly ajar. Mr Dorman sat down on the bed-settee, sighing as the springs took his weight. He stood his pigskin briefcase between his feet.

'I take it that your mother isn't at home, Leonard.'

'No, at work.'

Mr Dorman sprang the catches of his case and took out a packet of cigarettes. I passed him the ashtray from the top of the piano. He nodded towards the instrument's ebonised cabinet.

'Do you play at all, Leonard?'

'No, Mr Dorman. I'm not musical.'

'That's a shame, Leonard. It's a wonderful thing to have an instrument.'

Mr Dorman took his reading-glasses from a felt-lined case and hooked them over his small ears. The bridge had been broken and repaired by a wad of Sellotape which shone like polished amber between his eyebrows.

59

'Shall we make a beginning, Leonard?'

I passed him my six red exercise books.

'Have you any idea when you'll be returning to school?'

I shook my head. 'The doctors won't say.'

He nodded, turning the pages of the books. 'You must place your trust in your doctor, Leonard.'

He leafed through each book in turn, bending closely over them, breathing smoke from his nostrils. He flicked spent ash into the glass ashtray. When he was finished he stood them in a pile on the arm of the couch. I looked through the net curtains at a lorry parking at the kerb opposite. The driver applied the air-brakes and then jumped down from his cab. Mr Dorman cleared his throat to show that I should pay attention.

'Are there any particular problems?' he asked.

'No,' I said.

He put on a look of surprise. 'None at all?'

'No, Mr Dorman.'

He looked at me through his spectacles and then took them off. 'Always remember that maths and English are the foundation of your future progress, Leonard. Everything else you can catch up with later.'

'Yes, sir.'

He turned to the side to pack the things in his case. As he moved he made a rubbery squealing sound on the leather of the couch.

'Well, are you going to show me out, Leonard?'

'There's still the tea,' I said.

He laughed as he walked to the door. 'I make five or six calls in the course of a morning, Leonard. If at each one I drink a cup of tea . . .'

'That would be six cups,' I said.

Mr Dorman hurried along the hall to tap at the living-room door with his fingers. My aunt and he talked quietly for about five minutes. I waited near the front door and could not hear what was said. My aunt touched her hair nervously. When he said goodbye to her she did not smile but only ducked her head.

I unlocked the door with the key on its twine and held it open for him. He turned to me on the step. 'Some boys use illness of the body as an excuse to neglect the mind, Leonard.

You seem to have avoided that pitfall so far.' He adjusted his collar and then tugged at his jacket. The smell of tobacco was released from the folds of his clothes.

'Well, we'll say goodbye for now, Leonard.'

I shook his orange fingers and closed the door. Through the mottled glass panels I could see him leaning against the entry, putting on his cycle clips.

'You wouldn't think a fellah would be capable of a thing like that,' my mother said. 'Especially not that particular thing.'

She whispered in my aunt's ear and then took off her coat but not her overall.

'Not that especially,' my aunt said, nodding.

'What thing?' I asked.

'You'd be surprised what a fellah could do,' my aunt told my mother.

My mother laughed. 'Well, you are the expert on fellahs, Irene.'

'And what do you mean by that?'

'What's happened?' I asked.

'One of the patients,' my mother said. 'He *bumped* himself.'

'Bumped?'

'Bumped himself off. It's the full moon, you see: you have to be careful.'

Aunt Irene nodded. 'You have to watch your step with it, Leonard.'

'Only you can't tell him about the moon,' my mother said. 'He's the expert on that!'

'But what's happened?'

'It was in the toilets, the gents . . .' my aunt said in a whisper.

'A fellah wouldn't do it in the ladies, Irene. And spare him the details.'

'Mr Dorman called,' my aunt said with a smile. 'He was asking for you.'

My mother poured herself tea. She watched the cup fill with a look of disgust. 'Those tubby little fellahs with small hands and feet! And when he looks at you it seems he has no eyelashes or just something like pig-bristles.'

'He's a chain-smoker,' I said.

Aunt Irene pulled a face. 'There's nothing fouls the air like stale tobacco. I had to open the window after he'd gone. He didn't want his tea, either.'

'Well, what did he say?' my mother asked impatiently.

'Only that Leonard was making progress.'

'Everyone makes progress. It's where you end up that matters.' She stared at me as she eased off one shoe and then the other. She let them fall under the table. 'Do you know where you might have to go, Leonard?'

'Yes,' I said.

'Well, where then?'

'You shouldn't ask him that,' my aunt said.

My mother lowered her chin. 'He must tell us. He must speak it out, you see. To make sure that he understands.'

She stared at me until I felt myself start to tremble.

'Only don't make him say it!' my aunt pleaded.

Seven

The Poles fled war, tyranny and an increase of gravity. They set out from the Baltic port of Danzig, threaded the oily straits between Malmö and Copenhagen and sailed for Skagerrak and the North Sea. They stood in their coats and round caps on the deck of a steamer with rust-red sides, feeling the clanking beat of the engine through their thin-soled shoes. The black smoke from the funnel barrelled over their heads.

Once a week or so my aunt walked me to the chemist's to be weighed. She guided me, serious-faced, across the wasteground and around the corner. She paused to adjust the set of her scarf and coat. The shop was faced in slabs of black stone as shiny as glass with the name incised in gold letters which seemed to be sunk below the surface like something bright seen under water. I could see the back of the scales set against the window. They were taller than a man and pillar-box red.

Mrs Column smiled at us from behind her displays. My aunt pulled off one glove but not the other. I watched her as she bought a card of perforated curlers and then a small piece of pumice stone. The pumice was a kind of aerated volcanic lava and the same stuff as the luminous rays which stretched for hundreds of miles across the moon's face. At the chemist's it was an off-white chalky-looking stuff with shiny flecks. My aunt used it for smoothing the skin at her elbows.

Mrs Column smiled at me as she wrapped it up. 'Well, he looks well!'

'Would you say so?'

'Only he hasn't much colour to him.'

My aunt nodded. 'He's very fair, you see. His skin has what you call a fine grain.'

I started to fidget.

'One thing is, he never stops moving,' Aunt Irene added.

'I think mebbe he's bashful,' Mrs Column said.

'Yes, he can be nervous in human company.'

'But we shouldn't speak of him as if he wasn't there!' Mrs Column said.

I said nothing but looked at the advertisements for laxatives and hair-lacquer.

My aunt paid for her purchases and dropped them into her bag. 'Anyway, Leonard, shall we see what you are?'

Mrs Column opened the hatch of her counter. I stepped up on to the rubber mat of the scales. The platform shifted on its rollers.

'You'll have to stand stiller than that,' Mrs Column told me. 'So that the instrument can come to rest.'

I could see my face in the mirrored front of the scales. A round window at the centre showed silver weights connected by a mechanism of hinged rods and gleaming blue-brown springs. My aunt peeled her other glove and unglued a coin from the palm of her hand. It left a small impression.

Mrs Column smiled. 'You'd think it was a gold sovereign, Irene!'

'I'm terrible for losing things,' my aunt said. 'You can have no conception.'

She dropped it into the slot. The scaled band spun quickly into a blur at the edge of the mirror and at the same time the silvered weights sprung apart on their hinged spokes, stayed at opposite sides of their circle for a second and then came together again with a noise like a musical chime.

'That means it's all balanced,' Mrs Column said. 'If you step off now, Leonard, it'll print the card.'

Aunt Irene sighed and pointed to my feet. 'He should have slipped off his shoes. Now it won't be right.'

'Shoes don't weigh much, Irene: you can always take off a couple of pounds.'

I stepped down on to the bristly green carpet. The scale spun back to show zero again and there was a vibrating thud inside like metal meeting metal. Then a small grey card flipped into the slot at the front. I took it between finger and thumb. My weight in stones, pounds and fractions of a pound was printed in bright red ink. Quickly I turned it over and read, *Our misfortunes are often blessings in disguise.*

'You'll be down to nothing soon!' Aunt Irene said.

'It doesn't work like that: it makes a curve, not a straight line. It might approach zero but it never gets there.'

She shook her head. I could see that she was nearly in tears. 'Your mother's right in one thing,' she said. 'You're too clever for your good!'

We crossed the wasteground in front of the old typewriter factory, cutting between the parked lorries. The damp mist had condensed into rain and a small smoky fire was burning against the blind side-wall of the building. Men in long overcoats stood before it, warming their hands at the tepid blaze. As we went past one of them lifted his head to squint at us and then started to laugh and beckon, as if he wanted to share a joke. He came towards us with an off-balance walk. His shoes were broken and laceless, dragging across the wet gravel. The front of his coat hung open on a shirt and torn trousers.

Aunt Irene caught my arm. 'Don't look: he's indecent! Don't let him catch your eye!'

The man called out to us but only a mush of noise came from his mouth. The fire crackled and gave up oily smoke.

'Never speak to those!' my aunt warned, tugging at me. 'They want only the price of a drink. Any kindness you do them goes to waste!'

She pulled me away from contamination. The rain was in our faces and twisted stubs of iron pushed out from below the ground, threatening our ankles. The man shouted at our backs until he started to cough. Now that we were so clearly running away the other men around the fire started to jeer and whistle. We came to the kerb and were forced to stop while a removal van went by, labouring up the slight hill towards the main road.

I pulled back my arm to break my aunt's grip. The men were losing interest in us now, arguing and laughing among themselves.

'They are *lunatics*, you see,' my aunt said. 'Worse than the ones at your mother's work because at least those can be

65

helped. Some of those were clever people to begin with: teachers and professors. Until they went mental.'

'*Mental*,' I repeated. We crossed Rosetta Street and walked towards the house.

'It's these Sputniks that have turned people's minds,' my aunt said.

'It's got nothing to do with that!'

She held her collar against the damp. 'Everything's funny now: look at what the weather is like! When they land on the moon then the world will end!'

I didn't answer. It was only the simple truth. I felt the pierced stone in my pocket and then the smooth card from the weighing machine. Ahead of us a lorry was reversing into a parking spot outside the Belle Vista. The driver leaned out from his cab, looking behind as he backed into the space.

'Only look how our hedge is dying,' Aunt Irene said. 'Ralph says it's too much rain.'

Then she frowned and pointed. I heard a high-pitched buzzing in the distance and looked up the damp length of the street. A jiggling column of darkness was coming towards us along the crown of the road.

'It's those lads!' my aunt said excitedly. 'The Polish lads, Leonard!'

The buzzing and rattling grew louder and I saw that it was a man in a black helmet and dark clothes on some kind of skinny motorbike. When we were almost at the house he raised his hand and called to us, turning sharply towards the kerb. The grind of the engine stopped and he coasted towards us in silence. The bike wobbled as it slowed. He grinned at us from behind his goggles and then pushed out a foot for balance. He walked the machine the last few feet to the kerb, his long legs astride it.

'Your mother says they're both on that thing sometimes,' my aunt whispered. 'They must be a menace!' She pursed her lips. 'I forget which one is which now: they have only *nicknames*, you see. They're foreign and their real names would break your jaw!'

The Pole was buttoned into a one-piece outfit of dark material with a greasy shine to it. It was studded at the breast with

66

enamel badges. He wore no gauntlets and only a pair of shabby grey plimsolls. He nodded at us and then hooked out the sprung stand of the bike with his toe and jerked the machine upwards and backwards until it stood leaning at the kerb. I saw how its engine steamed in the rain. A squashed cardboard box was roped with hairy string to the rack behind the long seat.

'Hello missis! And mister.'

The bike had a smell of petrol and hot rubber. There was a symbol on the petrol-tank which I did not recognise: a blue tilted bomb with feathered wings. I knew from that it was a foreign make. The Pole swung down one leg and stood fiddling with the strap of his helmet.

'This is Leonard, Eileen's son,' my aunt said.

He pushed his goggles above the peak of the helmet and then tugged it off. He had a smooth pale head with tight curls of dark hair at the side. He wiped one of his hands over his belly and held it out to me. His smile made deep lines at his cheeks.

'The son of Eileen,' he repeated with a nod.

'And you're Wally,' my aunt said with a trace of a question.

'Unfortunately not, missis! My name is Oscar.'

He took the flat of my palm briefly between his finger and thumb. There was dirt in the creases of his fingers.

'So I'm bringing some clothes, missis,' he said.

'I am a *miss*,' my aunt said. 'My sister might have mentioned where we keep the key.'

The Pole made a diving motion with his hand.

'You've got the idea of it!'

The Pole smiled at me as she bent to push her hand through the slot. His long teeth had spaces between them. He turned back to his bike and began to untie the cardboard box, hissing to himself as he plucked at the string. I went closer to the bike and squatted down to look at the engine. It was clicking as it cooled and a drop of black oil had collected under the curve of a pipe. It dripped on to the road and I touched its warm dark circle.

'He dawdles,' my aunt said at the door.

'But nothing holds him for long,' Oscar said. He carried his box up the steps. I rubbed the tips of my fingers together to get rid of the oil and followed him inside.

'Now did Eileen provide you with a key?' my aunt asked before the door of the middle room.

He nodded and took a tiny silver key on a ring from one of his pockets. He unfastened the padlock and slipped it off.

'You'll have to buy one of your own soon,' my aunt said. 'That particular lock belongs to the house.'

'Yes, missis.'

'*Miss*.'

The Pole nodded and let his eyes half close. My aunt stepped past him and opened the door with a bump of her elbow. Through the opening I saw one of the prints of Africa in its dark frame. More cardboard boxes were already stacked against the wall.

'I hope you'll find it suits.'

The Pole squeezed in sideways carrying his cardboard box. 'It's very welcome to us, missis.'

'Things are hard abroad still, Leonard. Things were hard here and are just getting better. We had to finish Hitler and then there was rationing for years.'

'The Russians finished the war!'

'Mebbe they did and mebbe it was when the Yanks came in. We were all allies then. We squeezed him from east and west, you see. He'd what you call *overreached* himself.'

I heard the Pole opening one the french windows to let in air. The room still had its sickly smell of bleach.

'They're moving their things in slowly,' Aunt Irene said. 'But they haven't much. Their names are not their real names. Those have more letters than the alphabet! I've not met the other yet. Your mother tells me he's a dummy.'

'Dummy? You mean he's deaf and dumb?'

She nodded. 'If he's deaf or not I don't know, Leonard. Only that he doesn't speak.'

'Those two are clucking over the Polskies like a pair of hens!' Ralph said.

He lay on his couch reading. On the cover of his magazine a woman in a lemon-coloured bra held a tiny black pistol. The sloping skylight let through just enough light and then a cloud passed over and woolly darkness welled from the corners of the room. He had kicked his slippers off and the slack end of a sock hung from the toes of one foot. His other, leather foot was bare.

'Poland is an ally of the USSR,' I told him. 'Part of the Warsaw Pact.'

'The communist bloc, you mean! Not that they had any choice after the Russians sent in the tanks, or was that Hungary?'

'They were liberated from the Nazis!'

Ralph laughed unpleasantly. 'They found they'd exchanged one dictator for another. No wonder they're coming over here! Those Poles are camped in the middle room now and the Rinses' nose is out of joint!'

'Their nose,' I said.

'And that pair in the back are at it like a pair of bunnies.'

'What are bunnies at?'

He ignored me. 'That lass is never twenty-one for all her make-up! There'll be trouble in this house: you don't need to be psychic.'

He shook his head. I strolled over to where the aircraft hung on their threads from the sloping part of the ceiling. He had finished the Messerschmitt and arranged it at a diving angle.

'One is deaf and dumb,' I said. 'They call him Wally.'

Ralph laughed. He nodded as if he had expected this. 'And the name of the other?'

An impulse made me want to keep it secret. 'He told me but I forget.'

'You forget?'

'It's a foreign name.' I looked at the tanks. The fish circulated restlessly in their murk with sudden eddies and quickenings in their movements, as if they were being chased by something invisible. Ralph sniffed and turned a page of his magazine. *Diary of Hitler's child-bride. As used by sportsmen and naturalists.*

'You should chuck those fish,' I said. 'My mother says they're unhealthy.'

He didn't bother to look up. 'What does she know about health? Because she works in a bloody hospital?'

The woman on the cover held the miniature gun in both hands. Her breasts pushed from the top of her brassière and her mouth was red and frightened so that you wondered if she'd have the nerve to shoot.

'It's only a nut-house anyway,' Ralph said.

'*Mental hospital*. I have to borrow another candle.'

He pretended to be surprised. 'I gave you one only a week ago!'

'More like a month! Besides, I need two. For his birthday soon.'

He sighed and shut his eyes. 'Birthday, is it? Then mebbe you should send him a card.'

'I don't know where he lives.'

'Well, that's no obstacle: you just write, *Care of Kremlin, Moscow*. If he's so famous here he must be well-known over there.'

'He'll have his own place somewhere.'

'Better than this dump, I bet.'

'They named a town after him: *Gagarin*. The place he was born.'

'Like Milton Keynes? Maybe he lives there.'

'Then there's Star City where the cosmonauts train . . .'

Ralph leaned back, losing interest. 'So he's lucky then: he can have his bloody pick!'

I opened the glass doors of the wall cupboard. The inside smelled of dry bread. I took a fresh candle from the box.

'I didn't say you could help yourself,' Ralph said. 'You take things for granted.'

I lifted the front of my sweater and dropped the candle into my shirt pocket. He watched me, frowning.

'Why do you put it in there? You're the kind of person who is naturally secretive.'

I sat down in the armchair. The light changed quickly until it was almost dark. Ralph read on by the glow of the two fish tanks, making noises in his throat. He pinched his nostrils between finger and thumb. I heard a noise above and looked up to see the pale belly of a pigeon through the wired glass of the skylight. It disappeared with a circular flap of wings.

'Why don't you fix that window, Ralph? So that you could open it.'

'Why should I open it? What's there that's outside?'

My mother blew out her breath and put down a suitcase fastened by a thick leather strap. She pushed her fist into her side.

'You must have listened to me struggling with the thing!'

My aunt raised her hands. 'I had no idea, Eileen. You should have called to us ... And who does that belong to?'

My mother shook her head. 'Let me catch my breath before the interrogation!'

She took off her coat and overall. For two minutes she drank tea in silence as if she had earned her peace. My aunt went over to the suitcase. She lifted it an inch and put it down again quickly.

'You see how it's heavy!' my mother said.

'Why, the bottom's nearly out of it, Eileen!'

The suitcase was made not of leather or card but of some kind of tea-coloured matting. Pieces of it pushed out like ends of straw. I could see that the clasps were broken so that the belt was the only thing keeping it closed.

'It's some of their things,' my mother said.

My aunt looked horrified. 'I couldn't carry that a yard, Eileen! And you shouldn't cart their stuff for them.'

'He's working tonight and I said I'd take it back for him. I was given a lift anyway.'

Aunt Irene shook her head. 'You shouldn't be so obliging, Eileen. They're *foreigners*, you see. They might start expecting us to fetch and carry for them.'

She stood staring at the case. A break at one end had been repaired by a patch of black insulating-tape. 'You can judge a man by his luggage,' she said.

My mother sniffed. 'Years ago, mebbe. Now people are fortunate to own a cardboard box.'

'Does it belong to the dummy one?'

'As the other one is here already ...'

'But you said he asked you. But how can he?'

'He talks with his eyes, Irene, and his hands. You have to use your understanding.'

My aunt looked at the case as if she would see inside to its contents. I stared at it too. The fact of belonging to a man who could not speak gave it a special weight and strangeness.

'So what was the matter with their last place?' my aunt asked suddenly.

'What place? They've been laying their heads where we keep the bedding!'

'Why, Norris told me they had a room somewhere!'

'It was a room. Besides, what does it matter?'

'Why, it puts a different complexion,' my aunt said. 'I would have had second thoughts. Mebbe you've all deceived me!'

'Deceived or not, they're here now: they've given me a fort-night in advance,' my mother said.

Aunt Irene looked shocked. 'Then where is it?'

My mother laughed. 'Don't be so mercenary, Irene! I'll give you it in a minute.'

She went on with her supper, chewing her sandwiches slowly, dipping their corners in the pickle on the edge of her plate. My aunt could not seem to settle but paced about the room picking up small ornaments and folded pieces of paper. She nudged the suitcase with just the tip of her toe.

'We can't leave this in the middle of the floor. It'll have to go into their room.'

My mother put down her cup so that it made an off-key musical note with the saucer. 'You can't just *barge in*, Irene. The fellah might be in bed by now.'

'His light's still on.'

'Or he'll be having a wash or something.'

'Then we'll leave it just outside the door.'

My mother rolled back her eyes. 'Where people would fall over it?'

'What about us falling over?'

I put down my book and got up from the table. 'I could move it.'

I tested the weight of it. The handle was a single leather strap. The contents shifted as I lifted and I thought I heard the chime of glass.

'*Yes?*' Oscar asked.

I opened the door just a fraction.

'Please,' he said more loudly.

He sat in the easy-chair under the ceiling lamp in a part where the shade did not make a shadow. The shade's hanging fringes gave the edges of the room a ferny shadow which moved slightly in the draft from the door. The packing-cases were still stacked against the wall. The Pole had taken off his motor-cycle outfit and wore slacks and a bleached vest. He was barefoot, his ankles crossed.

'Leonard,' he said, as if it were a word it intrigued him to pronounce.

I edged in with the suitcase and put it down against the skirting. He did not rise to help but laid a book cover-up on his lap. The blood tingled in the tips of my fingers.

'So his clothes are here but not himself!' the Pole said. When he raised his eyebrows the skin of his forehead formed a ridge like the edge of a close-fitting cap.

'My mother brought it.'

He nodded. 'She's a kind woman. Is your aunt as kind?'

'I think so.'

'You think so? Well, that's good news, Leonard.'

He caught his nose between his finger and thumb and tugged at it so that it made a loud crack. He leaned back, his hand resting on the book he was reading. It had a shiny plastic cover, black and grey. I tried to read the title. Usually I could read things upside-down but some of the letters were written peculiarly.

'There's a library nearby for the Polish seamen,' he said. 'And this book is a *roman*, a romance.' He put his head to one side. 'Which is not to say about love but means really just a story.'

I nodded. 'So I'll go now,' I said.

The Pole sat with his eyes half closed. 'Do you read a book sometimes, Leonard?'

'I prefer non-fiction.'

'Non-fiction?' He frowned. The creases went from the bridge of his nose to his shining scalp under the light.

'Books which give you facts.'

He pursed his lips, thinking for a second. 'You see, Leonard,

73

with a book like this, a story, you sit in your chair and underneath the world turns one way and you turn in the other ...
And your thoughts turn in a third.'

I felt confusion come over me. 'Yes,' I said.

'You should remember this, Leonard. About the purpose of
a book.'

Oscar nodded to himself, watching me. I started back
towards the door which I'd left a foot open. As I turned away
from him I felt something in my ears like drums beating without noise, a disturbance in the air which made no sound.

Eight

Gagarin passed the night before his flight in one of three wooden cabins grouped in a grove of poplar trees. He and his understudy Titov lay on narrow cots in the single room. The radio played softly, folk music and popular orchestral, but the men were already asleep, breathing soundly, their faces towards the ceiling of birch-bark. Mission director Anatolevich stood outside the lit window with its small rustic panes and gazed in at the young men. He lit up a cigarette of powerful Caucasian tobacco and paced the cinder path which ran between the cabins, raising invisible dust, turning on his heels again and again. He paused to consult the luminous dial of his watch and heard a sound above him. It might have been a night-flying bird or the settling of a bough but suddenly his heart began to beat strongly, in a series of shocks, battering against the wall of his chest. He glanced up and saw that the stars were just visible through mist beyond the tops of the trees.

Susan stood in the angle of the hall below the big electric meter. I heard the hum as the notched disc spun above us. She put her finger to her lips. Except for her elaborate pile of hair she was my own height. She carried about with her a system of very fine invisible wires which brushed me gently at a distance and made a spark and a small flow of current. I had just returned with the dog and I held on to the lead as if it were an earth. The dog lifted his head and coughed. His sides trembled. The dog smell lifted from him in a body.

She smiled around her finger and signalled upstairs with her eyes. I heard my aunt talking with the stops and chokes in her voice she made when she was angry or upset.

'It's those on the landing,' Susan said. 'Your auntie's laying down the law!'

She touched my shoulder for a second, laying on only the polished tips of her fingers. She had on a pale blue dress with short sleeves and a broad shiny white belt fastened with a silvery clasp. She rubbed her bare arms to smooth the goose-flesh. I knew she must mean the Rinses.

We listened together, staring up into the twist of the stairs. 'There's no need for language!' my aunt called with her voice shaking. 'I'll give you language if you like!'

Mr Rinse's voice was quieter, so that you could hardly hear. 'You make me forget myself . . . Only a saint wouldn't swear . . . And she's not a well woman . . .'

My aunt said, 'Why, I'm ill myself, Wilf. With all the worry over this place!'

Susan put her mouth only an inch from my ear. Her breath was sweet and powdery. 'And *she'll* be listening, you see. But she lets him do the work!'

We listened to the argument above us. A loose banister rattled as the voices came around the bend in the stairs. 'She can hardly breathe some nights,' Wilf was saying. 'If you could listen it would break your heart!'

'You shouldn't laugh, I know,' Susan said.

She rocked her body, holding herself. I started to giggle too, until I couldn't stop. I let go of the lead and the dog ran the length of the hall and scuffed his paws against the living-room door. Wilf was coming downstairs now. Susan held my arm just above the elbow. My eye caught the shine of the lacquered buckle of her belt.

'The room is no business but my own!' Aunt Irene called down from the landing. Her voice was stronger now, as if she knew she had won. Mr Rinse stopped on the lower flight. It must have been his dinner break because he had on the sagging dark suit he wore for work. I could smell the oils and varnish which saturated the stiff cloth. He looked at me and quaking Susan directly. His round dark eyes were sad as a dog's. He lifted his head and called upstairs, half to my aunt and half to his hidden wife.

'When I get home we're packing our bags!' he called. 'We're *going*!'

He stamped down the rest of the stairs and passed us without another glance. Susan was still having trouble controlling her breath. We stared at one another, afraid to turn. I heard Mr Rinse swear to himself as he fought with the lock. He slammed the front door behind him. The draught of it whooshed through the house and then there was silence, though there might have been a noise behind it like a ringing bell.

Susan took her hand from her mouth and let go of my arm. There was a numb place where she had held me and then the blood began to move. Her made-up eyes were still bright and excited. I saw that the curve of her lashes did not end but just became fine and intangible. I dropped my glance. She wore no shoes and I could see her small bunched toes through the smoky nylon of her stockings.

She put her hand on her chest. 'All for that poky room!' She opened her eyes wide and then smiled to herself, showing the tips of her teeth.

'*She'll* have put him up to it! He won't do anything by himself, you see: he's the sort who only wants a quiet life.'

'He said they were going,' I said.

'And you were listening?'

'Why, the poor lad was just in the hallway,' Aunt Irene said.

My mother shook her head. 'They'll never leave this place, Irene. They've become *familiar*, you see. They wouldn't know where else to go.'

'He was raging at me. He clenched his fists,' my aunt said.

My mother laughed at this. 'Raging or not, you're twice his size!'

'Oh, I wasn't afraid, El. It was just shocking behaviour in a man.'

The Rinses were quiet after that. Their room was closed like an egg with something developing. I listened for voices and silences. Muriel gave me a sad smile when we passed on the landing but did not speak. She sighed as she shuffled to the bathroom in her loose slippers. The Poles came and went, working a complicated system of rotating shifts. I did not see them but only sometimes in the early hours heard the squeak of their padlock.

My aunt and mother conferred in the master bedroom. They sat at their table in the Albemarle and cautiously laid dominoes. Betty Guisewood sang at the hissing microphone. Mrs Kruger pounded the Bechstein, round-shouldered, her broad bra-strap showing through the lace material of her blouse. The night shift from the dairy stood at the bar in their white jackets, laughing and joking, a swift drink and then back again.

Raffle Night. 'Help the cure for cancer!' The moon almost full with the line of shadow passing through the Sea of Crises. The fat shine of it under clouds. The hens made soft night-time noises and gave off their smell of burning feathers. They scratched and called as the moon came fully out into an opening. I saw a man sitting with his legs drawn up, his back to the rockery against the side-wall of the garden.

It was the other one, the dumbo. He stood up, rubbing at his knees. He had a cigarette in his hand. He was much shorter than his friend, about my height or less. I knew it was him from his appearance of foreignness, though it had a familiar side which I could not place. He stood out of the moonlight in the shadow of the bushes. He flicked ash from the bright end of the cigarette.

'Hello,' I said.

He lowered his chin to me. I remembered then that he could not speak. I'd forgotten only for a second. Instead he started to cough, putting his fist to his chest and making a hacking sound. The white shape of his face was like having a word on the tip of your tongue. He looked at me crosswise for a second, squinting as if he was troubled by a bright light. The moon slipped into a cloud so that only the edge of it was visible and then it cartwheeled out from the other side. The hens squabbled, stirring their smell. Wally made a noise in his throat, half like a laugh, and raised his hand.

I felt my face turn hot. He stared at me, holding something up to the light between his finger and thumb. I took a step towards him, peering at it. It was a smooth egg with a froth of feathers.

*

78

I waited in my room. The moon went behind the houses. It felt like little hooks freeing themselves from my skin. Gagarin aimed his narrow test-pilot's stare and the shadows of the craters swivelled. Sea of Crises, Ocean of Storms. Only a short time seemed to pass until I heard the noise of the key as it was withdrawn on its twine. I sat up. The flame of the candle was withering in the bottom of the saucer, choking on its wax.

I stepped to the door as the candle failed. The light lurched about for a second and then the shadows collided. A greasy smell seeped into the air. The lino was cold against my feet and I could feel the icy heads of tacks.

I stood listening as she climbed the stairs. I waited for the flick of the switch on the small landing outside her door. In the 40-watt light her hair would be coppery and loosening from its grips.

I thought of this as I kneeled in the dark. I pictured her coat of imitation ocelot, the smoke-coloured stockings with the dark seam at their backs. Her face was turned half towards me as she looked for her key in her white leather bag. She lifted it to the Yale, stretching slightly, raising one heel so that her foot slipped half out of her patent shoe. I thought of this in anticipation. I held my breath and leaned towards the eyepiece of the lock.

A mist of rain fell on the garden. The sky withdrew until it was distant and white.

'They had a row. At work. She took a taxi home.'

'A taxi! He's no right making her upset.'

'Mebbe he is more upset than she,' my mother said.

My aunt scoffed. 'You mean that he is sensitive?'

'A man suffers in silence,' my mother said. 'Like a dumb animal.'

'A lovers' tiff, you see! They'll be billing and cooing tonight.'

My mother shook her head. 'He looks at you like something in pain. He holds it all in. He has those dark eyes that make you shiver.'

Jeff and I walked through the streets of warehouses. I waited while he lifted a leg or stopped to sniff among the bruised fruit.

The old smooth cobbles broke through the tarmac of the road. Crates and sacks were stacked in rows along the kerbs, attracting clouds of small agitated flies. The warehousemen laughed and called behind the darkened entrances. Radios played the same song. A forklift high with onion sacks manoeuvred from a side-street. Something bounced from the roof of the cab and went to pieces in the gutter. The driver swore and turned in his seat to spot the culprit.

I led the dog into an alley guarded by bollards. The sky shone above the river at its narrow end. Jeff began to whimper and tugged me towards a long shape lying half in water. I shortened the leash and pulled him by. The light caught the oily top of the puddle and I saw the blind nose of a rat.

The river was oil-coloured with a glassy belly as if it were straining upwards against the tension of its surface. A green municipal caravan was parked half over the kerb of the embankment, its back doors open. A black kettle stood above a flaring gas-ring just inside. Men were filling sacks from a slipping hill of sand, working without urgency, pausing to talk and ease their limbs. The storm-gates of the pier were already closed. The dog faced the water, forelegs braced but his hindquarters nervy and skittish. He lifted his muzzle to test the dangerous air.

'Hey . . .! Hey Leonard!'

I turned around. Fat Derek was standing by the glass front of the Marine Café, calling to me with his hands around his mouth.

'*Leonard . . .!*'

When he saw that he had caught my eye he began to beckon urgently. I thought of walking on but then knew that it was already too late. I went towards him, dragging the nervous dog. When I was a few yards away a man in a tea-stained apron stepped out of the door of the café. His face was red and shining. He made a grab for Derek's arm but he dodged away, laughing. The man pointed at him with a shaking finger.

'When I get you I'll kick your arse!'

Derek sneered from his safe distance, hands in his pockets. The men had stopped work to watch, laughing and leaning on their shovels. They cheered and whistled as he started a twitching dance, raising his arms, shaking his fat hips. Jeff began to growl. He rolled back his eyes with their ghostly rings. A small old woman with white, close curls like the head of a cauliflower looked around the edge of the café door. She had round, colourless eyes in a net of wrinkles. She stared at Fat Derek's belly-dance and then at me, curling her lips. She reached out and tugged at the sleeve of the man.

'Don't upset yourself, Jack! You'll make no impression on these hooligans!'

I felt myself blushing. I turned my back and walked away with the dog. Fat Derek had already dodged ahead. He signalled to me from the other side of a hill of sand. When I looked back the man had gone inside and the door was swinging shut. A cat slept behind the café window with its back pressed against the glass.

'His tea's like piss! He makes it twice from the same leaves!'

Derek drew on a stub of cigarette, holding it carefully between his fingertips. As we walked by the newspaper stand he pointed to a magazine in the rack.

'Look at the tits on that!'

He smiled at me sideways when I didn't respond. Then he squatted down to stroke the nervous dog. I stared at the folds of fat on the back of his neck. The stone was in my pocket, heavy against my thigh. The dog started to growl like a quiet engine.

'What's its name?'

'Jeff,' I said.

'That's not a dog's name!'

'That's what he's called.'

He stood up. He pulled a face and rubbed his palms on the belly of his sweater. 'Its back's full of scabs!'

'It's only losing its hair,' I said.

'*Yeah*? Are you sure it doesn't have lice?' He laughed with the side of his mouth. 'So did you find your shoe then?'

I decided to play innocent. 'What shoe's that?'

'What shoe!' He grinned. He drew on his cigarette. It was now down to an impossible length, only a scrap of damp paper and tobacco between his fingers. 'You never found it then?'

'No.'

I started to walk on but he followed me, pretending to be surprised. 'So you couldn't find it . . . And I didn't even chuck it far!'

'It went into the bushes.'

'I'd have found it for you if you'd asked me!'

'Only you ran off,' I said.

He kept pace and then overtook me. He shook his head. 'Only cause we were late for something.'

I didn't answer. I pulled the dog after me.

'Look!' Derek said.

He stood in my way so that I was forced to stop. He pointed ahead, wrinkling up his face. There was a line of warehouses with their windows blocked with corrugated iron and then the entrance to the old dock.

'Do you want to go in there?'

'What for?'

He kicked at some loose grit. When he blinked the dark line of his lashes was almost lost in his fat face. 'Just for a walk, say. Or I might want to show you something.'

He put his hand on my shoulder but I twisted away. The dog skittered sideways to avoid my feet and gave a snapping bark.

'It's nervous that dog!'

'Only because he's not well.'

'They bite when they're nervous!'

'He never bites because his teeth are rotten.'

He kept his eye on the dog. 'So are you coming, then?'

'Why should I?'

He smiled to himself as if he thought I was afraid. I had taken the stone from my pocket. It was the exact size to fill my fist without being seen.

'You're not coming then?'

'No.'

He let his eyelids droop and then slowly turned his back on us. With his shuffling walk he started across the road. The entrance to the old dock was guarded by a chain looping between leaning iron stanchions. He straddled it and stopped on the other side to look towards us. He beckoned with a jerk of his chin and when I did not respond he shrugged and walked on, his shoulders rounded, his hands bunched in his pockets. His back signalled contempt and indifference. I watched him until he disappeared between the walls of the tall buildings.

The men were working on the jetty again. The scrape of their shovels came back off the river, charged with distance. Jeff fidgeted, crooning to himself. My hand that held the stone began to tingle as if I were gripping it tight enough to stop my blood. I wound the lead around my other fist and stepped from the kerb.

We cut between the warehouses to the disused quay. Long weeds with small yellow flowers grew from below the shuttered windows. The arms of winches angled from the upper storeys, frozen with rust. Fat Derek grinned back at me sly-eyed and then broke into a weaving footballer's shuffle, his fat sides shaking. He kicked something flopping into the air and spun around, his arms raised.

'*GOAL!*' he screamed. '*YESSSSS!*'

I looked ahead. The boneless body of a rat lay in the gutter. Jeff whined and lunged forward against the tightness of the lead.

'There's a *million* of the bastards!' Derek said. 'The council try and poison 'em but there's always millions more.'

He slipped ahead of us again. We came out on to the dockside. Its stone blocks were set with iron rings rusted solid at different angles. You had to be careful where you put your feet. A vinegary smell came from the trapped water. It had a grey film of dirt and then oily colours below.

'That bollicking boat!' he said.

'What boat?'

He pointed with his toe.

'It's a barge,' I said.

He rolled his eyes. 'I know it's a barge. Doesn't matter *fuck*!'

It angled out from the side on a fat cable tied to one of the rings by a fraying knot. It was narrow and low-sided. Its hold made a long pit in the water.

'You *lost* it then?' Derek asked.

'Lost what?'

'Your *shoe*. You lost your fucking stupid shoe, stupid!'

I felt his spit strike my cheek. He stared at me with his mouth half open. He pushed his hand into his pocket.

'You smoke fags?'

'Sometimes.'

'What do you mean *sometimes*?'

'I mean only sometimes and not others.'

He let his jaw hang as if I'd said something stupid. Then he took out an oblong tin and worked at the lid with his nails. When the seal was broken he pushed it towards me. In the silvered inside I saw a pinch of loose tobacco and a few flattened cigarette ends.

'Do you want some?'

'No thanks.'

'No thanks!' he mimicked, making his voice go high. Then he started to look half desperate. 'Look, you said you smoked!'

He held the tin closer to my face. The butts were dark with spit and strands of pale tobacco pushed out of their ends like the hair from old men's ears. Derek pulled out some cigarette papers from a compartment in the tin's lid.

'A fellah gave me this. He said I was a *cunt* to smoke . . . Look, I'll roll you one if you like.'

'It's okay,' I said.

He looked annoyed again. 'What do you mean it's okay? You mean you don't want one?'

'No.'

He nodded, still delving into the tin. There was a little wad of silver paper. 'My mother knows yours. She asks things about her.'

'What things?'

'Things like, does she have a fellah?'

The barge swung towards the side so that I could see down into its hold. There was dried mud at the bottom with thin weeds growing through it. Derek pointed.

'You can find things on them. Brass and bits of scrap. It's worth *money*. The wood's rotten sometimes: you kick it and it just falls to bits.'

He stepped closer to the edge and leaned over. A black iron ladder was set close into the side of the dock.

'We could go down there.'

I watched him as he rolled a cigarette. His fat fingers and curving thumbs seemed expert. He put it in his mouth to light

84

it. His face swelled with pleasure as the tab started to draw. He looked into the tin again, searching through it with the tips of his fingers.

'Look, you can have this if you want!'

He unrolled the ball of silver paper and took a grey pill between his finger and thumb, holding it up to me. It was thick and glossy-faced, about as wide as a pencil. A line scored across its front divided it exactly into two.

'What's that for?' I asked. At this time pills meant only medicine to me.

He lifted one shoulder. 'It just makes you feel *okay*. Don't you want it?'

'No.'

'We could split it,' he suggested.

'No.'

He clicked his tongue and let the pill roll down into his palm. 'She says things go on in your house anyway.'

'Your mother does? What things?'

He turned away, secretive. My hands were full with the stone and the dog. He spun back quickly and slapped my mouth with his open palm. I felt the pill on the back of my tongue and had to swallow. It was a hard-edged gob travelling down. The dog reared up, pushing against my leg with its front paws.

'Makes you feel fucking *okaaaay*!' Derek shouted.

He opened his mouth to laugh and I hit him with the stone. Then I had to let go of the dog so that I could uncurl my fingers from it. They tingled. They were striped red and white like meat. Fat Derek dropped the tin so that it spilled its tabs. He went down on one knee, bending slowly over, his hands covering his face.

'You've put my eye out!' he complained.

'I didn't even touch your eye!'

'You have, you bastard! You've fucking *blinded* me!'

He started to sob. The barge swung towards us with its cargo of mud. I put my hand on his shoulder but he shrugged me off. The dog started to bark and dozens of gulls flew over my head. They circled the dock, screaming, as if they were unable to settle, as if the water had turned too tight for them.

85

I was sick by the side of the Pilot Office. I put my fingers in my throat while a lorry upended another load of sand on to the promenade. The sand kept its shape for a while and then slipped forward with a hiss. I seemed to bring up nothing but water. The dog lapped, whining, its tongue curling back. On its pale upper surface I saw for a second the pill with the line on its front. Then it disappeared.

Nine

The dog paced between the living room and the kitchen, panting and rolling his eyes, his sides twitching. Aunt Irene sat at the table, co-ordinating the rent-books with the picture calendar.

'That animal is heading for a fit, Leonard.'

She closed the calendar and hung it back on its hook. The dog turned in the kitchen and came back into the living room.

'Do you think it's pining for something?'

'I don't know,' I said.

The dog lifted a hind paw to scratch itself in front of the fire. Aunt Irene slipped a rubber band around the rent-books and snapped it into place.

'I'll show you something,' she said.

'What?' I asked.

She stared at me. 'Never mind *what*! *What* is uncouth.'

She followed the dog into the kitchen and came back with the cycle lamp and a small black key on a loop of string. I knew it was the key to the cellar.

'Is it the water?' I asked.

Jeff came back into the living room and blundered against her legs. She laughed. 'This animal will wear through the rug!'

The cellar door swung inwards over a flight of wooden steps. Even before she shone the lamp I could smell the water in the darkness. Jeff sniffed and whined. We had shut him in the living room.

'*There*!' she said. She was proud and aghast. In the light from the lamp the water was clear for an inch, and then a milky yellow as if clouds of fine powder were floating just below its surface. The clouds had a slow movement to them, a change and turning of shapes. The water was deep enough to cover the lowest of the cellar steps, and as I watched it withdrew a fraction and then slipped forward again. It must have been a foot higher during the day because there was a brown tidemark like a coastline against the whitewashed bricks of the wall.

'It must be six feet deep!'

'More like three,' I said.

'You must always contradict!'

An iron rail was set into the brickwork, running down into the water. I pushed beside Aunt Irene so that we both stood on the small platform at the top of the steps. The lamp made the surface of the water shine and light was reflected up on to the walls. The cellar ran part of the length of the hall and then beneath the Poles' room. Something big and striped was floating belly-up just under the water.

'It's like nothing in memory,' Aunt Irene said. She clicked her tongue and pointed the lamp at the floating thing. It disappeared at its edges so that you could not see its exact extent. There was another dim shape floating below it at an angle.

'They're coming up for air, Leonard: those old mattresses! They've been down there since the war. Your mother and I never wanted to touch them!'

We watched as the first mattress began to turn in the slow current of the water. It released a flock of sliding grey bubbles. A corner of it pushed above the surface for a second, the slick cloth shining. The lower mattress caught its agitation and began gently to swivel beneath it.

'You'd think they were dancing wouldn't you? We carried them down with a couple of camp beds. In case of the bombs. Your mother barked her shin and you should have heard her swear! But that was wartime for you.'

I climbed down a couple of steps. Closer to the water the air was cool and smelled faintly of metal polish.

'Eileen says there'll be rats,' she warned.

'They'll all have drowned by now.'

She shook her head. 'A rat will swim for miles! Nothing will kill it except poison.'

She nervously shone the lamp into the angles of the walls. I went down another step.

'Think of what might be floating there!'

'It's only water.'

'Come back up, Leonard!'

She took a step down towards me. I was standing just above the water now and I squatted down, holding on to the iron rail. I glanced back at her over my shoulder. Her face was narrow and tight above the lamp. I turned to the water again and stretched out my arm until I touched its surface with the tip of my finger. It was not as cold as I'd expected. My shadow stretched as my aunt pointed the lamp. I heard her nervous breath above me.

The high tide meant that the powers of the sun and moon were in alignment. In the early hours Norris and Susan kissed in the light from the landing. He wore his narrow dark suit. He pushed his hand into her hair to loosen it. She whispered and searched for the key in her red bag. He put his lips to the side of her face. She leaned back her head. He spoke to her slowly. Her tortoiseshell clip slipped on to the collar of her white coat.

Jeff guarded the body of a rat in the dusty corner by the rockery. Saliva rattled in his throat and his eyes were dark and hot-looking. Their white circles appeared clear and shining.

'An animal is *savage*, Leonard! All its instincts are that way and even if it tried to be different it couldn't be. Some people are the same.'

My mother made sandwiches in the kitchen. She slipped thin square slices of ham between the halves of buttered bread. This was for work, where she would never touch the canteen food after an outbreak of amoebic dysentery. She cut the sandwiches into quarters, pressing down the blade with her thumb, and wrapped them in a brown paper bag and then in plastic. I went back outside. The window of the upstairs flat was open and there was a radio playing inside the rooms. The dog toyed with the dead rat, growling and raising dust.

'He's still playing with it!'

I looked up from the square of grass as Susan crossed the dimness of their bedroom. Her arms were round and freckled, darker than her face. A bracelet shone as she closed one half of

89

the window. She kept her eyes averted from the garden and the busy dog.

'You'd eat a rat if you were starving,' Norris predicted.

'You think you're hilarious. Only other people might not!'

The radio went louder. Norris stood bare-chested at the window, dabbing at himself with a white towel. He rubbed his palms together and then smoothed back his hair with them. He saw me and winked, making his long face lopsided. His eyes were small and bullety without his glasses.

The flood was gone by the afternoon of the next day. It left just an inch of pale mud on the floor of the cellar. Norris and one of the Poles, the tall one, went down with a paraffin lamp. They manoeuvred the saturated mattresses up the steps and then through the side-door into the yard. The mattresses had turned the colour of dark tea. Their covers tore under the strain of handling, and grey ticking gone to paste spilled out. A brown shower flew up slower than water when the men threw them down on to the paving. The second mattress fell edge-wise, rolling over the first and lying across.

Aunt Irene watched from a safe distance. She kept her hands clasped over her belly.

'We'll get the council to dispose of them, Leonard. A health hazard, you see.'

I watched the Pole as he lit a cigarette. He let the match burn on for a couple of seconds, frowning into the flame. He wore his motorcycle jacket with the enamel badges and the waxed fabric was shiny with wet. Behind them the curtains were still drawn across the french windows of his room. Drops of dirty water made tracks down the glass.

'Have you seen the other one?' Aunt Irene whispered. 'Or rather, you never do . . .' She laughed. 'He's what they call the sleeping partner.'

'*Wally*,' I said.

'Take them some tea,' she said. 'The Polski doesn't take sugar.'

She tipped three spoonfuls into Norris's mug. 'You can't fathom a man not taking sugar,' she said.

'It might be his health.'

'You can see he's as well as anything.'

She went over to the kitchen cupboard and took down a flat bottle from the top shelf. She flicked back the cap.

'Johnnie Walker,' I said.

She took a tiny nip herself, closing her eyes. Her lips seemed to just touch the mouth. Then she added some to the tea and handed me the mugs. 'Don't tell them. Let them taste it first. That way it'll be more of a treat.'

I carried the tea out to the garden. The whisky sweetened its steam. Norris and the Pole had scraped the mud into buckets and were now digging it into one of the dusty borders. They worked in their singlets, two bony men of a similar build, although the Pole was taller. The sun was out, its heat concentrated by lenses of bottom-heavy cloud. My aunt had released the chickens into their wire-netting run.

'Our Leonard,' Norris said.

Oscar nodded. He stared at me for a second and then reached between his feet for a fistful of mud. He held it out as if he wanted me to taste it. It glistened and I caught the saline whiff of it from three feet away.

'Like the Nile,' he said. 'That was the wealth of the Pharaohs.'

He rubbed the mud between his hands and let it fall in sparkling flakes.

'Oscar here will blind you with science!' Norris said. He sniffed at his tea. The lenses of his glasses were specked with mud. 'It's got a dot of whisky, I think.'

Oscar sipped, closing his eyes. 'You must thank your mother,' he said.

'My aunt,' I corrected.

He nodded. 'Believe me when I say you have two mothers.'

Norris looked between us and then sat down on a flat stone of the rockery. He clasped his hands together and flexed his arms until their joints clicked. His shoulders were made up of sliding hollows. 'This one is also a reading man,' he told me.

Oscar smiled and then frowned, seeing something. He squatted to pick at the turned soil and held up a broken piece of crockery, part of a plate with blue figures. The broken edges were stained dark from the soil. He brushed the dirt away with his thumb and studied the pattern.

Norris looked at it over his shoulder. 'You can find all sorts if you trouble to look. Things that go back years. I found a pair of old dentures once. They were human teeth set in leather. It makes you sick to think. Things that are buried work their way back to the top, you see.'

Oscar did not seem to be listening. He threw the fragment into the hole they had made. They finished their tea and started to dig again, turning the wet mud into the soil of the border which was half dust and stones. They had tipped the last bucket when the Pole stopped and raised his hand.

'This'll be another of his ideas,' Norris said. 'You wait and see.'

We watched as the Pole crept towards the dog with long-legged stealth. Jeff was sleeping with the dead rat almost between its paws. When the Pole was a yard away it began to whimper and twitch.

'It chases rabbits,' Norris said. I saw the shine of a gold tooth at the side of his mouth.

Oscar very slowly bent and delicately took the tip of the rat's tail between his finger and thumb. He straightened slowly, staring at the dog. Jeff's eyelid fluttered but it did not wake. The nose-heavy body of the rat hung like a pendulum from the Pole's fingers.

'The poor dog's lost its dinner!' Norris said.

'It wouldn't have eaten it,' I said. 'Only played with it.'

He put his hand on my shoulder, staring into my face with sad, magnified eyes. 'It was still its dinner.'

Oscar strode back across the garden and flicked the long body of the rat into the remaining hole. Then Norris and he set to work again, turning the soil quickly and energetically as if they wished to finish. They laughed when the blades of their shovels clashed.

'You can't argue with compost!' Norris said. 'You could grow anything on this spot only now it would have whiskers.' Then his eyes went sharp. He nudged Oscar's arm and nodded towards the house. 'Your other half is about!'

I looked along the yard. The curtains of the french windows were still closed but the light was on behind them.

'He makes his *toilette*,' Oscar said without bothering to

look. He began to flatten the soil with the back of the shovel. It rang against a stone. The noise seemed to take flight, travelling the length of the garden to collide against the walls of the surrounding houses. It seemed magically amplified.

Norris put his hand to his ear. 'Somebody's impatient!'

'Talk of the devil!' she said.

I knew at once that it was Fat Derek's mother. She had the same build and a smooth face as if it were blown up from behind. She stood in the hall just in front of the open door, blocking the light with her body. My aunt stood before her in her Paisley housecoat.

'What can you mean the devil?' Aunt Irene asked. She looked very slight against the woman's big arms.

'I am Mrs Dolbey,' the woman said. She pronounced every word so that there would be no mistake. 'Your lad has blinded my son.'

She sighed and changed her position slightly, turning more to the side as if the sight of me pained her. She wore a short beige coat with blue buttons. Three gold rings on one hand were sunk into the flesh of her fingers. My aunt turned to me but with her hand still holding the edge of the door.

'Did you do this terrible thing, Leonard?'

'No,' I said.

'Are you sure? Mebbe it was just a lark.'

'I didn't,' I said.

Mrs Dolbey pointed at me. 'He's *lying*! You've only to see his face!'

Then she stood waiting, her big arms folded. Her fingers plucked at her elbows. Strands of rusty-red hair had escaped from the tight band of her cap.

'It isn't like him to tell a lie,' my aunt said. 'Not when we've brought him up to be truthful.'

Mrs Dolbey clenched her fists. 'My son's face can't lie if it wanted to! His eye is out to *here*. His father took him to the infirmary last night and he might have to be operated on!'

'Poor lad,' my aunt said.

Mrs Dolbey took the chance to push against her. She reached past to snatch my arm but I dodged further down the hall. The door to the middle room was open and the dummy stood in the doorway in a pair of grubby striped pyjamas. He made as if to step out into the hall but then hung back. One of his eyes was still closed with sleep and he stared at me with the other one, half turned. I knew him by something this time, something that I saw in him at once, like a picture making itself before me.

My aunt and Mrs Dolbey struggled in the doorway for a minute. My aunt hung on to the handle and Mrs Dolbey could not break her grip. After a minute she stepped back and disengaged her arms. She looked towards me. Her big face was red. My aunt swallowed to recover her breath.

'There's half a dozen fellahs I could call!'

Mrs Dolbey laughed. 'I'm certain that there is! But don't worry cause I'll not touch him. I only want him to tell the truth. Well, what is the truth, sonny?'

I looked towards the Pole again. He was standing near to me now but the miraculous resemblance had disappeared. Fat Derek's mother stared over my aunt's shoulder and gave me a sad, clear look.

'His face is as good as an admission!' she said. Then she stared past me at the Pole. 'Is this his dad?'

'How can it be his dad?' my aunt said. 'This gentleman is working nights and you've disturbed him.'

'Then mebbe I should speak to his dad.'

'His father is dead,' my aunt said quietly.

'And you're his mother?'

'I'm his aunt but I've nursed him from a baby,' my aunt said. 'I know that he's as mild as a lamb!'

Mrs Dolbey shook her head. 'According to my Derek's eye, he's a bloody savage!'

'That lady said you were handy with a stone.'

'A pebble it might have been,' my aunt said. 'Besides, you can't credit her.'

'You could let him give an answer, please!'

She waited. 'It was more a pebble,' I said.

'*Speak up*!'

'Between a pebble and a stone,' I said.

My mother nodded. 'Ah, you see, we are getting somewhere now.'

'The lad is only upset,' my aunt said.

'He can't hide behind himself all his life, Irene.'

'What do you mean *behind himself*?'

'That is the lowest form of deceit,' my mother said.

I felt the tips of my ears become like hot coals.

'He stole my shoe,' I said.

'What?'

'He stole my shoe!'

'The sort of low behaviour they have,' Aunt Irene said. 'God knows what kind of fellahs they'll turn into.'

'The lad's eye!' my mother said. She sat down at the table. She had not unbuttoned her coat and the blue hem of her over-all showed underneath. Aunt Irene leaned over her with her palms on the table. She spoke softly close to her ear.

'She'll be exaggerating, Eileen. She'll want money from us, that's all.'

'Only what if she goes to the police, Irene?'

My aunt blew out her cheeks with almost a raspberry noise. 'That sort will never go to the police! You see, they have too much to hide.'

'But then if he goes blind?'

'Blind! He'll have nothing but a black eye! Besides, I'd stick up for the lad if he was a murderer!' She closed her eyes for a second and then leaned over my mother more closely, as if she were shielding her from my sight. 'He's going for his check-up tomorrow. We can't have him upset.'

'If he can injure people then he can go on his own.'

'I will then!' I said.

'Why, I'll go with him,' Aunt Irene said.

'No!' I said.

'No,' my mother repeated softly.

Aunt Irene shook her head. 'You would turn against the lad.'

'Only he's disappointed me,' my mother said.

'You'd want him to stick up for himself.'

'Only not like that.'

She stared at me over my aunt's arm. Her eyes were shiny like the silver-white shine of fish.

Two men fought on the wasteground, waving their fists in wild arcs, their feet splashing through water, their long coats encumbering their legs. For no reason one of them fell on to his hands and knees in the dirt. When he tried to get up he could only roll on to his side. He lay half in an oily puddle, growling in frustration. His opponent laughed and there was a cheer from the other men standing close to the blank wall of the warehouse. One of them kicked a bottle and it rolled from him in a curve.

I turned around and saw my aunt. She was already crossing the street towards me, carrying her tartan shopping bag. She pretended not to see me, staring towards Mrs Goffrey's hotel where a group of men were standing outside the doors. I ducked between two parked lorries. When I reached the pavement there was already a queue of about twenty people in front of the bus stop.

I joined the end. I knew that my aunt would be crossing the wasteground, passing close to the drunken men. I kept my eyes to the road. The 43 came after about five minutes and I found a seat upstairs near the front. The air inside the bus was steamy and smoky and the windows were blanked with wet. I cleared a small circle with my finger, just big enough to see through.

She was standing near the back of one of the lorries, her bag in one hand, the other hand hanging loosely down. She looked towards the bus as it drew away from the kerb. She was surrounded by shining pools of water. The two men who had been fighting stood a few yards behind and to the side, close together so that their shoulders were almost touching. My aunt peered at the bus, frowning. She turned her head to follow as it left the kerb and angled out into the road. But her eyes were always missing me. The men watched her, smiling.

We stood close together in the lift. Dr Munro smiled at a woman who had straight light brown hair and a square face. She did not smile back, only blinked her eyes. A little girl of about eight stood in the corner, leaning back against the wall

96

and staring down at her feet braced against the floor. Her hair was tied back and her white ears were veined with purple. She sniffed when she saw that I was watching her and I saw her nostrils open and then close.

The doctor saw her first. I waited on the bench, my hands in the pockets of my coat. It was cold. After a couple of minutes a mouse came up the corridor, keeping itself close to the wall. It seemed to vanish for a second and then I spotted it running along the bottom of the door opposite, changing its direction as if searching for a way through. I got up to look closer but this time it really did disappear. I spent a minute looking but couldn't see where it might have gone. When I went back to the bench I found that by sitting sideways on its end and leaning forwards and down I could see through the keyhole in Dr Munro's door.

At first there was nothing but the corner of the doctor's desk. Then the girl stepped across it. She was dressed only in green pants and I saw her thin arms and the knobbly line of her backbone. The pale shapes of the bones moved under her skin.

I took my eye away. The doctor was talking but I could hear only odd words. Eventually the woman and the girl stepped out of his office. They walked by me without speaking. I stood up. As they walked towards the lift the woman held the girl's hand very tightly in her fist, holding it in the air so that the arm was stretched upwards, the girl's fingers bunched together in her fist.

He weighed me on the machine. The numbers flicked over and then stayed still. I dressed again in front of the electric fire.

'You're alone today, Leonard. Isn't your aunt at home?'

'No,' I said.

He looked at me as if he were about to ask me another question but then only nodded. 'I'll give you a note for your mother. I take it that your father is no longer present.'

'He's dead, Doctor.'

He looked down quickly at his papers. 'Oh, I'm sorry, Leonard. You see, I formed the impression that he was only absent.'

I stared out of the window while the doctor wrote. He

breathed quietly down his nose. There was a white sky with a thin dark cloud like a bar stretching across it. Dr Munro's pen scratched and squeaked as if he were rapidly covering the paper but when I turned around there were only a few large words sloping across the page.

He smiled up at me and then folded the note twice and slipped it into a shiny brown envelope. He drew his tongue along the flap and sealed it and then sat for a second with his pen poised above the envelope's blank front. He did not write.

'Was the girl ill?' I asked.

'Which girl?'

'The one who was here.'

He shook his head. 'Not really ill. She has a similar problem to your own, Leonard. You see, it's no longer quite so uncommon.'

Ten

I held the envelope up to the sky while I waited for the bus. The sun came out from a cloud and I could see the shape of the words under the brown paper. The queue began to push forward as the bus arrived. The conductor counted heads as they stepped between the folding doors. He stopped me with a palm against my chest as I mounted the step.

'Sorry, son.'

'Let him on!' a man called from behind. 'He's hardly a half!'

The conductor lowered his hand. There was already a press of people in the aisle. When the bus began to move I was thrown against a woman's side. She gave a little cry and then laughed, glancing at me sideways.

When the conductor came I could not find the money.

'Where are you going to, son?'

'*Town*,' I said.

'All the way? That's sevenpence, then.'

He waited with his fingers on the keys of his machine while I searched through the pockets of my duffel-coat. I found a stiff handkerchief and bus tickets from previous journeys. I was hot suddenly.

He leaned to look at me closely. 'Are you okay, son?'

'He got on at the hospital,' the woman standing beside me said. 'He doesn't seem steady on his feet.'

They both stared at me while I pulled different objects from my pockets: a fluffy throat pastille, a rubber in the shape of an emu, the broken end of a pencil. I felt a sweat break out over my body like tiny pin-pricks.

'He's not well,' the woman said loudly. 'You can see that!'

The conductor stared at me. 'Are you feeling okay, sonny?'

'I think so,' I said.

'You don't feel sick, do you?'

Some of the other passengers began to turn around in their seats. I felt another flush boil up into my face. There was a hot glob of something in my throat which prevented speech.

The conductor rolled back his eyes. 'You shouldn't board a bus if you're feeling poorly! You ought to consider other people!'

There was a shrinkage away from me among the people standing in the bus. The blood burned in my face and my eyes were watering. The conductor reached out and pulled the bell-cord three times. The bus squeaked to a stop alongside a line of parked cars and after a second the middle doors folded back. He guided me towards them with his hands on my shoulders. 'Make way!' he called. 'This lad is ill . . . You'd be better off walking for a while,' he said in a quieter voice. 'And it's not even far now. Do you know where you are?'

I glanced out at the cars and nodded. 'Yes.'

'That's a lad!' He kept hold of my arm as I climbed down from the platform. 'You take deep breaths as you're going along and you'll feel right as rain. When you're sure you're better then you can catch another bus.'

He stepped down to guide me to the kerb and then got on again and quickly rang the bell. People were twisting their necks to look at me through the windows. The white hand of a baby was spread against the glass. The bus drew away with its doors still open to let in the air.

Inkerman Street. The sign was on the side of a house. I knew the way home from here, or at least the general direction. As soon as I began to walk I found the change in my pocket, slippery silver and copper in the folds of my handkerchief, there suddenly with the contrariness of dumb things. Further down the street I saw an archway between two houses with a board painted in glossy black above it. One of the double doors under the arch was open on a dark entry. *Spearpoint*, the board read. *Undertaker*.

Spearpoint. I liked the sound of the word and repeated it to myself as I went along. A shiny hearse was parked facing me on the other kerb. I could see the dark shape of the driver behind the reflections in the windscreen. His window was wound down a couple of inches to let out cigarette-smoke. The street was quiet except for the passage of traffic on the main road. A ginger tom lay full-length on a windowsill, sleeping with its head on its paws. There was a smell of damp coal and then the street took a sudden right turn and the houses on one side were replaced by an embankment with steep allotments behind a chain fence. I knew that my way lay on the other side of the track and looked ahead for a footbridge. A white enamel bath stood upright as a sentry against the wall of a shed of old doors and corrugated iron. Beside this a man sat on his chair reading his paper, holding it out before him. He looked at me over the top of it as if he were about to say something. A train was coming slowly up the line, a squat diesel pulling a string of black shuttered carriages. It passed over his head with a hollow racket of wheels.

When the last carriage had gone he raised his hand and pointed after it. His unfastened cuff hung loosely from his wrist. A dozen yards away a pair of striped bollards guarded a wedge-shaped cutting in the shelf of the embankment. He grinned at me and nodded. Then he turned back to his paper, ducking his head as if he wanted to avoid being thanked.

'Thanks!' I called, all the same.

I reached the tunnel as the last noise of the train died. Sloping walls of grey concrete converged to a vacant half-circle the height of a tall man. The air inside was cold so that I could see my own breath. The floor was broken into loose chips of gravel and the curved walls were lined with green tiles, a wet shine to them. A bulkhead light burned at the mid-point of the roof.

At the other end identical bollards stood before a dome of green space. The playing-fields opened out with their low fringe of houses, odd lights already in their ground-floor windows, the lamps along the road coming on. A kids' playground stood to one side of the exit. The sandpit was flooded at one corner and beads of water shone on the ironwork of the rides. A small cabin stood to one side of the swings, like a sentry box with a sloping iron roof. Its door was padlocked and the shutters were up on the windows. I walked past it carefully. I noticed that it was slightly out of vertical to its concrete base. There was space inside for one man standing.

I heard a high shout. A boy of about my age was racing across the fields on his bike, standing over the saddle, his knees pumping. I watched him as I passed between the threepenny-bit and the copper belly of the slide. He called again, raising his arm, signalling ahead of him. His tyres left a dark line across the grass. The tarmac of the playground gathered to a path pointing between swan-necked lamps towards the houses. I could see more kids now, about half a dozen of them running in a close group about fifty yards from me. They laughed and shrieked as if they were delighted or afraid.

A woman stood against a tree, so still that I hadn't seen her, dressed in a plaid headscarf and a green raincoat belted against the air, waiting while her dog squatted straddle-legged at the side of the path. She nodded her head towards the excitement. 'That bugger'll kill somebody soon!'

She was about forty or fifty, a strong, frowning face. One lens of her spectacles was blanked with a circle of white cardboard. She held on to the slack lead and nodded towards the dark moving shape of a motorcycle. It was speeding along the fringe of the field close to the houses. Its rattle and chatter carried on the wind.

'He's *barmy*, you know! He's a regular nutcase!'

She gave me an expectant look. When I didn't answer her face fell into a bottom-heavy shape and she turned away, grumbling to herself and pulling the lead tight across her body. The dog was dragged behind her, scattering dark berries of turd. I walked on but she called to me, nodding towards the commotion. 'Hey, they say he's a bloody *German* or something!'

She pointed as the kids screamed and scattered. The motorbike had turned and was heading across the grass towards them, its engine barking as the rider changed gears. The boy on the push-bike appeared again, pedalling hard, his breastbone almost touching the handlebars as he fought the drag of the mud. He looped towards the path of the other rider, anticipating his line until they were approaching head-on. The other kids were younger, the boys still in short pants. Their voices were like a nail on glass. The motorbike rider sat up-right, short-bodied. He did not wear a helmet and I saw the flying ends of his pale hair. I was so sure that he was about to hit the cycle that I closed my eyes. When I opened them a second later I saw the motorbike leaning into a curve so tight that it almost slid on to its side. Its tyres scooped up mud and turf. The rider brushed the ground with his foot. The engine stuttered for a second and then caught its rhythm again. A cloud of blue exhaust drifted across the field.

He was heading away from me now, slowing, the engine losing its pitch, turning loose and chattering. From its foreign shape I knew the machine of the Poles. The rider looked about, head erect, his arms and shoulders relaxed. He wore a sagging brown jacket, trousers which had ridden up on his calves. I stared after him until he reached almost the perimeter of the field.

'Hey!'

I turned. The kid on the push-bike was freewheeling towards me, both feet on the same pedal. He made a noise in his throat and spat on to the grass. Snorts of excitement pushed from his nose. He jerked his chin.

'Fucking coppers'll have him, you know!'

'Yeah?'

He nodded. 'Yeah! He's a mad get!'

He wiped his nose with the back of his hand. It was Derek's friend from the cemetery, the one he'd called Alec. There was a graze across his knuckles. The legs of his trousers were soaked and splattered with mud. He spat again and looked past me towards the playground. The sentinel box stood among its rides. I wasn't sure if he'd recognised me.

'That bike's *shit*,' he said, nodding towards the Pole.

'It's okay.'

He looked contemptuous. 'It's foreign shit! It's not even Japanese!'

He smiled to himself, half turned away. The angles of his face were strange and sharp, as if it had been broken and put together again. His eyes went narrow.

'Did you *bash* him?'

'Who?' I asked.

'*Who!*' He looked away again, sneering. 'The *fat bastard*! Did you give him *this*?' He pushed out his fist, punching the air. His knuckles were white and skinny, hard-looking like the ends of bones.

I didn't answer. He shrugged, wrinkling his face. The lines spread from his nose like a map being drawn from the centre outwards. The noise of the motorbike dropped suddenly so that we both turned to look. The Pole glided powerless for a few yards and then stopped, pushing his heel into the mud. I already knew that it was Wally, the short one. He stood beside the bike and hooked out the stand with his toe. He squatted down to poke carefully at the engine. The younger kids were gathered in an edgy group to one side of him. They pushed and dared one another, nervously giggling.

'D'yer know him?' Alec asked.

I nodded. 'He lives in our house.'

He stared at the Pole as if he hadn't heard, his eyes snakish and attentive. I wanted to attract his attention again, surprise him.

'He's deaf and dumb,' I said.

He only rolled his eyes. 'I know he is, shit-face!'

He started to push his cycle towards the embankment. I noticed that he was limping, dragging his right leg. When he was a few yards away he made a noise like a fart with his lips. I walked on, shrugging myself into my duffel-coat.

The light was fading now, darkness lifting from the damp grass like a mist. The Pole had restarted his bike. The exhaust went black and oily as he turned the throttle. The kids jeered and danced, keeping their distance. He grinned towards them and slowly remounted, swinging his short leg over the seat. He sat still for a while, revving the engine gently, and then pushed the bike forward to release it from its stand. The kids gave a shivery wail as he started towards them, slowly at first, trailing his feet for balance, then accelerating. I could see his broad face now and the flop of his reddish hair. His cheeks were smeared with mud.

The kids broke their group as if their safety lay in separation. The Pole seemed as if he were about to pass them by but then turned and chased a couple. He went close to one, kept pace for a while and then reached out with his heel and pushed him gently. The kid slid shrieking into the mud. Wally did not glance behind, heading away from me now. The kids watched him with their breath in a cloud. The one who had fallen picked himself up and wiped at his clothes. His face was white and clenched, as if he was crying. Then I noticed the moon a quarter full and transparent, very small in the sky above one of the isolated trees. Wally turned again, throttling back the engine. He saw me standing alone and gave an open-handed wave.

I held on to the iron struts beside the seat. The roads leaned this way and that. My hands and face were numb in the rush of air and I could feel the heat of the exhaust near my bared ankle. The hood of my coat filled with wind, bobbing behind me like a surplus head. The bike's engine seemed to be eating its own parts in a terrible metal digestion.

Wally turned towards me, grinning from the side of his face. The mud was crusted on his cheeks. The journey had seemed to stretch for dangerous hours but now it snapped back again so that I realised it had taken only minutes. He had cut the engine and we glided towards the kerb.

Rosetta Street was still in forward motion as I climbed down. My legs were stiff and shaking. When the Pole dismounted he was the same height as me or just a fraction smaller. He drew the machine back on to its stand and clapped his bare hands together to restore their circulation. Then he curled his fingers as if he were still working the throttle. He made the wet rattle of the bike in the back of his throat, so accurate and metallic that it surprised me.

I laughed and he seemed shy for a second, smiling down at himself. He aimed a scooped palm to the front door. I climbed the steps and drew out the key on its string. The hallway was dark, with brown light gathered at the top of the stairs. I could tell from the slack feel of the air that my aunt was out. I caught sight of my smeared wind-chapped face in the long mirror of the hallstand.

Wally stood beside his door, grinning at me. His small teeth had gaps between them like the teeth of a zipper. He massaged his face with his palms, dislodging dried mud. The resemblance came and went, one face changing into the other and back. Some of the lines were the same, but not others. The bike trip had left me feeling full and empty at the same time, as though the wind had forced its way inside me. Wally gave his door a blow of the elbow and then pushed his head around its edge. He made a noise in his throat almost like a bark and then stepped inside and reached back to tug me into the room by my arm, as if he were producing a piece of evidence.

The curtains were closed and the light was on. Oscar sat in the bed in his shirt, smoking the last inch of a cigarette. A book rested face-down on the covers. Wally tugged at my sleeve, smiling with his ruined teeth. He waved his hand towards me as if he wanted to bring me to his friend's attention. His throat twitched and he made a small noise like the beginning of a question.

Oscar sighed. 'Because of a shock in his youth he can't speak. Maybe I'll tell you about it one day, Leonard. Meanwhile we have to follow his signs and noises.'

He coughed and laid his hand on his chest. The ashtray on the small table beside the bed was full of stubs. He pushed aside the covers and withdrew his bare legs. He sat on the side of the bed, frowning towards me.

I followed his eyes. My shoes and the hems of my trousers were covered in drying mud and there were long splashes of it on my coat.

Wally whistled and shook his head. He stepped up to the basin in the corner and turned on the tap. He made a face over his shoulder as he let the water run.

'He thinks that the water is always cold here,' Oscar explained. He leaned sideways to look closer at me. '*Ay!*'

Wally began to whistle to himself. The sound startled me, as if a dog had begun to sing. He drew the long notes into trills, some foreign tune. He washed his face and hands and then dried himself with a grey towel. His hands were small and quick-motioned. The other man started to dress, picking his clothes from the floor beside the bed. He tugged on his trousers and fastened the leather belt with a sigh.

'I think we'll make you new again, Leonard!'

He pushed his feet into backless leather slippers. He picked up the book from the bed and showed me the spine.

'I try to train my speech with this. Do you know this story?'
Dombey and Son, I read. 'No.'

He sighed and sat down on the edge of the bed to pull on his socks. They were a net of holes at the toes. Wally leaned against the sink with his arms folded. He'd washed the mud from his face now. Oscar's cigarette had gone out and he relit it with a match.

'So, from where did he kidnap you?'

'I'd been to the hospital. To be weighed.'

He raised his chin to button his shirt up to the throat. I noticed that his collar was frayed at the back. 'It's a special type of hospital?'

'No, what they call general.'

I couldn't help but stare for a second at the face of the other man. When he looked at me curiously I turned my eyes away.

'In our hospital people stay for a week and then for life,' Oscar said. 'So it's more dangerous than general. We have *old* people there. Sixty and seventy. *Ninety*. They suffer from mad-nesses . . .' He laughed to himself, remembering. 'I tell Wally that you watch the moon and he thinks because of this you are a lunatic. That's only my joke . . .'

He laughed. Wally watched us without smiling from the corner of the room.

'Please take off your shoes,' Oscar said. 'If your aunt should see you . . .' The corner of his mouth twitched.

I sat down on a corner of the big bed. The covers had been pulled back to show the striped mattress with its metal buttons. Wally opened the doors of the cupboard under the washbasin and pulled out a red linen bag. He threw it on to the floor close to me. Inside were brushes and a tiny tin of blacking.

'You say polish?' Oscar asked.

'*Polish*,' I said.

He jerked his chin and spoke towards his friend. The other man laughed. For a second he stood at the exact angle of the photograph so that I could almost see the helmet like a ghost-shape around his head. He turned back to the sink and began to soak a cloth under the tap.

'Wally wants to clean your coat. He feels that his poor skills are to blame. He practises only so far with the motorbike,' Oscar said.

I took off my shoes and my coat. Wally turned the coat in his hands to inspect it. A florin fell and rolled curling across the floor until he flattened it with his foot. He laid it on the mantelpiece, above the cold electric fire. The photograph my mother had found was leaning there against the wall. One leaf of the mounting had been torn away to leave a frayed edge of board but I could still see the brown marks where the sprig of lavender had stained the paper. I looked above it to one of the pictures of Africa and saw the Pole reflected as he bent over my coat. He looked up suddenly and captured my eye in the glass.

'Wally thinks that you look at him in a strange way,' Oscar said. 'He thinks that his poor teeth are to blame.'

'There's nothing wrong with his teeth,' I said.

Oscar laughed. He pulled on a seaman's sweater with holes at both elbows.

'The hens have gone off laying: something has disturbed them.'

'Mebbe a cat.'

'A cat with trousers, you see.'

'What do you mean?' my aunt asked.

'A cat isn't partial to an egg,' my mother said. She held out her hand. 'Have you something for me, Leonard? Like a letter or something?'

'It's in my coat.'

'And where is your coat?'

I went outside to the row of hangers in the hall and took the doctor's note from my pocket. When I went back into the living room my aunt was sitting with her chin in her hand. She looked at me sadly. 'You see, people are thieves, Leonard. Like a dog barks.'

'You'll make the lad maudlin,' my mother said. 'And he's enough inclined to that side of things.' She took the letter from my hand. 'Do you know what's in here, Leonard?'

'No,' I said.

'Well, do you want me to read it to you?'

'Not especially,' I said.

She sucked in her breath. 'I'm not angry with you, Leonard. You did a wrong thing but we'll let that pass for now.'

'He was what you call provoked,' Aunt Irene said.

My mother gave her an irritable glance. 'Only we shouldn't discuss that now,' she said. 'The reason I mentioned it was only to get it out of the way.'

'You see, he's the kind that meditates on things and you can never fathom his feelings,' Aunt Irene said. She put her hand on her side and sighed as if she had a pain.

My mother tore open the top of the envelope and tugged at the note. 'Only we can ask him, and draw out the truth!' She turned around to face me, planting her elbow on the table. 'If they wanted you to go in, Leonard. If they asked you. If that was what is in the letter. If you were ill, say.'

'Only I'm not ill,' I said.

'But say you were?'

Aunt Irene walked from one end of the room to the other and came back. 'These questions put a burden on the lad!'

My mother ignored her with a roll of her eyes. She unfolded the note and smoothed the paper with her broad upward-curving thumbs. 'But say you had to go into hospital, Leonard? Say they wanted you to. Only say . . .'

Eleven

I watched Mr Rinse bury the kitten. The sky was covered by felty-grey clouds as if the moon had been mixed to smoothness inside them. The hens made their calls and nervous noises inside the coop. He carried a shoebox towards an unused corner of the garden. He knelt and took a tablespoon from his back pocket.

I could not retreat without attracting his attention. I stood still in my duffel-coat against the back wall of the house. Mr Rinse tugged up some weeds and then began to dig with the spoon, displacing the soil into a pile. The spoon scratched against stones. He shifted position to ease his legs and turned half towards me. I saw the 0 of his mouth. We looked at each other for about a minute and a half.

'Is that you, Leonard?'

When I didn't answer he went back to his digging again. I took the working hunch of his shoulders as permission and went closer. I stood behind him and watched as he broke the soil with the edge of the spoon and then scooped out the loose stuff with his cupped hands. The soil under the ground smelled richly of damp and roots. After a few minutes it seemed a big hole for a small box.

Mr Rinse smiled at me over his shoulder. 'You have to make it *deep*. In case something comes sniffing.

'Is it that cat?' I asked.

'Why, we can't hide anything from you, Leonard! It just caught something and died, you see. You can't expect an animal to live just in a room. Especially a smallish room like ours.'

'No,' I said.

'No,' Mr Rinse said. He frowned.

'Is missis upset?' I asked.

He nodded. 'You'd have to be inhuman not to be.'

He took hold of the box. The white card shone between his dark hands.

'Could I see it?'

He shook his head. 'Well, I don't know about that, Leonard.'

'Only for a second,' I persisted.

He gave a little laugh. 'Okay. Only not too close, in case the fleas jump!'

He lifted one side of the lid so that I could see inside. The kitten was curled tightly in the bottom of the box except for its stub of striped tail which was straight and rigid-looking.

My mother sat with her feet in a washing bowl. Pine-scented steam lifted from the sudsy water. She sighed at the relief. A blue towel warmed on the line above the fire. The dog closed its circled eyes, passing as I watched it into sleep.

'Always be scrupulous about your feet,' my mother said. 'Especially the crevices between your toes.'

'Especially those!' Aunt Irene repeated. 'I'm sure he must know that by now, Eileen!'

My mother took down the towel and dried herself carefully. The water in the bowl was milky with disinfectant. She put her head on the side to listen and then pointed to the ceiling. The shadows moved in the room. The electric light was making a circle on its cord.

'We shall have to speak to him,' Aunt Irene said.

I watched as the lamp made smaller circles. There was the tremor as a door closed upstairs.

'Those black eyes of his,' my aunt said. 'You feel he's capable of murder.'

My mother patted herself dry. 'Not here he isn't.'

There was a loud footstep and the lamp started to swing again. We could hear shouting, two voices.

'He should pull up his socks,' my aunt said. 'Bearing in mind that he's two weeks in arrears.'

My mother listened. Her face was alert and frowning.

'If he hits her then we'll have to say something,' Aunt Irene said. 'If he strikes her, that is.'

My mother nodded. 'If it's a serious clout. Not just a little tap, like.'

'If it's something more than a tap . . . If it's only a tap then it's just between them,' my aunt said.

My mother sprinkled talc on to her toes from the tin and began to massage each one carefully between her finger and thumb.

'But with his big hands he could break her nose or something,' Aunt Irene went on. 'A fellah sometimes doesn't realise his own strength.'

'Or give her a black eye or cauliflower ears.'

'Or break her arm or her leg. Or damage her internal organs.' Aunt Irene turned to me. 'You must never hit a woman, Leonard!'

'Though a woman can sometimes injure a man,' my mother warned. 'They can do terrible damage with their nails. They can put a man's eye out!'

'Or kick him in his weakest spot,' Aunt Irene said. 'But the thing is, I can't understand about the rent. How can they be so far behind with both of them earning? All that overtime and its not as if they drink to excess.'

My mother turned the top of the talc to close up the little holes. 'There's other things besides drink, Eileen.'

My aunt looked interested. 'Oh, and what are those?'

The noise upstairs stopped for that night but then started again on the next. The sisters listened for signs of serious violence. Then there was quiet again until we heard their key in the lock.

Aunt Irene lifted a finger. 'Mebbe they're going out for the night. Leonard, you should take a look and give your eyes a rest from that telly! Don't seem to stare but see if she has any bruises.'

My mother sat at the corner of the table sticking saving-stamps into a small book. 'Oh, he'll hit her where it doesn't show, Irene. Besides, you shouldn't use the lad for your key-holing.'

My aunt stared at her through the mirror above the mantle-piece. '*Keyholing*,' she repeated. 'And what do you mean by that?'

My mother licked a stamp and stuck it in its square. She brought down her fist on the page.

I waited outside the old fellah's door. Susan laughed as she came round the bend of the stairs. '*Don't!*' she said. Her red-brown hair was combed and pinned into a tall column which glistened with shellac under the lamp. She wore her short artificial white fur coat with the square red buttons and then white ankle-length boots with a pierced design at the toes and shiny white enamelled buckles. She paused on the middle steps and smiled at me with her white, even teeth.

Norris reached over her to show his palm to me. 'The man!' he said, grinning. 'The man himself, I mean. The *professor*!'

Susan laughed, looking down at herself, spreading her arms. Norris's glasses flashed. He wore his narrow dark suit and his shirt was unbuttoned to show a thin gold chain and a tiny crucifix against his pale chest. An oiled lock was teased down on to his shining forehead. He gripped Susan's waist with both hands and lowered his face into the angle of her neck. He took a vacuuming sniff and then sighed as if it were a breath of sweet-smelling air.

'The other night,' he said. 'When I saw you with the little fellah. You were both doing some gardening.'

'Mr Rinse?'

'That's right. Husband of Mrs Rinse. He hasn't spoken to us lately . . .'

Susan's eyes were made up with trails of mascara at the end for the Queen of the Nile look. She made them wide. 'Imagine, he's still sulking about that room! The poor fellah thinks we were behind it!'

Norris clasped his hands around her waist. She laid her fingers against his wrist and I saw a single bright-white ray flash from one. This was just after the invention of the laser.

'I don't know why!' Norris said. 'As if we'd put his nose out of joint like . . .' He laughed. 'And that woman is prodding him from behind.'

'Stoking the fires of conflict,' Susan said. 'Though you shouldn't say too much.'

She slid her look along the sloping ceiling above her. Norris put his finger to his lips and looked sly and pleased with himself. They stepped down into the hall. I saw that he was wearing the patent shoes I had retrieved from the garden, buffed until they were brilliant as fresh-poured tar.

'Is there life on the moon?' he asked.

'Not yet.'

Susan pushed her hands into the broad fur pockets of her coat. 'You shouldn't tease him, Norris.' She looked at me shyly. 'We're going dancing!'

'We'll get something to eat afterwards,' Norris said. 'What you call a meal, like. We're *celebrating*, you see.' He gripped Susan's wrist from behind. '*Show* him then!'

Susan struggled against him. 'No need to break my arm!'

'Sorry, I'm sure!'

Norris adjusted the hang of his jacket in the hallstand mirror. He grinned at me for sympathy. One of his big front teeth was chipped at the corner. Susan held out her hand with the fingers limp. The stone shone with its narrow light.

'It's diamond and platinum, Leonard.'

'It wasn't out of a gum machine,' Norris said. He gave me a placid wink. 'If you can't beat 'em then you've got to wed 'em!'

Aunt Irene clapped her hands. 'Diamond and platinum!'

'Then you can forget the rent for another few weeks,' my mother said. 'Besides, she should get it tested: it might be zircon and white-metal.'

She opened the cigarette-box. The chimes played. She took out a cigarette and bent to light it against a hot coal.

'But a wedding in the house!' Aunt Irene said. 'You can't be mealy-mouthed about it. I wish them every happiness myself!'

She stared narrow-eyed at my mother's back.

I had hidden the stone near the wall under my bed, away from my mother's examination. I took it out sometimes to admire its fingernail gloss, the complicated threading of the veins of red mineral. I put my eye to the hole through its centre and watched the movement of candlelight on the lunar formations, the swivel of a mountain shadow, the twitch of darkness in the well of a volcano. I went for walks. I was nervous now of the streets near the river and went instead on slow circuits through the town. I led the dog through the crowds of shoppers. He sniffed at things, as if they were other than they appeared. He groaned to himself and started to stumble over kerbs. One day when we came back the Poles' bike was lying on its side in the road.

'Bike?' my aunt asked.

'The *motorbike*!' I said out of breath. 'It's been in a smash!'

She nodded. 'Ralph says it's a fire hazard. He says it should be towed away. It was the one with the bad teeth. The short-arse.'

'You mean Wally?'

'If that's his name. He goes barmy on that thing!'

'Is he injured?'

'How can you ask him when he can't speak? It is more like shock mebbe.'

'Is he in the hospital then?'

She shook her head. 'I think he's only gone to bed.'

I listened at their door and heard not even breathing. I went outside into the street again. There was broken glass on the road and the smell of petrol. The bike's front forks were twisted and the headlight was smashed. I went closer to look at the speedometer, hoping to read the speed of the crash. The glass was shattered and the pointer had returned to zero. There was a strong smell of petrol.

Aunt Irene watched me from the step. 'Don't go close, Leonard: it might flare up!'

'It's not even smoking.'

'But all it needs is a spark!'

'He must have been doing sixty! Seventy-five!'

'Then that's why he came a cropper.'

'Then he's lucky to be alive,' I said.

She started to look anxious. 'Do you think he might be worse than he seemed? Can shock kill a person?'

I walked around the bike. The broken glass scraped under my shoes. 'I don't know. He should have gone for a check-up.'

'He could have broken his neck and not realised,' my aunt said. 'I've heard of it happening.'

'A hairline fracture,' I said. 'Or mebbe a clot on the brain. He should have an X-ray!'

She twisted her hands together. 'Will you go and see, Leonard? Ask him how he is?'

'He's *dumb*!'

She put her hand to her forehead. 'Well, just go in there and take a peep!'

'But what if he's *dead*?'

The Pole made a frothy sound of breath. There was a sweet smell and when my eyes adjusted to the dark I saw a bottle on the small table by the bed. Wally's head was covered with just his short-fingered hand pushing palm-up above the edge of the quilt. I went closer. His fingers were curled except for the smallest which was pointing towards the head of the bed, trembling slightly against the pillow.

I touched the cold side of the bottle. There was about an inch of drink left in the bottom, a clear liquid as heavy as a lens. Its smell was strong and grainy as if it were constantly evaporating, filling the air. His breath stopped and I waited for it to start again but it didn't. The draught lifted the hem of the curtains and changed the light.

'There's some tea for you,' I said.

The Pole said nothing from under his blankets.

'He needs a doctor's note or he'll get no sick pay,' my mother said. 'Anyone can see he's ill but it has to be in black or white.'

'Black *and* white, Eileen.'

My mother took a slip of paper from the pocket of her overall. 'If he signs this it'll keep them happy for a while.'

'But where's the other one?' Aunt Irene asked.

'He won't be back until late.'

'But it's his friend that's injured! You'd think he'd rush here!'

My mother clicked her tongue. 'He's *angry* with him, you see. With his goings-on. So he'll get no sympathy there. Has he eaten since it happened?'

'Only two biscuits,' I said. 'He even left his tea.'

Aunt Irene lifted the corner of the curtain. 'He has his light on at least.'

My mother poured black tea from the bottom of the pot.

She cut a thin sandwich of ham and pickle crosswise on the plate.

Aunt Irene frowned. 'He might still be in bed, Eileen!'

'What if he is? I see men in bed every day of my life.'

'It's different in the hospital: there's other people about. You'd better leave the door open.'

My mother arranged the things on a tin tray. From the living room I saw her tap on the Poles' door and then push it open with her hip. She disappeared inside. My aunt cleared the table, scraping the plates together, making clicking noises with her tongue. I moved to the couch to be further out of range.

My mother was in the room for about fifteen minutes.

'I think he's starved of conversation,' she said when she came back.

My aunt stared at her.

'I'm joking,' my mother said. 'Only he seemed grateful for the sandwich.'

'It must break his heart,' my aunt said. 'That he cannot express himself.'

'He can make himself understood.'

Floods, wars and accidents you could blame on the moon. You could lay them at its door. I spied at the Pilot Cosmonaut through the shivery tunnel of the stone. I looked at myself in the wardrobe mirror, lifting my arms. The flesh ran from me like water. Wally lay sick in his bed while the men on the wasteground fought and swore. *Lunatics*. Then they made peace and tipped the bottle. The fire shone along its side. *Glug*! *Glug*! *Glug*! The river lifted again and the rats left their sewers. Stars turned. The dizzying, sun-reflecting disc swung into sight like a long shout.

I sat up as the glass broke. The pieces fell through the dark. '*Cow*! *Cow*! *Cow*! *Cow*!' Norris called. Their voices snapped. I got out of bed and stood still, listening. The sisters stirred behind the wall with soft hen sounds and movement. I opened my door and saw Mrs Rinse in her nightdress, standing in a bar of light from her room. She turned to me and smiled. The gas stove scented the air with cold fat.

'There's murder going on,' she whispered.

I went closer to the head of the stairs until I had a clear view of the small landing. Norris's door was closed.

'He's killing her!' Mrs Rinse said.

Mr Rinse stood behind her now in the too-big trousers of his brown suit. His braces hung from their waistband. He rubbed his hands together with a rasping sound. He leaned forward and spoke close to his wife's ear.

'Don't involve yourself, pet. Let the buggers do for each other!'

Things had gone quiet now. The light was on in Norris's room. The gap below his door shone in the dark of the landing. There was a movement above my head. I looked up and saw Ralph standing on the flight leading to the attics. He wore his tweed overcoat over striped pyjamas. He gripped his rubber-tipped stick half along its length, like a club.

Another window burst. The house seemed to loosen around the noise as if a tight cord had been cut. The door of the master bedroom opened and my aunt and mother came swiftly across the landing in their dressing gowns, stepping so close together that they touched at the shoulder and hip, pushing by without a word and leaving a scent of skin lotion.

I saw that my aunt's long feet were bare. My mother wore her fur-trimmed slippers. They climbed the short flight to Norris's door. Aunt Irene searched through her string of pass-keys, sliding them like beads. My mother turned and stared. She frowned back at us so that her eyebrows were a single dark line.

'I'll stay here,' Ralph called. 'For if there's any trouble like.'

She didn't answer but waved her hand, signalling that we should return to our rooms. Aunt Irene had found the Yale key. She turned it in the lock. The light came on in the hall and I looked down and caught the eyes of one of the Poles in the curve of the stairs, I didn't know which. Norris's door opened on a slab of shivery light. The women went inside and shut it behind them.

Twelve

'She's chucked him again: she's playing cat-and-mouse!'

'He has to learn to master his feelings!'

'She gave back the ring. She's flighty, you see, and never twenty-one.'

'He says he had to break something. It was the glass or her!'

'He mortifies his own flesh! His hands are cut to ribbons.'

'Worse than ribbons! But you can't excuse him.'

'I didn't say that word! He must mend his ways.'

'He says he'll fix the windows.'

'Does he? With his hands like that?'

I held the ladder. Wally climbed one-armed, a sheet of glass under his other elbow. He leaned out from the line of the ladder. There was a missing rung and he had to stretch to span the gap. The sun caught the side of the pane and the light wedged along the wall. He carried a claw-hammer tucked into his belt. He whistled to himself, compressing his lips, squeezing out the high sounds. The grazes on his face were healing into scabbed skin.

'It's funny the way he can only whistle,' Norris said.

He pushed glass splinters and chippings of old putty into a pile with the broom, working gently and carefully because both hands were covered to the wrists in a criss-cross of bandages. The Pole reached the top of the ladder and we watched as he balanced the glass on its bottom edge and leaned it into the frame. The silver heads of small nails poked from between his lips. He took them one by one and hammered them with a single blow into the rebate, so that they clasped the glass. When it was secure he took a slab of putty from his back pocket and unwrapped it from its greaseproof paper. He tested its condition with a press of his thumb and,

119

satisfied, started to whistle again, drawing out the ends of the notes into warbles.

'The Polish Nightingale!' Norris said. 'It's a pity he's simple.'

'No he isn't.'

Norris winked at me, a slow slide of lid behind the magnifying lens of his spectacles. 'Simple or not, he's happy as Larry.'

Wally separated a piece of the putty and began to knead it with both hands, pinching off small pieces to press them elsewhere. He made a shape between his fingers, working at it with small gasps of breath, his body jerking on the ladder. He stopped to hold it up to his face, looking at it closely, wide-eyed. He gave it the finishing touches and smoothed it with his thumbs. Then he brushed his lips against it and flung it down. It landed with a smack on a slab of paving close to the ladder. It was a putty-man with a starfish shape of arms, head and legs.

'More tricks than a barrel of monkeys!' Norris said, laughing.

I nodded, watching the Pole. He was making another figure, shaping it confidently as if he had learned from the first. When he had finished he whistled between his teeth and showed us the five-pronged shape and then threw it so that it landed a yard away from the first. This one had the triangle of a skirt. He gave his small-town cosmonaut's grin and then turned back to the window. He squeezed a white worm of putty from his fist and began to press it into the rebate with the back of a kitchen-knife. He smoothed it with the side of the blade and then scraped away the excess, scooping it into his cupped palm. Norris stood the broom against the wall and picked up one putty-figure and then the other, unpeeling them from the paving. He lay one on each palm, staring down at them, blinking behind his heavy glasses. Then as the Pole worked above he started to press the figures together between his bandaged hands. I could smell the linseed oil as he squeezed.

'You see, Leonard?'

'See what?'

'The more you care for someone then the more she's maddening to you. It's the price you pay, like, because everything has its ticket. Do you understand me, Leonard? Do you under-stand what I'm saying to you?'

He rolled the putty between bis palms until he had made a smooth ball. Then he laughed and threw it backhanded into the air. 'Allyoop!' He caught it and showed it to me, holding it between his finger and thumb. It was between a golf and a cricket ball in size. He passed it from hand to hand. The putty figures had lost their shapes so that they were only scorings on its pale surface.

'It was nice out today: it was like spring.'
    'You can never trust it.'
    'They say the year has become unjammed.'
    'I'll believe it when I see it.'
    'You were always a doubter, Eileen.'
    'Life has taught me that.'
    'You think that it's only you?'
    'I think the best time is July myself.'
    'I can take or leave it. But October isn't bad, or May. When things start to change. When there is some movement in the weather.'
    'December can be nice if it's crisp and dry. Then there's Christmas . . .' She sighed. 'Will we ever see snow again?'

The river slipped under the house. It was not as deep as before and had a sour smell. I shone the cycle lamp. The top of the water was yellow and treacherous.
    'It's flooded again,' I told Ralph.
    'Think I don't know? So what's the colour of the water?'
    'Yellow,' I said.
    He nodded to himself as if this were significant. 'I expect the Polskies will be down there.'
    'Only it isn't so deep this time.'
    'That won't deter them! You see, they'll make themselves *in-dispensable*.'
    'Wally fixed the windows,' I said.
    'You see!' Ralph's shoulders twitched. He sat at his table, facing the big tanks.
    'Maybe he isn't a Pole,' I said.

'Then what would he be?'

'Maybe a Russian.'

He laughed. 'One of your Soviets! It comes to the same thing: they're all *Asiatic*.'

'What's Asiatic?'

'You should know these things. They're neither one thing nor the other. They have narrow little minds.' He stared at the fish. The water had grown cloudy again. 'They won't stop moving tonight. They can sense the flood, you see.'

'The Poles?' I asked, to tease him.

'The *fish*, Leonard. Even the bottom feeders. Even those you never usually see. And the rest are in a frenzy!'

He took up his stick and shifted awkwardly from the chair to the couch. He stretched out his sick leg to massage it where the false limb was spliced to the real, pulling a face. 'And I can feel it too!'

'In your foot?' I asked.

He rolled his eyes. 'Foot as used to be.'

'You mean it hurts?'

He considered for a second. 'It isn't what you'd call pain. More a *sensation*, you could say.'

He moved up to his knee, pressing with his fingers and thumbs as if he were searching for points of tension. I watched their movement, the flexing of his hand. I couldn't prevent a question. 'But what does it feel like?' I asked.

He stared at me and then shook his head as if he could not answer. I turned away and walked over to the two tanks. The fish made rapid darts through the brown water. A speckled catfish was climbing the front of the tank, eating a clear trail through the green algae with its pale sucker-mouth like a devouring spiral.

'Like what?' I persisted.

Ralph sighed and leaned back against the creaking couch. 'It feels just like *glass*, Leonard! Like a glass bowl when you ring it.'

I read at my desk: *A space-schooner leaves the orbit of the Earth to begin the long haul to Ganymede, a moon of Jupiter rich in precious ore. Captured by solar-sails soon the radiations of the Sun may be harnessed to provide a means of propulsion on long space-flights. With this bountiful source of energy man may at last be freed from the chains of gravity.*

I heard a tap against my window and blew out the candle. I closed my book and breathed quietly in the dark. I could hear nothing but the faint beat of Ralph's air pump. Another sparrow-beak of gravel hit the glass.

Tap!

I lifted the corner of the curtain and stared down into the street. At first I could see nothing but the tops of parked lorries. The captive water on their tarpaulins shone with the reflections of street lamps. Then Susan stepped back from the path and showed her white face. She beckoned and put her finger to her lips.

Music seeped from below Norris's door as I crossed the landing. My aunt and mother were out. The Rinses slept in their big bed. I went downstairs and opened the front door.

'Is he in?' she asked.

I nodded. 'He was playing records.'

She swore and looked along the street both ways. No one was about. She came up the steps so that we were both standing in the cover of the doorway. She sucked in her lips. 'I have to go, Leonard. I mean, *leave* here.'

'Why?'

She closed both her eyes. 'Don't ask me *why*, Leonard. I have to, that's all. I have to look after myself. I have to get my bag,' she said. 'It's got *things* inside.'

'What things?' I felt mystified and stupid.

She started to bite her lip. 'It doesn't matter what things exactly. It could be keys or money or a letter, say, or just anything which I might need. Isn't that enough? It doesn't have to be something special, does it? I shouldn't have to go through all this, Leonard! You should be able to help without my having to stand here and explain these things!'

'Sorry,' I said.

'*Shit!*'

She leaned against the doorway, tipping her head back. She wore her blue coat with the collar, glossy red knee-length boots which caught the light from the lamps. Her scent filled the entry like the smell of half-sucked sweets.

123

'Is your mother in?' she asked. 'Or your Auntie Irene?'

'They're at the Albemarle. You could go there,' I suggested.

She shook her head. '*He* might turn up. And then everything would happen! He's in love with me, Leonard: he can tell when I'm around. He just *picks* it up!'

'You mean like radar?' I asked.

She stared at me. 'Like what?'

'Radar,' I said.

She put her hands over her face. I thought she was crying but then saw that she wasn't. I could see the shine of her eyes between her fingers.

'Look, I could get your things for you,' I suggested. 'I'll just go up and *ask* him.'

'No, he can be sarcastic when he's in a mood.'

'He seemed okay today.'

She shook her head. 'You can't believe the way he changes, Leonard. He is a sort of Jekyll and Hyde.' She took hold of my arm, gripping it through my sweater, just above the elbow. 'No, I'll send for them tomorrow. I'll just have to walk the streets tonight.'

I knew that had to do with prostitution. *I'd sooner walk the streets*, my mother said.

'We could go to the pictures instead.'

She blinked again. When her eyes closed her long lashes meshed together. 'I've no money,' she said.

'I could pay for you!'

She looked pleased but troubled. 'How could you?'

'I've got some money. I've been saving up for something.'

She smiled. 'But are you sure you don't mind?'

'We could see an X,' I said.

'I'm not sure about that. I'm not watching anything *dirty*!'

'It's not dirty, it's more horrific.'

She looked down the street again. There was still no one around. 'Okay, then, but hurry up! I don't want to hang about.'

I went upstairs to get my coat. Norris's door was open a few inches now. He stood in the light with his back to me, combing his hair with a long steel comb.

*

124

I felt awkward in the lit foyer with its mirrors. The woman in the booth stared at me. 'You're never sixteen, love!'

'Of course he is,' Susan said from behind. 'It's just his fresh complexion.'

The woman laughed and gave me the tickets. The hall was nearly empty and we sat halfway along a middle row. We were late for the start of the picture. It was in Japanese with subtitles.

'It's a kids' film!' she complained.

'It's an X.'

'It doesn't matter. It's still a kids' film.'

We watched the last two-thirds of *Godzilla versus the Thing*. Godzilla was a dinosaur who came from the sea and ravaged the cities of the coast. The Thing was a gigantic caterpillar which hatched from an egg in a mountain valley. The Thing was monstrous but peaceable, vegetarian. It wriggled to the lowlands. Great organ chords sounded as it powered southwards. Meanwhile Godzilla plucked up a locomotive and shook out the people like fleas. He caught them between his opposed finger and thumb and crammed them into his terrible jaws.

The creatures met in an empty baseball stadium outside Yokohama. Godzilla attacked with tooth and claw and the fight was fierce. The Thing at first had the worst of it. It thrashed and hissed and green liquor spurted from its wounds. It fought bravely but its mandibles seemed too weak to penetrate the lizard's crusty hide. Godzilla struck again and again, roaring and salivating. The Thing began to retreat, twisting back on itself to defend its soft body. It was losing strength now and its movements were becoming slower. Suddenly its compound eyes seemed to glaze.

'It's *dying*!' Susan whispered.

I could see that she was moved. Godzilla snarled and beat his breast with his foreclaws. The green blood was gushing from the Thing in a dozen places. Painfully it began to turn until the end of its segmented body was facing the dinosaur. It quivered, summoning the last of its strength. A thick white liquid began to squirt from a kind of nozzle in its tail. The big chords played. Godzilla roared in shock and outrage as the

125

liquid struck his body and turned rapidly into nets of silk. Soon the dinosaur was powerless, suffocating in a white mesh of cobweb. It staggered in a helpless circle and then fell with a great bellow.

I tried to hold Susan's hand but she moved it out of the way. 'I want to *go* now,' she said.

We left by one of the fire-doors and then walked without talking through the town together. People were coming out of the pubs and standing in queues in the fish-shops. Stalls were selling chestnuts and hot-dogs near the station.

'I thought that was *horrible*,' Susan said.

'It's only a film.'

'Watching those poor animals die! Is that the kind of thing you like?'

'It was *Japanese*,' I said. I felt hopeless. I felt like crying.

She stopped near the bus stops. 'I'll say goodbye then.'

'But where are you going?'

She faced away from me, in the direction from which the bus would come. I could already see it in the distance with the lamps shining on its windows and bodywork. 'I going home to my dad's. I don't want to but I've got to for a while. He said I'd always come back, you see. And he was right.'

She dabbed at the side of her nose with a handkerchief. My stomach went liquid with pity. 'But what about Norris?' I asked.

'Norris will stay a special person for me, Leonard. Norris will always be in my heart!'

She kissed me on the cheek and then started to run for the 73. Her heels clicked faster in the drifting steam of the hot-dog stands. She called out, pushing through the crowds as the conductor rang his bell. The bus started to draw away, its fat tyres hissing. I saw the long seam of her stockings as she leapt for the tailboard.

Thirteen

Norris kept to his room and did not go to work. 'They'll be sacking him,' my mother said. 'You can only go so far with them.'

We sat in the kitchen listening to his footsteps upstairs. He made a soft noise as if he were in his stocking feet or wearing slippers. He paced to the limits of his rooms and then back again.

'He was an orphan,' Aunt Irene said. 'A Barnado's boy. And now it's hard for him to be with someone.'

Susan's father called. He was a short, square-built man in railwayman's uniform. He stood in the hall and would not leave. I watched him from the living-room door.

'I want to speak to him,' he said, looking up the stairs.

My aunt and mother barred his path. 'We can pass on any messages,' my aunt said.

My mother nodded. 'And barring that we can call the police!'

Susan's father started to shout. 'Call 'em then! And I can turn that bugger in!'

He pointed. Norris was coming down the stairs with a cardboard box. His face seemed thinner and longer, the skin tighter on the bone. He had not shaved and his oily hair fell over his forehead. The bottom of the box had split so that he had to hold it with an arm underneath.

'Else there might be murder!' Susan's father warned.

'Eileen, go into the street and bring a policeman,' Aunt Irene said.

My mother stared past the man at the open front door. 'Only what if there isn't one?'

I came up the hall from the living room. The dog followed me and started to growl and snap.

'I could go.'

My mother hissed at me. 'Get back in there!'

'You should make that bugger *clear out*,' Susan's father said. 'I'll take him by the scruff of the neck for you!'

He put a hand on the banister as if he were about to climb the stairs. My aunt snatched at his arm.

'You'll have to go, mister! Take her things and go!'

The railwayman pulled against her. She had a grip on his sleeve. The dog lunged forward, snapping, and I caught hold of its collar. I looked at the Poles' door and saw that the brass padlock was clasped on its staple.

'You leave her alone!' my mother warned. 'She's not a well woman.'

He stared at her, surprised. 'Why, I've never laid a finger!' He looked about as if he was confused, as if he had just come to himself and realised his situation, the sort of company he had fallen into. 'She said there were all sorts here! She said it was like the bloody UN!'

'You keep a civil tongue!' my mother told him. 'There's such a thing as the law of slander.'

Norris held out the collapsing box. A fold of light flowery material was poking through the open bottom. Then a little gold case fell on to the stairs and opened in a puff of powder. Inside was a mirror and a pink padded tongue.

'Here, take 'em, mister,' he said. 'If there's anything missing then I'll send it on.'

The man looked him up and down. He turned thoughtful for a second. His cap was at an angle on his head and he set it right. 'A lanky trollop like you,' he said quietly. 'My daughter was a virgin when she entered this house!'

My aunt laughed down her nose. 'Well, we can't return that, mister!'

Then Susan's father roared and made as if to mount the stairs. I had the feeling that every door in the house was opening. Frightened and curious faces looked out from everywhere. I heard Mrs Rinse's intake of breath and then Ralph's mismatched feet as he descended from his attics. Norris used the box to shield himself from the other man. His sleeves had become unrolled and the loose cuffs flapped. The box's cardboard sides were squeezed between his arms so that the seam gave completely.

My aunt put her hand to her mouth. 'Her dresses! They'll be *ruined*!'

Tiny pencils and gold bullets of lipstick spilled on to the stairs. Then a roll of underthings. A small alarm clock bounced into the hall, ringing. Susan's father's feet were caught in the folds of fabric. He kicked out at them, stirring a smell like a make-up counter.

'As it turns out, she was never twenty-one.'

'Never even eighteen, you see. There's such a thing as the age of consent.'

'Never even sixteen: it could be a crime!'

'Would you say so?'

The sisters took a cigarette each from the inlaid box. They paced the confined spaces of the kitchen, crossing and recrossing the space between the sink, the cupboards and the gas stove. Jeff began to pace with them, following them with his head down, turning as they turned.

'We can't be blamed if people are liars: we should ask him to leave after this,' my aunt said.

My mother drew on her cigarette. The air was turning thick with smoke. 'You can't kick him when he's down!'

'I'll kick him when he's up as well,' Aunt Irene said. 'She was what they call *intact*, you see. We could be prosecuted: there's such a thing as a disorderly house.'

My mother opened the door of the oven and then slammed it shut on its black iron-scented well. 'That could never stand up in court, Irene! Reason is, how could he prove that she arrived in that condition? She looks eighteen if she's a day and you could see that she wasn't shy with men.'

'No,' my aunt agreed. 'You couldn't call her *shy*.'

I walked Jeff through the town to the pet-shop. Mr Webster was standing by the counter in his khaki coat.

'Have you seen this?' he asked.

He took a biro from his pocket and turned it upside down. A

woman's black swimsuit drained from her until she was naked.

The fat girl who worked at the till rang up no-sale and took out some change. 'Which one of you is the bloody schoolkid?' she asked.

Mr Webster stared at her hands but said nothing. He slipped the pen back into his pocket and pointed to the dog.

'And how are his worms? Have you counted them lately?'

Jeff hung his head, nervous at the attention. His tail trembled. The white circles in his eyes shifted.

'That animal's in terrible condition,' Mr Webster said. 'Have you taken it to a vet?'

'No,' I said.

He tutted to himself. 'Then you ought to! It's an act of cruelty keeping a dog like that.'

I looked at the gerbils for a while and then bought a box of worming tablets and a sachet of fungicidal rinse. When I got back to the house my aunt and mother were standing before the open door of the cellar. My aunt held a cup and saucer carefully between both hands.

I stared down into the dark. 'Is it flooded again?'

'Not yet!' she said.

My mother was holding the cycle lamp. She shone it along the cellar wall and down the steps. I let the dog go and squeezed between the two women.

'Norris is down there,' my mother told me. 'He says life isn't worth living.'

'You have to keep trying, that's all,' my aunt said. Then she cupped her hands and called down into the body of the cellar. The closed space made her voice sound strange and musical. '*Norris*! We've made a pot of tea for you!'

We listened but there was no answer. 'Tea won't bring him back,' my mother said. 'He's too far gone for that!'

My aunt shook her head. Beside herself, she started to sip from the rim of the cup.

I looked for him but from where we stood you could only see the area near the foot of the steps. The concrete floor was shiny with damp. 'But it won't be high tide for hours yet,' I said.

'He says that he's prepared to wait. He says he'll sit there and let it cover him,' my mother said. She went down a couple of steps, shining the torch.

'Can you see him?' Aunt Irene asked in a whisper.

My mother crouched slightly to peer below the level of the hall floor. 'No, I think he's hidden himself in a recess.'

'We can leave him the tea anyway. Mebbe it'll tempt him.'

'He'll see sense eventually,' my mother predicted. She climbed back up and clicked off the torch. There was darkness in the cellar except for the light from the open door. She turned on the top step and called down again. 'We'll leave it just inside the door, Norris! Don't let it get cold!'

I told Oscar about it when I met him in the hall. He carried a bag which chimed with glass.

'It's his choice like it's his shoes,' he said.

When the news came on at six the tea was still untouched. A circle of scum had formed on the top. Later in the evening I saw the shine of flames through the dimpled glass of the front door. I ran back into the living room.

'There's a fire outside!'

My aunt was shampooing the dog in the zinc tub. With his hair wet, the dog looked skinny and reduced. The grey foam smelt powerfully antiseptic. My aunt nodded as if she'd expected the thing. 'It's her father: his revenge, you see.'

'More like that bloody bike ablaze,' my mother said, standing up. 'It'll be kids, you see!'

Outside the bike was burning in a curl of yellow flames with oily smoke above them. People were already standing in the doorways of the houses opposite and a couple of tramps watched from the wasteground.

'Run to Mrs Goffrey's,' my mother ordered. 'But don't go too close!'

I felt the heat on my face as I went out. Things were cracking and popping in the flames like tiny sealed bottles. I squeezed through the skinny hedge into next door's front garden and then stepped out on to the pavement. I could smell the burning rubber of the tyres. I turned to watch for a second. The fire was reflected in the windows of the houses.

I knocked on the second door of Mrs Goffrey's hotel. After half a minute she came wearing a white dress with no sleeves. A sparkly brooch was pinned to its front. She stared at the blaze, her mouth open.

'It's a bike,' I told her. 'A motorbike.'

She put her hand to her mouth. 'Then it might explode!'

She beckoned and led me along the hall. There was a smell of food and tobacco. A door was standing open and a man laughed as we went past. She led me towards the back of the house and pushed open a door of dimpled glass backed by pleated net curtains.

'A *fire*,' she said. 'Then what we need is 999!'

I stopped in the doorway. A man sat on the couch pouring Guinness from a bottle, tilting the glass so that it slid smoothly down the side. A record player was on, a woman singing. 'There's one for you, my love,' he said.

'You know I hardly ever drink,' Mrs Goffrey said. She crossed the room to a cream telephone sitting next to a bowl of fruit. I could not tell for certain but I thought the fruit was artificial.

She scooped up the receiver. 'A bike's caught fire,' she told the man over her shoulder. 'This is Charlie, Leonard. One of my relatives.'

The man sat in his shirt sleeves. He was dark and slack-looking. He wore gold cufflinks and a light blue tie with gold threads in it loosened from his collar. His hair was combed back over a thin patch and he had gold rings on both hands.

'What's on fire?' he asked.

'A bike,' Mrs Goffrey said. 'A motorbike apparently.' She tucked the receiver under her chin and dialled. 'It's an *emergency*,' she said.

The man laughed and winked at me. 'Then you've come to the right spot!'

He stood the filled glass on a beer mat on the coffee table. The end of the song died away and then the music started for another. 'The fire brigade, please,' Mrs Goffrey said into the phone. Then she held it away from herself. 'There's no one injured is there, Leonard?'

'Not yet,' I said.

'Kids, it'll be,' the man said.

Mrs Goffrey shook her head. 'I hope it's nothing serious . . . I hope the whole street isn't ablaze.'

'Kids, it'll be,' the man repeated. He clasped his hands in his lap and then looked down at his wristwatch.

'I'm glad it's just a bike and not a whole house ablaze,' Mrs Goffrey said.

'A *motorbike*,' I said from the doorway.

Across the street the fire was almost out. Ralph and Oscar were carrying buckets of builder's sand from a pile along the road and up-ending them over the wreck of the bike. It was already covered and grey smoke was filtering through the mound.

'Don't breathe it in, Leonard,' my aunt warned from the doorstep. 'It'll blister your lungs!'

The smoke was blowing along the road away from the house. Ralph had tied a plaid scarf over his mouth but the Pole's face was bare. He coughed and wiped his eyes. The neighbours were still standing at their open doors and there was a group of lorry-drivers in front of the wasteground.

'They've come to spectate,' my mother said.

Ralph pulled the scarf below his chin. 'It's only natural curiosity.'

She looked sideways at him. 'Nosy buggers, you mean! There's always an audience when you're in distress . . .'

Oscar said nothing but looked down at the bike. The smoke was still dense, rising from the heated sand and then sailing down the road in a body.

'That thing ought to have been removed,' Ralph said. 'Bloody days ago! You only have to phone the council.'

'They've phoned the fire brigade,' I told him. 'They'll be here as soon as possible.'

'And you can't always blame kids,' Ralph said. 'Kids get blamed for everything but it's adults who are supposed to be responsible.'

Oscar's face was grey from the smoke. He coughed and then spat. 'It's that bloody *short-arse*! Short-arse little get!'

My aunt closed her eyes. 'There's no need to profane.'

'I'll kick him in his short arse,' Oscar said.

Ralph shook his head. 'Some people would make a saint swear!' He set his mouth but I could see that he was pleased.

The fire had burned out by about nine. A few minutes after that the fire brigade came and poked about in the rubbish.

'Aren't you going to take it away?' my aunt asked.

One of them took off his helmet and laid his gauntlets inside. 'That's not our job, sweetheart. We just make sure that nothing's still burning.'

'Only I'm not your sweetheart,' my aunt said.

The men switched off their revolving lamp and climbed back into the cab of the engine. In the living room my mother put on her reading glasses to study the tide tables in the paper. 'He'll choke on that stuff before he drowns,' she predicted.

'I couldn't take another drama tonight,' Aunt Irene said. 'A fine fellah like that and the balance of his mind is disturbed. By nothing but a child!'

My mother folded the paper. 'She's no baby, Irene. She has what any woman possesses.'

My aunt was thoughtful for a while. Then she took a glance at the picture calendar. 'And what shall we do about Thursday?' she asked. Thursday was rent-night.

My mother looked surprised. 'You can't expect him to pay for a week in the cellar! And if he stays down there he might not last until then.'

Aunt Irene lifted a leaf of the calendar to reckon backwards. 'He's three weeks behind already, you see. And his rooms are available to him whether he uses them or not...'

My mother shook her head. 'I can't think about rent at the moment, Irene. I'm tempted to have a cigarette, you know. After all this my nerves are in tatters!'

We watched the TV in the living room. High tide was due just after eleven.

'You could toddle up to bed now,' my mother said at ten thirty-five.

'I ought to stay here,' I told her. 'In case of emergency.'

I pictured myself running to Mrs Goffrey's again, the man with the gold rings pouring drink from his seat on the couch. A drowning.

My mother pointed to the door. 'You can go upstairs, Leonard! We'll call you if we need you.'

The water moved under the house like a balance shifting. At the time of high tide my aunt and mother began to call down into the cellar. I could not hear the words but only their mournful drawn-out tone. When I could stay still no longer I went out on to the landing to overhear.

I was leaning over the top of the stairs when Mr Rinse hissed at me from his doorway. The noise made my hair bristle. He stood in his pyjamas, a plaid scarf knotted at his throat to repel the night air. I hadn't seen him in almost a week. He looked sick and alarmed and stepped slowly out of his room as if he were entering hostile territory. He closed the door carefully behind him.

'What is it, Leonard?' he asked in a whisper. 'What's going on?'

'It's Norris. He's in the cellar to make away with himself.'

Mr Rinse smiled with the side of his mouth. 'That tart's left him then?'

'Susan,' I said. 'She wasn't sixteen.'

He must have thought that I was talking too loudly because he put a finger to his lips. 'She's *poorly*,' he said. 'My pet. She's not the same since that argument. It's terrible when foreigners come between people! She always respected your auntie, you see. *And* your mother. Especially your mother . . . *Listen!*'

I listened. Faintly from inside their room I heard a rattle like a few peas being shaken inside a box.

'That's what's left of her poor breath,' Mr Rinse said. 'Every night I listen to it and wonder if I'll find her in the morning.'

'Find her?'

He stared at me as if words were too big for his mouth. His face was shrivelled and brown with dark threads of varnish in the creases of his cheeks. 'You know what I mean, Leonard. Don't you? You do know what I mean, I'm sure!'

I went downstairs. My aunt started to call again, drawing it out like the soft call of a bird. My mother glared at me as I stepped into the hall but then only tightened her lip. Aunt Irene was leaning in the doorway of the cellar.

'It isn't even water, Norris. It's only *filth*!' She glanced back at my mother who stood just behind her. 'All this for a daft young tart.'

'She's upset his equilibrium,' my mother said. 'Some fellahs tread a knife-edge and anything can tip them.'

She stared at me for a second, frowning, and then beckoned and drew me into the elbow of the hall.

'What's happened to the tide?' she asked almost with disappointment. 'You see, I shone the lamp down there and the water was only up to his ankles although the paper said high tide.'

'Some high tides are higher than others, Mam.'

She stared into the angle of the wall. The meter hummed above us, its little wheel turning. 'So that means he'll be okay tonight?'

'Unless he drinks it.'

He was still there in the morning. Wally was home from work and took down tea and sandwiches. As he came up with the lamp I looked down and saw him for a second at that special angle so that his face shifted into the cosmonaut's. I watched him turning into himself again as he climbed back into the daylight of the hall. There was mud on his shoes and he removed them before he stepped into the living room. I noticed that his holed socks had been darned with matching wool at the heels and toes. My aunt saw it too and blinked. Wally put his hands on his chest and made a pantomime cough. Then he smiled with his crippled teeth, looking towards the kitchen where my mother moved backwards and forwards across the open doorway. He lifted his flat hand until it was above his mouth.

'When the water rises, like,' my mother said, coming into the room.

Wally glanced at her through his lashes.

'Until he drowns or asphyxiates,' my aunt said.

The Pole sipped tea on the couch, looking about the living room. He seemed uncomfortable for a while but then settled back. The grazes on his face had healed so that the skin was only mottled. He sipped again and made a small movement with the cup, opening his mouth as if a word were lodged there.

136

'*Sugar*,' my mother said.

'He's got a sweet tooth,' my aunt commented. 'And you are his interpreter.'

My mother brought the bowl from the table and stirred another spoonful into Wally's tea. Wally nodded and smiled. He held the small cup between his big hands, bending over it.

'Are they still fallen out?' my aunt asked, meaning he and Oscar.

My mother watched the Pole's scalp as he sipped his tea. 'They never talk at work, now. What they do in privacy I don't know.'

'Then he's lost his only friend,' my aunt said sighing. 'I think he can be sarcastic, that Oscar. He has what they call a clever mouth.'

'A reader,' my mother said.

In the afternoon I went into the cellar alone. I climbed down three steps and left tea and biscuits on the fourth. When I ducked my head I could see a candle burning in a saucer and the reflection of the flame in Norris's specs.

He called out to me in a cheery voice but with a croak to it. 'Now then, Leonard! How's the moon and stars?'

'Still the same,' I said.

He laughed and then coughed about six times. As my eyes adjusted I saw how the candle flame chopped the darkness into swivelling blocks.

'Are you still taking your O-levels?' Norris asked.

'I think I will be.'

'You need to *know* so, Leonard. You have to be definite about your future.' He coughed again and then recovered his breath. 'You keep up with your studies, Leonard, and don't let things force you aside. For God's sake don't end up like me.'

'No,' I said.

'And you should try and eat more.'

'I do eat. It's my blood that causes it. The corpuscles.'

'Oh,' he said.

'And you'll never drown yourself in this place, Norris.'

I heard the springs shift as he leaned forward on the edge of the bed. Though I could see him only vaguely I felt his attention. 'So why is that?' he asked.

I left the tea behind and went down the rest of the steps. The floor of the cellar was covered with a skin of drying mud which stuck to my soles.

'Your feet must be cold,' I said.

He laughed to himself. 'They're like blocks of ice, Leonard.'

I stood where the candle threw most light. I squatted down and drew a circle in the mud with the tip of my finger. It wasn't quite a circle.

'That's where we are,' I said. 'The Earth.'

'The *Earth*,' Norris repeated.

Next I drew a smaller circle for the moon and one for the sun on the fringe of the light.

'You see, it's the combined action of the sun and the moon which drags at the water. At full moon or when it's new, then it and the sun are in alignment with the Earth. Their gravities combine to pull the oceans into a bulge before and behind the Earth.'

'Yes,' Norris said. He was listening as though his life depended on it.

'The water stays still more or less while the earth turns inside it, so that the bulges sweep past any point twice a day and cause the tide. That's the high tide, what's called the *spring* tide.'

'And that's the highest you can expect?'

'That's it,' I said. 'But then other things come into it such as wind, rain and ocean currents. When all these combine you get a flood tide . . .'

Next I drew the circle of the moon in a different alignment, so that it was to one side of the Earth relative to the sun.

'After that the two bodies move out of line and the tugs of the moon and the sun start to counteract one another. When the moon is in its first or third quarters then it's just about at right angles to a line between the sun and the Earth and that makes for a specially low tide, a *neap tide*.'

'Like now,' Norris said. '*Neap*. And how long will it take to be spring again?'

I sat down on the bed beside him. The mud was tightening on the end of my finger. 'Well, if a lunar month is twenty-eight days then it's three-quarters of twenty-eight. That's about three weeks. And unless we get another lot of rain the floods will be over by then anyway.'

Norris put his hand on my shoulder. 'Thanks, Leonard. It's not exactly good news but it's nice to have it explained to you.'

'You could get a book out of the library,' I said. 'Read about it yourself.'

He smiled and shook his head. 'I'd just never have the patience.'

Just after the six o'clock news we heard him climbing from below. My mother was at work. My aunt and I waited in the hall with soup and warm towels but he walked past us without a word and went up to his room. His hair was spiky and grey with dust.

Fourteen

I thought then that Norris was lost and that I had contributed to his defeat. Me and the tricksy moon. After that he worked only nights. I'd hear him leaving just before I went to bed. When we met in the hall he'd smile at me but with only one side of his face only. I watched him as he locked the front door from the outside. His white fingers returned the squat key through the slot of the letter-box. It swung on its twine, chiming against the panels.

'The graveyard shift,' my mother said. 'Ten till eight. They're like *zombies* in the morning!'

Another letter came from the hospital. *Give Blood*, the envelope read. She read the note and then threw it on to the coals. It curled as it burned.

'He'll need two pairs of pyjamas. One to wear against the other. We can bring them back and wash them here.'

I sat at the table spooning cereal. Aunt Irene cut into a rasher of bacon. She was more advanced in her breakfast. She looked surprised.

'Surely they'll have proper facilities in a place like that?'

My mother had eaten separately, at an earlier time. Now she made herself ready for work. She took her imitation-pearl earrings from a shell-topped box and clipped them on to the long lobes of her ears.

'I know these places inside out, Irene. You can't trust them with laundry. They'll lose things or give him things that are still damp. It's the same with the food.'

My aunt put down her fork. 'But you can't be always finding fault, Eileen. Sooner or later we have to put ourselves in their hands.'

She vacuumed the stairs in her blue housecoat, moving the

chromed body of the Hoover from step to step. She would work her way up to Ralph's rooms.

'Your mam,' she said. 'There is something about her you must know.'

'What?'

'She *punishes* herself, you see.'

She vacuumed the middle landing. 'He's got a hi-fi now,' she told me.

'Who?'

'Norris has. Bought it new. Well, that's not a crime, is it? To spend your own money? No one to waste it on now ...'

Ralph applied the transfers to a newly finished Focke-Wulf. First he soaked them in a saucer of luke-warm water until they floated away from their backing papers. They were the swastika, the lightning bolts and the black crosses.

'This is always the last thing, Leonard. You have to learn how to wait in life.'

The transfers floated belly-up, crimpling the water. Carefully he took each in turn on a fingertip and transferred them to their places on the painted wings and fuselage. He took care to align them correctly, adjusting them with just the slightest touch. Quickly they lost their shiny surfaces and turned dull and matt.

He winked at me. '*Cleaves*, it says in the Bible. As Adam did to Eve.'

He nodded to himself, as if long-held suspicions had been confirmed. The transfers trembled on the blunt tips of his fingers. He took a breath and applied the squadron numbers of the plane and then the tiny swastikas on each side of the tailfin.

'Only he never goes out!'

'It's not a crime to work and save. And be careful with money.'

'I am only saying,' my mother said.

'Oh, I wouldn't contradict you, Eileen!'

'You see, he needs someone. Of his own age. Flesh longs for flesh, you see.'

'To complete itself, you mean? Only it's a case of once bitten.'

141

'And only his hi-fi now: Cliff and Elvis! I think he dyes his hair, not all over but in parts. Not dyes it. *Touches it up*, like. Just the grey bits.'

'It's not a crime to dye your hair.'

At five thirty a.m. Moscow time Yevgeny Anatolyevitch entered the cabin and woke Gagarin and Titov. The two men ate a light breakfast of chopped meat, blackberry jam and coffee and began to dress. First came a soft, sky-blue suit of underwear, then a protective bright orange overall along with gloves and boots. The white cap with its built-in earphones was next, and finally the airtight helmet. The coach which was to take them to the launch pad was already manoeuvring in the confined spaces between the trees. The driver blew his horn as the doors folded back. The two men hesitated on the rustic porch until Gagarin stepped aside, ushering the other man forward with a courteous wave of his arm. Touched, a little tearful, Titov let himself down the steps and led the clumsy walk along the path.

'Drink something with me,' Oscar said.

He took a very small glass from where it balanced on the arm of the chair and lifted it until he barely touched it with his lips. The colourless liquid at its bottom moved in a slow way as if it were much heavier than water. There was a clear bottle on the rug to the side of his feet, bottom-heavy with liquor. It did not have a label.

'Is it strong?' I asked.

He shook his head. 'You don't talk about strength, Leonard. You talk about *purity*. It clears the brain and your thoughts become *single*.'

He raised the glass again to show me. The liquor gathered the light from the lamp and sprayed it out again in fine rays. He looked over to the other side of the room.

'Wally?' he called with a twitch to his mouth. 'Don't you wish to join us?'

His friend was asleep among the covers of the bed, turned on his side away from us. His hand lay on the covers with the palm showing. When I listened I could just hear his shallow breath.

'My friend whom I no longer love,' Oscar said.

Wally made a noise because of an obstruction in his throat.

Oscar laughed. 'Now he gives us his farmyard! Everything's to be found there, Leonard: horse, dog, swine, sheep and cockerel!'

'Why can't he speak?' I asked.

He reached above him to take another of the small glasses from where they stood in a row on the mantel-piece, turning it between finger and thumb, nodding, his eyes half closed. I wondered then if he was drunk, but it would have been a quiet sort of drunkenness and not boisterous as in the Albemarle. He tilted the bottle carefully and let some of the drink slip through its neck.

'You see, his family were poor, Leonard. And poor people love the priest,' he said. 'And the poorer they are the more the priest moves like a king among them.' He glanced over at the other man, almost invisible in the bed. 'And this priest was very proud, tall, with stern eyes. Here, Leonard!'

We drank from the glasses. The spirit fell in a hot gob and burst in the middle of my belly. At once I felt its sly disguise of drunkenness. We sat quiet for half a minute except for Wally's breath. The electric fire made clicks of expansion.

'What happened to the priest?' I asked.

'Ah! He lived in a house behind the church. On a hill, you see. With only a housekeeper from the village. A very holy woman who was unfortunately simple-minded.' He took a sip from his glass. 'You see, Wally was to be instructed in points of doctrine. For some special reason of the church, some special matter. Some evenings after school he went up to this house with his books to learn from this proud priest. One especial night . . .' He pulled a face as if he did not care to continue.

'And what happened?'

'What? Wally would tell you that.' He put his head on one side as if he were listening for a signal. I saw something in his eye, a light which moved from behind something dark, shone for a second and then moved back again. 'So your father is dead, Leonard?' he asked quietly.

'Yes,' I said.

He poured more spirit, tightening his lips as he controlled

the bottle. He left it unstopped to let out the grainy sweetness.

'So you were unlucky in this matter?'

'I suppose so.'

He nodded at the space between his feet. Then he looked again towards the bed.

'This fool cannot settle himself without being first drunk. Thoughts which he can't understand disturb him. Then he lies like an animal in its dirt . . .' He looked into my face, smiling. 'Leonard, I've a very sharp knife which I took from the kitchen, small but with a fine edge. I steal these small things only for sport sometimes. Your good Sheffield. *Sheffield*, you say?'

'*Sheffield steel*,' I said.

The sisters played dominoes in concentrated silence, drinking bottled Guinness from shiny-sided glasses. Maeve Guisewood sang at the microphone over the slam and slither of the pieces. The night shift at the dairy was about to begin. The men tipped back their pints at the bar. Dolly Greenbanks pushed through the crowd calling, 'Help find the cure for cancer!'

'Nothing could be finer than to be in Carolina,' Maeve Guisewood sang to the club-footed rhythms of the Steinway.

Norris opened his door still dressed in his work clothes but with his long hair brushed back and oiled. He did not look surprised.

'I could hear you, Leonard.'

'Only I wasn't making a noise,' I said.

He smiled. 'When someone stands quiet then I know it's you.'

The new hi-fi stood on a wheeled table in front of the window. It was silver-grey and black with a brushed shine to it like the coat of a pedigree dog. The tall loudspeakers were veneered in blond-coloured wood.

'Was it expensive?'

'You have to pay for quality, Leonard!' He pointed to the name in letters of raised gold on the veneer. *Bang and Olufsen*. Since his nights in the cellar his eyes seemed to be set more deeply. 'And it's not just a hi-fi: it's a *radio-receiver*!'

He pressed a silver button and a clear panel shone with smooth green light. The glass scale was calibrated in both metres and megahertz. The names of the stations were etched in neat italics. Then music, loud and startling, welled up in the middle of the room – strings and a piano like a cat walking in the air. I went closer, stepping through cones of sound. *Hilversum*, I read. *München. Lisboa.*

He smiled and turned down the volume. 'You should sit back and listen, Leonard. There's music from all over the world.'

'From where?' I asked.

He waved his arm. 'From anywhere you want!'

'From the Soviet Union?'

He ducked his head. 'When I said everywhere I was thinking more of the Continent. You'd need an outdoor aerial for places further afield than that. Mebbe I'll ask your mother if I can fix one up on the roof . . .'

He sat back and stretched out his legs. He wore no shoes but his socks were startlingly white. The *Radio Times* was lying open on the glass-topped coffee table.

'I thought about things while I was down in the cellar, Leonard. Your thoughts seem to go everywhere in the dark.'

'What things?' I asked.

'Things in general. Things you don't find the time for usually. I decided in the end that everyone has a sort of *path*.'

'Like fate, you mean?'

'Not exactly like fate, though fate would have a place in it. I meant more your future which you have to follow. It's always out there in front of you somewhere but it isn't always clear. What they call *obscure*: there half the time and the rest not. Like when sometimes you can only see a thing if you look at it sideways. Do you understand me, Leonard?'

I didn't answer because I wasn't sure. The music still came through the air towards us, winging on its strings.

'*America*,' Norris said. 'I have to go there. That's where it lies for me. I saw that when the water was around my ankles.'

'*America*,' I repeated. When you said it out loud it sounded like a place which didn't really exist.

'That might not seem like much of a destination to you, Leonard.'

I didn't want to offend him. 'It sounds all right,' I said.

He turned to the set again. He fiddled with the tuner and the illuminated needle tracked across the dial. The stations swished and crackled until he found a man's voice, powerful and mournful.

Norris smiled at me over his shoulder. 'That's someone I see as having *star quality*. If you believe fully in the things you're expressing then it comes across in the song.'

'Twenty-four hours from Tulsa.'

He nodded, pleased with me. 'That's it, Leonard. And there's another place I'd like to visit. See the reality of it. You see, most of these singers came from out on the country some-where. *Hillbillies*. What we'd call working-class over here. But they knew that the important thing in life was to struggle to realise your personal goals. You see, even if you don't manage it altogether then trying gives you pride in yourself.'

He settled back again, clasping his hands. We listened until the end of the song. *Never go home again*. I looked at the hi-fi receiver and thought about the moon landing. There was no atmosphere and the red flag would have to be stiffened with wire. The cosmonauts would wait quietly for Earth-rise and then start their broadcast. In Russian with a simultaneous translation into all the languages of the world.

'You think there's nothing those Russkies can't do! And who will it be, then? Who'll be the first up there – Khrushchev? Fidel? Mao Tse Tung? All those big commies would never fit in a rocket!'

'You know who,' I said.

Ralph laughed. He creaked himself upright in the wicker chair. 'They say your Gagarin died just after his flight. That he was sick when he came down and he'd vomited inside the cap-sule. He must have caught something up there, something floating around, some kind of space-bug. Or it could have been the effects of weightlessness. The human body's not designed for zero-gravity . . .'

'But I saw him! He gave me a photograph!'

Ralph shook his head. 'That would have been a double. Trained actor, you see. And they all look the same anyway.

Peasants. Alike as pennies. Who's to know if he really went up there? Some people reckon that he never left the ground.'

'What do you mean?'

'People have shown that the whole thing could have been done in a TV studio.'

'But he was tracked by Jodrell Bank! Scientists monitored the broadcasts!'

Ralph angled himself out of the chair, reaching for balance, levering himself upright with his hand against the back. He started to walk about the room, limping badly and grunting to himself as if his missing foot were giving him pain. *Phantom limb*. He seemed to be having trouble sleeping nowadays. In the night I'd hear his footsteps above me.

'You can't rely on what these scientists say! Half of them are Soviet sympathisers. *Fellow travellers*. That means they have no respect for the truth, you see. Everything is subservient to the state – the mentality of the ant-heap! Notice that we only hear of the successes, Leonard. God knows how many might have died in the process! They sent them up there in leaky tin cans, forced them at gun-point!'

I watched him as he crossed the room. I stared at his back with hate. His shoulder set the Dornier flying-boat swinging on its thread.

'He was the first to see the curve of the Earth,' I said.

'Oh yes? Well, Galileo knew about it. And the ancient Greeks.' He stopped as he reached the part of the room where the ceiling sloped low. He turned to me, half crouching, his teeth gritted. 'We used to get people like you at work. Spouting off! I wouldn't waste my breath arguing. I used to spit on the ground in front of them.'

He paced again with his stiff, swivelling step. I followed at his elbow, half a pace behind, pursuing him. 'They're saving him for the moon, Ralph. I *know* that. People predict it'll be by 1966, or 1968 at the latest – the fiftieth anniversary of the Revolution!'

'The blackest day in human history!' Ralph said. 'When I lost my foot they came for me in the hospital. They wanted my story for their propaganda machine, for one of their dirty arse-wipe rags.' He laughed and twisted his jaw as if he wanted to spit. 'I soon sent them running! That's all it meant to them, you see. A human life! An accident like that!'

He walked into the corner of a table and a half-completed model of a Heinkel bomber slipped towards the floor. He made a late grab for it and almost lost his balance but managed to catch hold of the edge of the chest of drawers. I picked up a loose wheel and an aileron. When I replaced them on the table I saw that his face was white.

Fifteen

The further from the Earth's surface the atmosphere extends, the thinner it becomes. It has no clear-cut boundary. At about 1,000 miles from the surface the atmosphere becomes so thin that it is difficult to distinguish from the airless space between the planets.

I saw the Poles standing on the wasteground. A fire burned against the factory wall, more smoke than flames. Wally and Oscar stood close together, but looking down and to one side as if they were deep in thought. Neither of them saw me although I passed within six feet and the dog coughed in the blown smoke from the fire. I looked back once and saw Wally with his hand on the lapel of Oscar's jacket, holding just the outside edge of it which he rubbed between his finger and thumb, half threatening and half coaxing.

I reached the house and went inside. Aunt Irene sat smoking in the kitchen with one leg stretched out on the seat of a chair. She blew out smoke and smiled up at me. The kitchen window was open by about six inches and the wet wind blew through the gap.

'You won't tell your mother, will you?' she asked.

'No.'

'Good. God hates a tell-tale.'

My mother came back at about seven. She sat on one side of the fender to massage her stockinged feet. Her toes looked bloodless and yellowish under the nylon.

'Don't ask about today!' she said.

Aunt Irene poured golden pear-halves in syrup from a tin. 'I won't then.'

My mother twisted her head. 'Because it would stick in my throat to tell you,' she said.

I sat on the couch reading *An Illustrated History of the Soviet Peoples*. It was already more than a month overdue. Because of its size and coloured pictures it would come into a special category of fines. I shielded the page with my arm.

My aunt came in with the pears and potted-meat sandwiches on a tray. She stopped suddenly in the middle of the floor. 'And who's this then?' she asked.

My mother shook her head. 'Was there a knock? Your ears must be larger than mine.'

They listened. The knock was not repeated. 'Well, mebbe he's changed his mind,' Aunt Irene said quietly.

I stared at the door. A heavy red curtain hung before it to keep out draughts. Suddenly the Pole pushed through – Wally, carrying a bottle by its narrow neck. He grinned about the room as if he were delighted to be inside it at last. His big-toed feet were bare.

'He's *drunk*,' my aunt said. She stepped away from him and turned down the volume of the TV. 'Tell him to go back to his room, Eileen!'

'Only I'm not his boss,' my mother said quietly.

Wally held the corked bottle over his head, gripping it with one hand by its base. It was full to the neck and the spirit condensed the light of the lamp into a bright column. He laughed in his throat, looking at us in turn. His striped shirt was open on the front of a woollen vest.

'If he wants to drink he can keep to his own room,' my aunt said.

My mother took off her coat at last. She folded it to show the gold lining and laid it down carefully against one arm of the easy-chair. Wally sat down on the couch, keeping the bottle upright in his hand. He smiled so suddenly that his teeth came together with a clack.

'He acts not altogether there,' Aunt Irene said.

Then the Pole pulled the cork with a twist of his wrist. He held the bottle under his nose and sighed, shutting his eyes. His bare toes clenched and unclenched on the rug.

'He knows more than you'd think,' my mother warned. 'He has a quick way of understanding with him.'

Aunt Irene nodded at the Pole's bare feet. 'We'll have to excuse his undress, I suppose. Turn a blind eye like.'

'At least he's clean enough,' my mother said. 'When there's English who live more like pigs.'

The Pole smiled up at her and slanted the bottle to tip it into an imaginary glass. The liquor trembled dangerously at its lip.

Aunt Irene stared at it. 'What's that he's offering? It's as clear as water.'

'Have you never heard of vodka, Irene?'

'But without a label it could be anything! Like those tins you buy as flood-damaged goods.'

I remembered the half-dozen rusting tins of pickled cabbage she had thrown into the dustbin.

'But then we can't make a stranger of him,' my mother said. 'When he's away from home.'

She went over to the sideboard and lowered the front of the drinks cabinet. The light came on inside showing a dark bottle of tonic wine and glasses of various sizes against the mirrored back. She took out three of the whisky glasses and stood them in line near the edge of the table. They had frosted sides and gilt rims and I usually only saw them at Christmas or birthdays.

Wally stood up carefully, gripping the bottle by its tapering neck. He seemed to move under a gravity which acted slightly from the side. He crossed to the table and quickly dashed spirit into the bottom of the glasses. Then he stood back, looking puzzled suddenly, as if he were keeping track of some difficult quantity. He clicked his fingers towards where I sat at the other edge of the table.

My aunt shook her head violently. '*Never*! Never while I live and breathe!'

'He had a drop at the funeral,' my mother reminded.

'That was an occasion. And only port-wine.'

My mother stood close to the Pole with her back to him. From the edge of my eye I saw him reach out to touch her waist at the back. For a second he laid the tips of his fingers where her spine would be under the cloth. My mother changed her position slightly so that his hand was left in the air.

'Spirits are treacherous,' my aunt said.

Wally held up his glass and my mother followed. They waited.

'You've made me an impediment,' my aunt protested. 'He's barged in here and now he stands between us.'

My mother laughed. 'You're so dramatic, Irene. You build these things in your own mind until they're mountains!'

Aunt Irene rolled her eyes in a troubled way but picked up her glass, holding it delicately between her thumb and finger, making as small a contact as possible. The Pole made a sort of ceremonial noise in his throat and the three of them raised their drinks.

'*Prosit*!' my mother said. 'Partners in crime!'

Wally tipped back his head and quickly returned his empty glass to the table, rapping its thickened bottom against the oak-veneer. My mother and my aunt sipped at the spirit. Their brightened eyes moved about the room.

At night a woman sat among the men at the fire. She drank from the neck of the bottle and wiped her mouth on her sleeve. The men laughed as the drink passed from one to the other and then one of them jumped to his feet and started to shout at the rest of them, waving his fists. Jeff laid back his ears and shifted against me, nervous and on guard. I touched his scaly back and felt the long growl locked in his body. A lorry was backing towards us from the direction of the main road, the driver leaning out of the open door of his cab to see behind, one hand turning the wheel. His headlights lit the brick piles making shining slopes and deep shadows. He blew his horn as a warning and after the noise had died I heard the thin bright notes of a mouth-organ. The man gesturing before the fire spun around to face it, frowning into the dark.

Fat Derek's friend stood in the gap between two parked cars, the shiny instrument clamped between his lips. He spat it into the grip of his fist and nodded his narrow head at me, grinning. He called out something, jerking his chin, and then waited, holding the mouth-organ against his chest as if it were his only precious thing.

I pulled at the reluctant dog. The lunatics still called and argued at their fire. The smoke drifted and my eyes started to prickle. As I went past his hiding place he stepped out and walked alongside, lengthening his stride to keep pace step for step. He wore a dark sweater with gold threads in it which caught the light from the fire. Something about him smelt like the gum on envelopes.

'What's your name then?' he asked.

I didn't answer.

'Secret, is it?'

I decided to lie. 'Jeff,' I said.

He stared at me, twisting his face. The dog growled at him and then lowered his muzzle and started to cough. He pointed down at it. 'That thing's *dying*! Why don't you look after it better?'

'He's only got a cold.'

'There's something in its eyes!'

'It's nothing.'

'My name's *Alex*,' he said.

'Short for Alec?'

He looked annoyed. 'How can it be short for Alec? It's not short for anything: just a name on its own.' He chewed something in his mouth, some word he was turning over. 'He's in the hospital now.'

'Who is?'

He rolled his eyes. 'Who do you think? The fat bastard! You smacked him with something. Right in the eye. And now he needs an operation.'

'Operation?' I thought of coming home and finding a tall copper talking to my Aunt Irene.

'On his eye. It went out of line and now he sees everything double!' He laughed in satisfaction, hunching himself around the hollow of his chest. 'You fixed him! Yeah!'

I felt panic-stricken. I wanted to run but only walked ahead of him. He caught up with me with quick, loose-footed steps. 'I only pushed him,' I said. 'My finger might have gone in his eye.'

He shook his head. 'He's got a big gob, you see. You can't trust him. And I'm not his mate anyway . . .'

We walked on in silence for a while and crossed the street. He made his shoulder brush the overgrown hedges.

'Hey, Jeff!' he said.

'What?'

'Will you see *him* tonight? The dumbo?'

'Dumbo?'

'You know. The Polski.'

'He's got a name.'

He turned back his lips. 'I know he's got a fucking name! Even that dog's got a fucking name!' He pointed down at the dog. 'D'you see him much?'

I shrugged. I didn't know exactly how to answer. 'Sometimes,' I said.

He looked suspicious. 'What do you mean, sometimes?'

'I mean, sometimes I see him and other times I don't.'

He nodded and seemed satisfied with this. 'Then next time you see him, give him this!'

He pushed the harmonica into his back pocket and rummaged. He opened his fist on a note folded around some change.

'What's that for?'

'Never mind what it's for: you can give it to him!'

He passed the money into my hand. The greasy note was folded around the slippery heaviness of the change.

'Give him it or I'll tell,' he said.

'Tell what?'

He laughed. 'I'll tell him that you haven't!'

The dog planted his paws and started to send out a string of barks. You could hear the noise bouncing back from the sides of the houses. At each bark I felt a wrench coming up the tightness of the lead. The dog's tail was curled between his trembling hind legs.

'Noisy fucker!' Alex said.

He started to walk backwards away from us, up the street towards the main road, keeping us in view, hands pushed into the pockets of his shiny pants. Still facing us, he started to skip and then run, his body jerking, his mouth open. He did not turn his back until he was almost at the corner.

'Wally?'

I tapped at the door to the old fellah's room and then tried the handle. It wasn't locked. The bottom of it scuffed against the rug when I pushed it back. I held the dog's collar while it snuffled into the dark.

'Wally?' I whispered.

Inside the room was a breath and a gap of silence and then another breath. I thought then that it might be Oscar sleeping there. I thought that Wally's breath would not be so shallow and regular but more dog-like, interrupted by scents and dreams. I held the warm money in my fist, squeezing it tight. A coin was pressed out between the folds of the notes. It fell with a crack and ran on its edge along the bare boards near the skirting.

'Who's there?' Oscar called out from the bed. 'What thief wakes me?'

He laughed to himself in the dark. I pulled the dog back into the hall and closed the door quickly.

Then I didn't see either of them for a couple of days. I kept the money in my pocket, transferring it whenever I changed my clothes. The notes turned moist and soft as linen.

'They work all the hours,' Norris said. 'Wally's got a new bike on the HP. A BSA.'

I shook my head. 'I haven't seen it.'

Norris laughed. 'He's always out and about, you see. Night and day. Maybe if you don't talk then you don't need to sleep . . .'

He stood before the hi-fi set with its veneers and silvered metal. He adjusted the tuner and a song came up. The voice filled the room with a tremolo like jellied meat.

'You know who this is?'

'Yes.'

We listened to the song in silence until the last notes faded.

'What did you think of that, Leonard?'

'It was okay.'

'Only okay?'

'It was *special*,' I said, more to please him.

He nodded as if he'd proved a point. 'He was born to a poor family, you see, but he knew he had the talent to become a star. The biggest star the world has ever known. People have to struggle over there just the same, you see: it's just that there's more opportunity.'

'Opportunity,' I repeated.

Norris turned away from the set and looked at himself in the round mirror behind the settee. 'He lives in a mansion with fifty rooms, Leonard! It's got a heated indoor swimming pool and a private cinema. It's more like a city than an ordinary house, but then it has to be because if he stepped outside the fans would tear him to pieces. *Love*, you see! They love him so much they forget that he isn't immortal. They think they can take a part home with them and it would be the same as the whole! There's that big house like a palace on a hill but inside of it there's this room like the inside of a one-room shack. Just a stove and a bed and plain furniture. That's where he spends most of his time.'

I tried to understand. I imagined the richest man on earth sitting at his plain table. I wondered what he cooked on his stove. Norris tried out different angles in the round mirror. He seemed satisfied with the way he looked. He whipped the steel comb from his back pocket and made a few passes through his glossy hair.

'With a sun-tan I could pass for a Yank,' he said. 'Only I need to practise the accent.'

'Got your ticket yet?'

He shook his head. 'First you need what they call a visa. You say it's only for a visit. You see the sights for a while and then vanish! *Blend in*, like. In a big place like that you can keep moving. You can be in Las Vegas one week and Oklahoma the next.'

'Chicago,' I said. 'Dodge City. You'll need money, though. You'll have to find a job.'

He fiddled with the comb, teasing at his forelock. 'Oh, work's no problem, Leonard, there's always something in catering.'

'She said, come into the toilet with me,' my aunt said. 'She needed to empty this bag thing, you see, a sort of bag thing she had to wear.'

I opened the kitchen door to let the dog through to its bowl. My mother sat with her eyes closed, upright in the easy-chair. Her face was pale and shiny.

'She's *asleep*,' I said.

Aunt Irene laughed. 'And I've been talking to myself! She

can't keep awake nowadays. She nods. *Worry*, you see. You must never think that she doesn't.'

I crushed Jeff's pills into shiny grey powder with the back of a spoon. I mixed it into the strong-smelling meat.

'He hangs about,' Irene said.

'Who?'

'A lad with an old face. He waits outside or at the corner. Sometimes he has a bike with him. He *fidgets*.' She laughed. 'Like a kind of monkey or . . . What's that little animal with a kind of ruff?'

'Marmoset,' I said.

'Do you know who I mean?'

'No,' I said.

'He's not one of those lads who stole your shoe?'

'No.'

The dog lapped suspiciously, testing with the tip of its tongue. The white rings in its eyes had thickened until they were like perforated discs above the pupil. Then it ate the mess of meat and biscuits.

There was another fire. I saw it from my room. I stood at an angle to the window and watched its red glow through the broken roof of the old typewriter factory. Whitish smoke drifted past the exposed timbers.

'Those tramps have broken in,' Ralph said later. He sat with his back to me against the shine of his fish tanks.

'The lunatics,' I said. It gave me pleasure to speak the word.

He smiled. 'They might be as sane as you or I.'

I went closer to the tanks. The fish were motionless one to the other but a slow tide seemed to be moving them left to right. Ralph had changed the water recently but even now it was not completely clear but contained moving clouds of fine particles which gave it a green tinge. The glass was beaded with tiny bubbles against its inside. The fish floated at odd angles, as if in a frozen explosion. Only when I looked more closely could I see the tiniest ripple of a fin.

'How do they keep so still?' I asked.

He sighed as if he thought this was something I should know. 'They have a swim-bladder. And what's called a lateral-line. Between the two they have control of their movement in three dimensions.'

'And don't they ever sleep?'

'Why should they need to? When they're tired then the water supports them.' He looked at me over his shoulder. 'I sit up here but my head isn't in the clouds. In the army you learn to use your senses. See and not be seen. Hear and not be heard. Would you like me to teach you?'

I shrugged. I watched the slow, sideways drift of the fish and wondered if it was because of the Earth's rotation.

'Is that a yes or a no?' Ralph asked.

'Okay,' I said.

He nodded and arranged himself more comfortably in the wicker chair, clasping his hands loosely in his lap.

'The first is to control your breathing. Breathe quietly and regularly through your nose but don't try to force it or hold it back. Breathe normally as much as possible. As you're a beginner it would help if you'd close your eyes.'

He lifted his finger as a signal. I lowered my lids on fish-smelling darkness. For a while I heard just the seashell hiss of silence which I knew was the blood in my ears and then faint movements and strainings. Around and below me a nearly silent struggle was taking place between the walls and the floors.

'Can you hear it?' he asked.

'I'm not sure.'

'Well, think of a blind man who has his sight restored. At first he sees just a jumble, like a TV gone wrong. It makes no sense to him. Then slowly he pieces it together: the sky, the ground, his own hand in front of his eyes.'

We waited. I listened. Gradually the house became the sounding board of its own doings.

'Whenever a door opens or someone crosses a room,' Ralph said. 'You can hear a conversation through two floors: not the exact words but the *slant* of it. You build on what you already know. You have to learn to *interpret*, use each piece of information. Like a picture made by joining up the dots. Take your Poles, for instance . . .'

158

I opened my eyes. My ears felt larger, sensitised.

'What about them?'

He cleared the phlegm from his throat. 'Sodding Armageddon is on the cards!'

Sixteen

Wally wore his dark sagging suit and high biker's boots, mud-splashed but with the shine still on them. He stood beside his new bike on the fields backing on to the railway. It was a glossy blue BSA with bright chromework and trim. He put his head on the slant to listen to the rise and fall of the engine. A ripple of clear warmed air jetted from the end of the exhaust.

I watched from thirty yards away, twenty. A white helmet rested like a skull on the bike's seat. He stood in a band of sun and then went into shade again, his shadow tugged back into the undersea green. He put out his hand to tease the throttle. The bark of the engine was as clear as a dog's.

The kids danced and clapped their hands, keeping their safe distance, daring one another with digs and kicks. The Pole was intent on the bike and took no notice. He looked once in their direction but then seemed to forget them. After a moment of quiet thought he hefted the helmet and lowered it over his head, lifting his chin to fasten the buckles. He lowered the curved glass visor and then straddled the bike, lifting his leg stiffly, like a dog. He leaned his weight forward, straight-armed, and pushed the bike into motion, guiding it with his feet. The engine caught a sharp, rising beat.

'*Duuuuumbo* . . . !' the kids called.

They ran through the mud, smeared legs pumping. He headed towards them. They shrieked as if they were excited beyond their bearing, belching out damp breath.

'*Dumbo* . . . ! *Dumbo Wally!*'

He sounded the high blare of the horn and picked his way through, overtaking each of them in turn but ignoring their screams and flushed, queasy faces, sitting upright and long-backed on the saddle and looking ahead. He rode past them, a moving point of noise and disturbance. He passed behind one

160

of the cropped isolated trees and then started to bring the bike around in a long curve, leaning his weight to the side, scooping out an arc in the saturated grass until he was almost facing me, so that if I stood still he would pass not far in front. I waited until I could see the faceless shine of his visor, then I took the money from my pocket and held it in the air, gripping it tightly with my fist.

'*Wally*!'

He might not have heard me because of the noise of the bike. He passed ten feet away, his jacket filled with wind. A piece of mud thrown by his back wheel caught me on the cheek. A dark bar of shade overtook him. Above the racket of the motor I heard the steady beat of a train. It was coming along the embankment, its carriages cut through with the white spaces of windows, gaining speed slowly against the drag of its own long weight.

The Pole turned and made towards it. The wet green of the fields seemed to be tugged behind him like a wake. I watched him become small, a dark shape except for the white shine of the helmet. He crossed the playground with its empty rides and then turned so that he was running close to the wire fence of the embankment, keeping pace with the train above him and then starting to overtake it.

I squinted after him. My eyes were watering in the wind. I had this feeling as if my stomach was upside-down, as if I had done a somersault. The Pole's bike turned on itself until it was narrow, just a black line against the embankment. The train was passing over his head, air and darkness mixing with the noise of his engine. Then there was just this scramble with the train over the top of it: light-dark, light-dark. The train clopped away, freeing itself, trading its weight for momentum.

The kids stood straddle-legged, catching their breath. I started to walk towards the embankment, following his tracks of torn turf with the black mud exposed, still with his money in my fist. One of the kids began to call after me in a high, pleading voice, as if he wanted to follow or was demanding an explanation. I ignored him and went towards the empty swings. The muddy shine of his tracks weaved a long *S* to avoid the sandpit and the iron steps of the slide.

'You'll need wings to catch that bugger!'

A man in a blue official raincoat stepped backwards from the narrow hut like a sentry box and padlocked the door behind him. He grumbled to himself as he pressed home the hasp.

'Next time he comes here I'll telephone the police. These fields are for recreation, not bloody wall-of-death!'

I stared at him. He had a long, bottom-heavy face topped by a dark cap with a peak. His coat was stained at the bottom with drying mud.

'People think this place is sodding Shangri-la, but there's a list of by-laws on the inside of this door as long as your arm — longer.'

He waved his keys at me. There were about fifty of different sizes on an iron ring.

'Aren't you able to speak then? Can't you make an intelligent comment?'

'Yes,' I said.

'Well, thank God for that!'

He looked at me sideways and then pointed to the scooped cutting where the slope of the embankment wedged into the tunnel.

'He went through there like a rat up a drainpipe! It's pedestrians only! It's marked on a board, though I don't suppose he can read. I keep telling them they ought to erect barriers. People'll be *injured* with idiots like him. They say he's simple, anyway.'

I started to walk away but he beckoned me with his finger. 'Hey, is he a bloody foreigner?'

'*Polish*,' I said.

His eyes were still on me as I crossed the playground. The shine of Wally's tyre tracks was already turning to a crust of dried mud. When I came closer to the fence I saw that the space behind it was filled with a scramble of weeds and brambles. Rubbish had been dumped among them and a double mattress lay like a swollen tongue across the slope of the embankment. The entry of the tunnel made a wedge of shadow and I felt its coolness fall over me. I could see the ruts left by his tyre in the loose gravel. The bollards at the tunnel mouth stood at a splayed angle as if someone impossibly strong had stood between them and forced them apart.

Inside, the overhead lamp seemed to have been broken. The daylight closed down quickly. The exit was an arch of white with a pool of white water below it. I could smell the bike's exhaust now. The fumes of unburnt petrol were concentrated by the low roof and my eyes started to sting. I stepped into a puddle and escaped it with a splash of cold water. I touched the money in my pocket as if it were a good-luck piece.

Something was coming now, from the other side. It covered the light from the arch – a collection of different dark shapes which jostled and overlapped. I went towards it, dragging my waterlogged foot. Just as I reached the middle of the tunnel I made out a woman holding a shopping bag in one hand and the arm of her small child in the other. I slipped up the hood of my coat as she came closer and stepped back against the wall to let her pass. She stopped as well and stared into the dark where I stood. The little girl tugged at her arm making soft noises like a kitten.

'Who is that?' she asked.

'No one, missis.'

Mrs Dolbey stared at me for a long time, shifting her angle. I looked towards the exit, wondering if I should run for it, but my legs had gone rubbery.

'Is it you then?'

'Who's that, missis?'

She came closer, bending down to me. 'So what about my Derek's eye?'

I tried to walk on but she stopped me with her hand against my body, still keeping a tight hold on the arm of the little girl.

'Hello, missis,' I said.

'Never mind hello when my son is nearly blind! I asked what about my Derek's *eye!*'

'I don't know.'

She stared at me. I could feel her amazement in the dark. 'What was that?' She bent over and gripped me by the angle between neck and shoulder, digging her fingers into the sensitive space. 'What was that you just said?'

'I said I don't know,' I said very quietly.

She stepped back but still kept her grip on me. 'So you don't know. Well, how is that then? How is it that you don't know? How can you nearly put my son's eye out and still not know!'

She lowered her face over me in the darkness. I could just make out the waiting 0 of her mouth. The little girl was becoming frightened now, leaning against the grip of her mother's hand. She started to call. The word was stretched by the long brick walls.

'*MAAAAAAAAM!*'

'Shut up for God's sake!' Mrs Dolbey said. She turned her face on me again. 'So you've nothing to say to me then?'

'No,' I whispered.

Her thumb pressed against my neck until I could feel a vein throbbing. She breathed into my face with a sweet smell of caramel. 'The Bible says an eye for an eye and a tooth for a tooth!' she said. She prodded me with her other hand, emphasising each word. I tried to turn away but she gripped me tighter, swivelling me back to face her. 'That's the word of the Bible!' she said, with more poking.

'Only in the Old Testament,' I said quietly.

'What? What's that?' She seemed distracted for a second. She half released me so that I was able to suck in a few breaths.

'It says that only in the Old Testament,' I went on. 'We did it in religious knowledge.'

She sucked in her breath. 'The Lord sayeth an eye for an eye and bugger religious knowledge!'

Then the little girl started to call again, pulling away from her mother's side. Fat Derek's mother turned on her and slapped her sharply on the back of her tethered hand. The child was silent for a second and then started a wail which seemed rapidly to fill the inside of the tunnel. The noise was amplified to a heavy shudder through the air and I realised that a train was passing overhead. Mrs Dolbey looked up at the arch of the ceiling as if she thought it was about to shatter. I pushed against her arm with all my strength and felt her fingers lose their grip. She twisted half around, trying to keep hold of me, and started to fall in a slide of wet gravel. The child screamed above the noise overhead as I ran from under the big body.

*

I ran. Across the playing fields, through the streets with their dog-leg corners. A car blew its horn. The smell of food came from a window. On the wasteground the fire was out against its blackened wall. As I opened the front door I heard their voices stop in mid-breath and knew that the argument had been confidential, a private matter between them. My mother sat opposite my aunt at the dinner table, her chin in her hands.

'Your mother has come home,' Aunt Irene told me.

'I was unwell, Leonard. I didn't want to but they insisted.'

My aunt made a just hearable noise inside her nose. She stared at me as I unbuttoned my coat. 'The lad has been running!'

'You can't stop nature,' my mother said. 'A lad is made to run.'

My aunt stood up from the table and carefully put back her chair, lifting its legs from the rug as if it might disturb my mothers thought. 'Is there anything you can think of?' she asked.

My mother glanced at her. 'What do you mean *think*?'

My aunt sighed as if she'd been misunderstood. 'I only meant I'm going shopping, Eileen. And what haven't we got?'

My mother started to laugh. 'Irene, you must know we have everything you could desire and more!'

'You're being sarcastic then,' Aunt Irene said. 'I thought that mebbe it would come to that.' She tugged on her gaberdine raincoat in silence and went out with the wicker bag she used for serious errands.

'That running,' my mother said. 'It's brought the colour to your cheeks. Maybe you'd enjoy dancing.'

'What?' I was surprised.

'You need an interest other than books, Leonard.'

I didn't answer. I went into the kitchen and fed the dog and gave him his powders while she assembled the vacuum-cleaner. She sighed as she worked. The vacuum-cleaner had many tubes and attachments which needed a strong turn of the wrist.

'Are you ill then?' I asked when I'd finished the dog.

She shook her head. 'It's not exactly *ill*, Leonard.' She plugged the flexible hose into the body of the cleaner and secured it with its spring clips. 'Do you know what is meant by the facts of life?' she asked quietly, looking up at me.

I felt my face turn hot. 'I think so.'

She wound the black extension lead into a loop between her hand and her elbow and then carried the cleaner into the hall. I stayed behind in the living room. After a while I heard her cleaning the stairs. The machine made a hollow knocking in their corners.

Then she called me. '*Leonard*! *Leonard*!'

I followed the fat black cable up the stairs. She was standing on the middle landing opposite the Rinses' door, holding the striped hose of the cleaner. She turned off the machine with her toe. I saw that her eyelashes were fluffy with stirred dust.

'I *am* ill in a way,' she said.

'Are you, Mam?'

'I've been given a lot of things to worry about at the same time, if you know what I mean. You know how that can get on top of a person and undermine their health. When that happens, then maybe a little rest is just what they need. Do you understand me, Leonard?'

'Yes,' I said.

'I'm telling you this because you're only young, but then you need to know of certain things to get your bearings in life or you'd take a wrong course at an early age. And then where would you be?'

'I don't know.'

'Well, it would more than likely be too late by then. It would be too late to begin again at that stage, wouldn't it?'

'Yes,' I said. I felt tears behind my eyes. My shoulder still ached where Fat Derek's mother had gripped it.

She nodded urgently, as if my understanding had been too slow. 'Then we'll go then, won't we? We'll go and find out and open our eyes for once!'

She let the hose and its silvered tube fall to the floor and then I followed her up the two flights to the top landing. She paused for a second to listen and then knocked on the door of Ralph's sitting room, rapping with her knuckles quickly and casually as if she did not really expect a reply. But she still waited with her head on one side for a few seconds.

166

'They meet out sometimes, you see. When she's shopping. That was why she was so anxious to depart. The shopping is only a smokescreen. To put other people off the scent. The cupboards are full of tins as it is. We've enough tinned pears to last a lifetime!'

'Where do they meet?' I asked.

She curled her lower lip. 'Here and there, Leonard. Everywhere you'd least expect. They sit and drink cups of tea and talk. What they find to talk about I couldn't tell you.'

She slipped her fingers into the small front pocket of her plaid skirt and tugged out a pair of brass Yale keys connected by a loop of string. She compared them and then slid one into the lock of the side room which was Ralph's bedroom.

'She doesn't know I've got these, Leonard. She thinks she lost them years ago.'

She lowered her head and pushed open the door. It was dark in the room and she felt with her hand to turn on the light and then stepped inside with a smooth, swift step. She left the key in the Yale with the other key hanging down.

'You can come inside, only don't move anything because he's got eyes like a fox.'

I kept my hands in my pockets. The thin floral blinds at the small attic window were closed on the day outside but there was enough light to see a narrow single bed and then a few pieces of furniture. The bed was tightly made, a rug of dark plaid stretched over the mattress and pillow so that they seemed sealed in a package. A mirror in a scrolled mahogany frame leaned back against the wall from the top of a marble washstand. There was a mixed smell of sour tobacco and sleep. A travelling alarm-clock ticked like a rapid heart.

My mother walked to the window and tugged at the curtains, uncovering slate-tinted light. 'Let's see what sort of fellah he is!'

The room was directly beneath the roof and the ceiling had many slopes and angles meeting in whitewashed wooden purlings. Its different spaces were filled with pictures scissored from magazines, pasted back against the plaster until they covered almost every inch.

'That's the kind of man she gives herself to! He's been collecting those for years: they pick up the habit in the army, you see. Dirty little minds and hands when they should be concentrating on the enemy!'

I looked at the breasts and bums. Some were in black and white and some in colour.

'They take *money* for it, Leonard. Lounging around naked when you can see that half of them should still be in school! He prefers 'em young, you see, but he's making do. He drove his wife away with his little ways – I've been told the story!'

She nodded, rehearsing it to herself. I was glad she did not say. I walked deeper into the room, passing under the different parts of the ceiling. It was every angle and corner of a woman's body in different lights and poses. After a while the stillness and dumbness of the pictures seemed to be wanting to say something, maybe a single word. It stuck between my teeth like toffee. When I lowered my eyes there was a walking stick standing in the corner near the bed. It was shiny knobbled wood with a broad rubber ferrule.

For some reason I wanted to defend him. 'He lost his foot,' I said. 'At work.'

She laughed. 'He never tells the full story. Only parts. Turns out he'd been on a spree with some mates of his. When they got back they started to lark around and he fell backwards off a scaffolding. They covered for him so that he still got some compensation.'

'But it was still his foot,' I said.

She closed the curtains again, whisking them along their rail. 'Irene lowers herself when she could do better. Love is blind, you see. She's a good woman but fixed in her ways. She thinks she has to settle but she's plenty of time. That man from the Mariners' was a single fellah. She could have had him!'

'He was sick on the carpet,' I said.

'That only shows a delicate stomach.'

'And the hearse-driver,' I said.

My mother nodded, narrowing her eyes to estimate the possibilities. 'Maybe him as well.'

Seventeen

'Like that box someone opened . . .' Aunt Irene said.

The sisters moved about their room, picking up small ornaments and then replacing them. I listened to the soft scuff of their heels.

'What box is that?'

'A sort of box what d'you call it. This box they opened and couldn't close again. There was something inside it too strong for them.'

I slid the cup over the roses on their gold trellis, keeping my ear to it. The paper had a soft, damp smell.

'You make no sense to me, Irene! I think that peg-leg has turned your brain!'

'An invalid,' my aunt said.

My mother made a buzzing noise with her lips. She sat on the side of the bed and began to massage lotion into the hard skin of her heels.

'When he's half your age and not all there,' Aunt Irene said. 'His eyes never fix on something but only wander . . .'

'Only they speak volumes.'

'You read in them whatever you want to, Eileen! I'm only warning. I suppose you're the laughing-stock at that work of yours.'

My mother coughed, smothering it with her hand. 'You can't begrudge me, though! Not when you've had your own pleasure.'

'If you can call it that,' my aunt said. She stared at my mother from the other bed. 'Only what they call an imbecile!'

'But not here; never under this roof!'

My aunt held up a finger. She stared at the wall that separated us. 'Ssshhh . . . !'

'Ssshhh, then!' my mother said, irritated.

I waited for a minute, knowing they could not stay silent. I moved the cup another foot over the embossed paper.

My mother began again. 'He makes the best of himself. Only he was struck by nature.'

Aunt Irene sighed. 'I'm not denying that. But the word is out now. Soon we'll be the biggest fools going. I'd sooner tell the lad than that!'

My mother stood up, agitated. She screwed the top back on the bottle so that the thread squeaked. 'Tell him what?' she asked, so quiet that I could not hear.

'Why, what there is. What things are and what they aren't. What things are other than they're made out to be,' Aunt Irene whispered. 'Among those things that concern him.'

'Not while I draw breath!'

'You'll give him up then?'

'Maybe I will or will not.'

My aunt kicked off her slippers. She lay back on the bed with her sharp face to the air. 'When all else fails you're left with the truth, Eileen. You have only that to resort to.'

'Where's the dog?' Mr Webster asked.

'He's ill and we're keeping him at home.'

He shook his head. 'That dog's a wonder!'

'What d'you mean?'

'Nothing . . . I've something to show you.'

We walked through to the back of the shop. Mice and hamsters scrabbled at the fronts of their cages and there was a sharp smell of shite. Mr Webster pointed to where a corner had been partitioned off with wire to make a large cage. A black spider-shape hung against the wire. When I looked closer I saw its wrinkled mask of a face.

'What you call a woolly monkey,' Webster said. 'Because of its fur.'

The monkey moved between its wire walls, hanging its body from the sling of its long arms, tightening the curl of its thick tail. Its small hands gripped the mesh. The flattened nails were black and softly shiny like flakes of dusty coal.

'Is it for sale?' I asked.

Mr Webster looked gloomy. He took off his spectacles and

polished them on his coat. 'We shall have to sell it in the end. First it has to have its proper injections.'

The shop was quiet except for the creaking of the wire cage. The monkey suspended itself between its stump of tree and the wire roof and shook its body, its small sharp teeth gritting. Its eyes were dull yellow under drooping leather lids. It began to scatter dark droppings.

'It needs to what you call acclimatise,' Mr Webster said.

I followed him back between the rows of hutches to the main part of the shop. The other animals made their racket. 'They don't understand patience!' he complained. 'Every time is their feeding-time!'

Trudy was reading *Reveille* behind the till. He leaned over to flick the edge of the page with his fingernail.

'Is that what I pay you for?'

'There's no one in the shop,' she said sulkily.

'There's this young man.'

She went on reading. 'You think you are Adolf Hitler!'

I fished in my pocket and took out the empty packet of pills. Mr Webster squinted at it and shook his head slowly. Parts of his neck stayed still while the others turned.

'I think he'll need more than those.'

He began to search through the medicines on the shelves behind the counter, considering several but then pushing them back into their places. Finally he chose a white and blue box. 'These are worming tablets combined with what you'd call a general purge.'

He handed it to me. The front of the box showed a jumping, frisking dog in silhouette. There was a rattle and crash from the back of the shop and I turned to see the monkey flinging itself between its wire walls. The wooden frame of the cage was bouncing and twisting out of shape from the impact of its skinny body.

'It'll escape,' the girl said. 'Like King Kong!'

Mr Webster laughed. 'It's only lonely. It'll get to know us.'

'It's *disgusting*! It *touches* itself!'

'And what parts does it touch?' Mr Webster asked quietly.

The girl closed her magazine, closing her eyes at the same time.

*

The clearing still held the last of the night. Gagarin climbed the steps to the makeshift podium. Before him he saw untidy stacks of breezeblock, thick cables coiled on wooden armatures, piles of steel rods with a coat of fresh red rust. The base's bureaucrats, the teams of scientists, the technicians who were to supervise the launch stood in loose groups before him, shivering, hugging themselves in their coats, smoking despite the proximity of the rocket. Their stomachs growled for coffee.

Gagarin lifted his hand and began to speak into the angled microphones.

'My friends and colleagues! At this moment the whole of my life seems to be condensed into one wonderful moment! Of course I am happy! In all times and epochs the greatest happiness for man has been to take part in new discoveries. To be the first to enter the cosmos! Could one dream of anything more? I dedicate my flight to the people of a communist society!'

He raised his arms aloft and then turned to enter the open cage of the elevator. The lattice gate was closed by an aide and he was lifted slowly, climbing the silvery hull of the Soyuz. He rose from the shadows of the tall pines into full sunlight and saw the forests with the lakes behind, the mountains. The sky was clear with only very far away some fleecy clouds.

'Do you understand what you read?' the woman in the library asked. 'I'm not suggesting that you don't, but I mean in its proper context. You'll find that sometimes you need to supplement your reading.'

She smiled at me. She wore ugly glasses but had small white teeth and a fresh smell came from her, welling up from the neckline of her sweater.

'We've a guest speaker tonight,' she said. 'A man who's just returned from Moscow. In the Soviet Union.'

Moscow! I felt something like a bird land on each of my shoulders, balanced identical birds made from vibrating fields of electricity so that just for a second I had the ability to fly.

'Aren't you taking the dog?' my aunt asked.

'It's cold for him, he's ill.'

'He's being a mystery,' my mother said. 'A mystery and an enigma.'

Aunt Irene laughed. 'Mebbe he has some girlfriend!'

'When his head is in the stars?'

'You shouldn't mock the lad. He's a youth now and needs some outside interests.'

I put on my coat and walked the half-mile. One of the double doors was locked back but the lights were off in the downstairs of the building. Inside a paper arrow pointed up the staircase. I climbed a flight and then had to walk past darkened stacks of books towards a partition of glossy painted wood and frosted glass.

It was the children's library. A man in uniform sat on a low upholstered chair in the half-light just outside the entrance. He puffed at a cigarette despite the no-smoking signs. A big bunch of keys lay on the low table beside him. He nodded at me but did not smile. Behind the partition was more cigarette smoke and about half a dozen people in dark clothes stood talking against a background of kids' books and coloured posters. *British Wildlife. Flowers of Fields and Hedges.* The conversation stopped for a second and then started again when I sat down on one of the low, uncomfortable seats. I looked for the girl who'd spoken to me at the library counter but she'd not arrived.

I waited, staring at the tall spines of the children's books. After five minutes another group stepped into the room. 'Did it have to be the children's library?' a man asked, laughing. 'Not that there's anything the matter with childhood.'

One of them women came over and shook his hand with both of hers. She had a sharp nose with small dark nostrils, greying hair tied back. Everyone in the room seemed to be taller than normal. 'It's a Wednesday,' she said. 'Never a good night. And the heating's been turned off.' She looked about. She gave me a quick smile. 'I think we all should sit down,' she said.

Most of them kept their coats on. The sharp-faced woman and the man who'd complained about the library remained standing. The woman clasped her hands together. 'Let me introduce Peter Hadlow who has recently returned from a year

173

in the Soviet Union,' she said. 'He agreed to be our guest this evening to describe conditions in that country and answer any questions.' She smiled and held out her hand. 'Thank you.'

She sat down. There was applause. Mr Hadlow wore a rough grey jacket patched with leather at the elbows. He stood behind one of the low children's tables and started to speak, pushing his hands into his pockets. He had a wide, smiling face and his voice travelled easily. After a couple of minutes I felt a sigh of air behind me and looked around. The girl from the lending library had come in silently and taken a seat at the back. She was searching through a black briefcase, taking out papers and files and then replacing them. When she had finished she glanced up at me and smiled but then frowned as she began to listen to the talk. Several times the speaker was interrupted by questions and she frowned more deeply, as if she found this painful.

'You have to remember Lenin's belief in the value of material progress,' Mr Hadlow said. 'And especially his observations on the role of technology and science in general. Dialectical materialism is itself a method of scientific enquiry and remains so even when it's applied to society.'

After about half an hour of this the attendant came holding his bunch of keys. He was still smoking but had put on his peaked cap. He crossed the floor behind the speaker and began to pull the cords which opened the high hinged windows.

'*Special Branch*!' one of the men said.

A few people laughed but then the tall lady stood up. 'I hope that was meant as a joke,' she said. 'But I think we should now allow Comrade Hadlow to rest his voice.'

When I heard the word comrade I knew that it would be special to me, that it would always be music to my ears. People began to clap but Hadlow raised his hand. 'I still have enough voice to take a few questions from the floor.'

The tall woman smiled and sat down. The uniformed man opened another high window with a squeal of the pulley and then stood with his arms folded against the bookcases at the back of the room.

When the meeting was over I left quickly and without speaking to anyone. I saw by a clock in a shop window that it was almost ten o'clock. As I crossed the road I heard sharp-heeled footsteps behind me. For a second I thought of Susan but then someone put a hand on my shoulder and I saw that it was the girl from the library.

We stood on the pavement together. A man in a long dark overcoat was waiting on the other side of the road. She waved to him with a quick flick of her hand.

'Thanks for coming!' she said. 'I hope you felt you gained something. We meet here once a fortnight. I hope you'll come again.'

'Yes,' I said.

'I'm very glad. If you visit the library then I'll keep you informed of special events like tonight.'

She smiled at me again. She wore a short coat of some kind of nubbly brown material and a small fur hat. I felt myself blushing and looked down at her legs. Her boots of shiny dark leather reached almost to the hem of her skirt, their laces were done up crosswise and tied with wide bows.

'Thank you,' I said. My fingers played with the lost objects in the pockets of my coat.

She leaned forward and kissed me on the cheek, pushing back the side of my hood, touching my skin lightly with her lips. 'People like you give us hope for the future,' she said.

I waited until they were sleeping and then turned to the chart. I read very softly the names of the formations: *Newton and Galileo, Kepler and Copernicus, Sea of Crises, Sea of Tranquillity, Sea of Storms*. I dripped a small pool of wax and then stood the candle in its saucer. There was an inch or so left. I looked at the cosmonaut with his sad quarter-smile and then blew out the flame. For a second the light seemed to stay caught behind the glass. Then it contracted to a small star which slipped fading towards the edge of the frame.

I crossed the landing, navigating by the smells of the stove. I stopped at the bathroom door to listen to the drip of the cistern and then climbed the short flight to Norris's room. There was light under the door. I tapped with the tips of my fingers and leaned closer. I heard a noise like a clearing throat and turned the handle.

Norris was asleep on the couch, his feet in their white bopper's socks resting on the arm, ankles crossed. His glasses were crooked on his face and a padded earpiece of his headphones was adrift from his ear. He made the sound I'd heard, repeating it. His eyelids flickered.

'Excuse me,' I said.

A lick of music came from the headphones. As the door hinged back I saw that Wally was sitting in the easy-chair, rolling a cigarette. He gave me a small smile and laid the cigarette-paper and scruff of tobacco on the arm of the chair. He held up his palm then turned it to beckon me into the room. There was a loose curl of smoke near the ceiling. One of the tall narrow-necked bottles stood almost empty on the glass table among loose threads of tobacco, spent matches, torn scraps of gold paper. Oatmeal-coloured pills were scattered. The top of each was stamped with letters and scored across with a deep line. There was also a folding knife, the dark blade turned back into its wooden handle.

Wally grinned at me with his mouth open. The jacket of his dark shiny suit was folded on the rug with its striped lining turned out. The lining was torn under one arm exposing grey ticking. He pointed to the other low chair and then got up to fiddle with the tuner of the hi-fi and turn the antennae of the aerial.

I watched him. The pile of the rug felt electrical under my feet. Wally pulled out the jack of the earphones and music racketed about the room. He giggled and turned the volume down hastily. He sealed his cigarette with spittle and sat down to light it.

Besides the bottle there were four empty glasses on the table. They were the ones from downstairs with the gold rims and frosted sides. I took the money from my pocket and spread the note on the glass table with the silver on top. The Pole nodded with his eyelids half closed. He might have been thanking me or only acknowledging what was due. He scooped the money into his pocket without counting it and then sat back for a minute smoking the thin cigarette, his face turned down. Then he delved into his pocket again and took out a dirty pound-note, holding it out to me between his finger and thumb. When

I made no move he stuffed it into the pocket of my pyjama jacket.

We shook hands, an agreement made in silence. His hand was cold except for the tips of the fingers. After that we had to drink together. The gold rim of the glass was chill against my lip and then I felt the spirit like a tree of heat, its flowery top in my mouth, its stem descending and then hot roots pushing further down. The hi-fi played its songs quietly. Norris twisted on the couch but did not wake. His spectacles became dislodged and fell on to the soft rug.

Then Wally took the knife and locked open the blade. Smiling, guiding it with his broad thumb, he brought its edge down on one of the grey pills. His hand trembled as he applied pressure. The pill split and the separated halves skittered over the glass top of the table until he stopped one with the flat of his hand. He opened his mouth and flicked it in. He showed me his pink tongue with the half-moon of the pill lying on it and then drew it back inside and swallowed.

'Take!'

The word was on his lips. He held the other half on his fingertip, giving me his spaceman's stare. I held it between finger and thumb. It was bitter. I bit it into powder, felt the sour paste in my throat. We drank some more spirit. We chimed our glasses. I felt the whoosh of heat pass over me. Wally leaned across the table and took hold of my arm just above the elbow. The door of the other room was open an inch to show a line of silver like a column of mercury. He led me to it, his hand light on my shoulder, and pushed it back.

'It's *okay*!' he said. He didn't speak. The room had a big bed and two windows, one looking to the side and then the arched casement looking out over the back garden. Both of them were filled with light which pressed flatly against their panes so that you could feel the strain on the glass. The light turned the room silver-white so that everything in it had lost its natural roughness and was smooth and slightly shiny. There was a silver line at the edge of everything which seemed to move slowly. I knew that this slow creep of silver was joined to the motion of the moon.

Wally crossed to the window and cleared a small circle of

the glass with the tip of his finger. Laying his hands on my shoulders he guided me towards it. I put my eye to the clear lens and saw a dark blue sky with a paler glow at its lower edge because of some bright planet which had just set. I saw the dark roofs of the houses surrounding the garden and then, behind them and slightly less transparent than the sky, a range of high, sharp-toothed mountains.

'What mountains are these?' Wally asked. Of course he couldn't speak. Then when I did not answer he took hold of my head between his hands so that I couldn't look away. I could feel the pressure of his fingers and the weight of his arms. I stared through the clear glass. The ridges of the mountains were impossibly steep, floating weightless above the roofs of the houses.

'*Don't you see?*'

He laughed softly behind me.

Alex counted the pills back into the bag to check them. One rolled and fell into the deep print of a tyre. He picked it out and cleaned it carefully on the sleeve of his jacket. That made him forget his count so that he had to start again. His hand had a fine, fast shiver.

'They're short!' he claimed.

'That's because of last time.'

He shook his head. 'If I can't trust him then we can't do business.'

'That's up to you.'

He looked for a second as if he was about to throw them at my face but then changed his mind and slipped the bag into his back pocket.

'Look, I want something different next time. Something else.'

'These are okay.'

He shook his head. 'These make you sleep, you see, and I want the stuff you can stay awake on.'

'What for?'

He started to laugh. 'Don't you ever go anywhere, Jeff?'

'I go for walks.'

'With that dog, you mean?'

178

'Sometimes on my own,' I said.

He started to hum to himself, making buzzing noises with his lips. He nodded towards the dark wall of the warehouse.

'Have you been in there?'

'Where the dossers live?'

He nodded. 'You have to be careful. You have to know them first. A bloke was cut up last week. With a bottle.'

'D'you talk to them?' I asked. I was interested now, impressed.

'They talk to *me*! You can find things out, you see. There's a bird who sits with them and drinks like a fellah. If you buy her a bottle you can feel her tits.'

'Have you?'

He curled his lip. 'Nah, she's filthy.'

Aunt Irene rubbed at her elbows with the volcanic stone. She frowned at the dog in its place close to the fire. A smell was lifting from it.

'It's time Jeff was put down,' she said. 'His existence must be only a misery.'

'The dog, you mean?' my mother said.

My aunt stared at her. 'Of course the dog!'

'You will have your revenge,' my mother said.

'And what do you mean by that? You can see he's in pain. He's half blind now and his organs are in a terrible state: his internal organs.'

The dog looked away from us to the hot, cindery spaces below the grate of the fire. His breath wheezed and his nose was dry and cracked. The white circles in his eyes had almost closed altogether to leave just a pin-head of clearness.

'Life begins and ends,' my mother said. 'You shouldn't interfere.'

Aunt Irene nodded. 'Only sometimes you must, Eileen. You see, even a pet is just a dumb creature. An animal reaches a certain stage, you see.'

My mother looked at the dog. 'And so does many a person.'

Eighteen

Wally kept pace with me on his BSA. I turned down Smedley Street and then crossed the road into Liddell Street. From the edge of my eye I saw him turn and then he was alongside of me again, weaving to keep balance, the noise of his motor rising and falling. A van overtook him and blew its horn. He held something out towards me – a clear plastic bag rolled up on to itself until it looked like a bar of lumpy silver. He rode skilfully with his arm stretched out and the machine just kept from stalling. I didn't look at him but listened to the petrol-starved sob of the engine.

I kept my savings under the carpet in my bedroom, smoothing the notes down carefully so that they would not make a bulge. One afternoon I met Oscar in the hall. He wore his slack trousers and a yellow pyjama jacket. Maybe he had heard me on the stairs and waited. I was on my way out but he stopped me with a hand on my arm.

'Does he give you money, Leonard?'

'Money?'

'Surely you know what money is!'

He looked down at me from his height, frowning as if he himself had become confused. From his appearance I did not know if he had just got up or was going to bed. There were bruise-coloured pouches under his eyes and dark hairs clustered on the underside of his chin. When I did not answer he laid his hands on my shoulders and started silently to shake me.

'I think he does, Leonard.'

I said nothing.

'*Leonard*!' he said with his teeth gritted.

'No!' I shouted.

He gave me a last shake of such violence that my teeth struck together. The ringing shock of it passed through the bones of my skull. He let me go, shaking his head. A snot pushed from my nose and I wiped at it with the back of my hand. He stood over me, opening and closing his mouth. I looked down the hallway to avoid his eyes. The beaded glass panels of the door netted the shadow of a passer-by and then released it.

'Leonard?'

'What!'

He leaned against the wall of the hallway, resting his shoulder against the ancient anaglypta. He shook his head and spoke softly and reasonably. 'Do you know that every time you lie then you let death into your body, Leonard? Each time you tell a lie to a well-meant question then death occupies a part of you like the Russians . . .'

I walked towards the door. I was still trembling from anger and the shaking he'd given me. Maybe I was ill as well. Fine rain had been falling all afternoon. Now it had stopped and the flat bright light in the hallway drew the shadows from angles and from underneath things.

Alex held a gleam of spittle in his mouth. He pushed out his lower lip.

'Why did you bring the dog?'

'Why not?'

'I asked you not to. Not for tonight.'

'What's special about tonight?'

He laughed. 'Aren't you coming then?'

'I don't know.'

He shook his head. 'Yes you do!'

He walked towards the dark middle of the wasteground, away from the lorries and the lights of the road, into the darkness near the side of the old factory. After a second I started to follow him, dragging the nervous dog behind me. Out of the light the fine rain turned invisible. There was a private angle where the broken stumps of walls met.

He whistled to himself and stopped. 'Do you know where we're going?'

'Yes.'

The heaps of damp rubble gave off a chill. The wall of the factory lifted out of the bricks. An iron sheet was levered out of a window close to the ground. Jeff's blunt claws scrambled and slid.

'Look, we have to lose him!' Alex said.

'Lose him?'

'Send him home. Tie him somewhere. They don't like dogs.'

'Tie him where? We can't just leave him!'

He kicked at something irritably. 'It's only for a while.' He pointed to a broken pipe pushing out from a slope of bricks. 'Tie him to this.'

'It's raining!' I said.

'I know it's raining!'

I looped the lead twice around the pipe and knotted it. I stroked the dog's damp head.

'You treat that dog like a brother!' Alex said. He went close to the side of the building and pulled at the rusting iron sheet, folding it back as if it were a curtain. There was a creak of pulled nails. The last light from the road showed me broken angles of wired glass.

I hung back. 'We haven't got a torch,' I said.

'We don't want a torch. They think it's the coppers if they see a torch.' He sighed. 'Look, just do what I say and we'll be okay.'

He turned the glimmer of his face away from me and then squeezed his head and trunk through the opening. He reached for something above him and pulled himself up, drawing in his legs carefully to avoid the ends of glass. I heard him jump down into darkness. For a second I thought of leaving him there, untying the dog and running quickly home.

He spoke to me through the opening. I could see only the mist of his breath. 'Are you still there, Jeff?'

The dog heard the name and started to whine.

'Are you coming then?'

I climbed up into the opening. The ends of my coat snagged on something but I pulled it free. There was a drop and then a heel-jarring collision that made me cry out. The floor was slippery with wet so that I almost lost my balance.

Alex caught me and held on to my arm. 'You make too much noise!'

'Sorry,' I said.

He mimicked me in a small squeaky voice. '*Sorry*!'

He laughed and moved away from me, out of the faint light from the window. The darkness ahead had a faint sharp smell of piss.

'Come on!'

'I can't see!'

He made a noise of impatience. 'Then use your hands.'

I could not see him now. I listened to the slither of his feet. The dog started to croon and yap outside. I felt shamed by its fear. My fingers found the side of a wall and I felt my way along. The floor was booby-trapped with broken glass and fragments of brick. After a while I walked into Alex's waiting back.

'Can you hear the bastards?' he asked.

'Who?'

He made a shushing sound. 'Just listen!'

I listened. My eyes were making shapes out of the darkness, filling it with formations of red specks like bloody moths. I heard a slow shudder like the vibration of a train which then changed itself into sound.

'They're *singing*,' Alex said.

It was somewhere ahead of us in the spaces of the building, not exactly singing, more a raw noise pumped directly from their lungs. I glanced up and saw misty shapes of light overhead, holes which seemed to extend upwards through successive floors. The darkness ahead of us ended in smoke with a red glow mixed smoothly through it like ink in water. My eyes started to smart. A mist of rain turned visible for a second as fine, shiny wires.

'They're *here*,' he warned.

I could see only a shape against the glow from the fire, leaning towards us: a man, peering at us through the smoke. He lifted his arm to point.

'*Wazfukka!*'

The singing stopped suddenly. I could still hear Jeff's troubled yapping. We waited. The man tilted slowly to one side until he was about to fall but then recovered himself with a jerk. He lifted his arms as if he'd performed a trick.

'He'll take us,' Alex said.

'Where?'

'Wherever they are.'

The building extended backwards further than I'd thought. Its rooms and spaces had been altered by the bombing. Isolated steel columns lifted into the mist and smoke. The walls were burnt to their framework of timbers and thick electrical cables hung like cobwebs, weighted by black junction-boxes. The voices started again but then lost their rhythm, turning into coughs and jeers. I saw the dance of the fire in a pit of debris lower than the general level of the floor. As if it were burning its way towards the basement.

Five or six of them were gathered to one side of the flames. The sideways movement of the bottle was like a current passing along a wire. It reached the end and repeated, shining with the fire. The man who had brought us here stopped and shouted something out, waving his arms. One of them picked up an empty bottle and held it against his eye like a telescope. I could feel the heat from the flames and then the dampness of the air on either side of me, as if I were a wafer of warmth between two coldnesses. Our guide took hold of Alex's sleeve and tugged at it gently. As we went towards the fire I could see his frowning, concerned face.

The woman stood up. She had been there all the time, drinking like the rest, wiping her mouth on her sleeve afterwards.

'Alice!' the man said. 'Beautiful Alice!'

He laughed. She made a gesture to push him away. The others watched them, smiling as if they were a familiar entertainment. The fire burned on broken ends of timber, dying down, more smoke than flame. One of them held out the bottle and the man who had brought us took it and tipped it back. When it was empty he dropped it vertically between his feet. It did not break but bounced on its base and rolled in an arc. He still held Alex's arm, tugging against it, his weight swinging.

'Steady,' the woman called.

She went between them and broke the contact of his arm. Her wide face had nothing about it which gave its age. Alex stepped back and adjusted the hang of his jacket. He pointed towards me.

'Not me: him!'

We walked to a place from which you couldn't see the others or the fire. The floor above sagged towards us, fraying into holes, its joists thinned by fire. Rain fell through the gaps, thinning out now. I missed the continuous sound of it. She stopped me in a spot where the light from over our heads was better.

'Is he your pal?' she asked.

'Yeah.'

'Do you like him?'

'He's okay.'

'Only he's *shit*,' she said. 'Some are gold and some are the other stuff. You have to learn to spot the difference . . .' She looked at me closely. 'What's your age, sonny?'

'Sixteen.'

'You're never sixteen!'

'I am,' I said.

She closed her eyes, smiling. Then she unfastened her coat. The two halves swung aside.

'Have you got something for me?'

'Ten bob,' I said.

She put her face to one side. 'Make it a quid!'

'All right.'

'All right!' she said, mocking, smiling. She undid buttons and then pulled up a layer of woollens and a grey vest. Her belly pushed towards me with its long fold of a navel. Her breasts were low and widely spaced, heavy. She laughed and tipped back her head.

'Are you staying over there then? Do you prefer your own company?'

I went closer, stepping over the rubbish on the floor. She laid her hand in the angle of my neck and brought me to her. Her skin was warm against my face and smelt of smoke and damp paper.

'These are a woman's tits,' she said softly. 'D'you like them?'

'Yes,' I said.

She laughed. 'Well, so you should!'

She put her finger to her lips and pointed upwards. I looked up from my cosy hollow of flesh and saw that we were standing below a big open space. It must have been exactly where the bomb had fallen, in the war, when my aunt's shoe was lost.

Clouds were shifting over it, rubbing against one another, turning, breaking into dark gaps which then oozed again with light. She still pointed, stretching upwards, making a humming noise in her throat. A mealy smell came from her body. There was a silver edge of cloud and then a bright fish-shape was released into the open.

Mrs Rinse's chest got worse and Mr Rinse took time away from work to nurse her. He stood at the stove in his shirt sleeves, cooking broth. Grey froth lifted above the sides of the pan. An atmosphere of menthol breathed from the open door of their room. The lines on his face were all downwards. Then Muriel called him from her bed. 'Wilf!' she shouted. '*Wilfred* . . . !' The broth boiled over and scorched on the gas-rings.

The smell, like burning shoes, lasted all week. Another letter came from the hospital. My mother tore it as she opened the envelope. Aunt Irene kissed me on the side of the face and then bent to pet the dog. The dog pressed its nose into her palm. She pushed it away and walked quickly into the kitchen.

I gave the dog its tablets. In the street I saw Oscar with Wally's bike. He was talking to another man and pointing at the engine. The other man wore overalls and a red tartan scarf knotted at his throat. He winked at me. 'And how's my favourite lad?'

Oscar crouched beside the bike talking in a quiet, slow voice. 'And this is the carburettor. And this is the wire which links the carburettor to the . . .'

'*Throttle*,' the man said. 'I can already see it's had some misuse.'

Later from my window I saw the man riding the bike up and down the street, going slowly and revving the engine. He turned around at the corner and steered the bike back through its own cloud of exhaust. Oscar stood at the kerb with his hands in his pockets. I watched for another minute and then went up to Ralph's room.

'The Poles are selling the bike!'

'Nothing about those lads surprises me.'

'But why? It's a brilliant bike!'

He closed his eyes. 'They shouldn't be selling it, because it's on the never-never. But then it's let the buyer beware.'

'He says it's been misused.'

'That short-arse Wally has no respect for machinery. And tell me one thing the Poles have invented!'

'The helicopter,' I said.

He sneered. 'You think you're clever but those boys are up to their eyes in it: their sword of Damocles is coming down fast.'

'What?'

'A sword that was hung on a thread. You only had to breathe.' He lowered his voice. 'It was the dumbo, you see. He was used by others. Cleverer than himself. Cleverer by far. But even those other people put their foot in it. Feet. Even they went too far!'

He laughed to himself.

'What's happened?' I asked.

Ralph shook his head. 'You need patience and humility, the same as in any walk of life. And to know when to cut your losses. When the war was ending, you see, the German rocket scientists went over to the Yanks because they knew where the future was.'

'Wernher von Braun,' I said. 'Walter Dornberger. But the Russians captured Peenemünde!'

He shrugged. 'They found technicians and a few drawings – the big birds had already flown.'

He pushed himself upright and then went over to the fish tanks. He stretched his arm along the length of one, as if he were measuring it against himself. He leaned his weight on his artificial leg which was pushed out at an awkward angle. In the light from the water I could see bright beads of sweat on his forehead.

'They *knew*, you see, Leonard.'

I felt the faint shudder as the front door was opened below. I wondered if the bike had already been sold. 'What, Ralph? What did they know?'

He looked at me cleverly, holding my eyes. 'Well, Leonard: that German brains and Yankee dollars would win the moon race.'

The room went quiet and dark with the light fading in the angled window. I felt something come over me like gravity.

*

187

There was an oily space where the bike had been. Norris gave up his job in the hospital kitchens. I was walking with the dog when I saw him on the top deck of a bus wearing a white stetson hat and dark glasses.

'I'm *going*,' he told me later.

'When?'

'Soon as I can fix it!'

'How long for?'

'Mebbe for ever. I might come back when I'm old and grey but probably I won't.' He laughed but then started to look uneasy. 'There's something wrong, you see. Something that isn't quite right.'

'Is it the Poles?' I asked.

He pulled a face, unhinging his long jaw. 'You can't just blame them, Leonard. The Poles are only the tip of it!'

We walked along the esplanade. The river was low, leaving glossy hills of mud with brown water running in the channels between them. Every few feet along the railings a gull faced exactly into the breeze. It was spitting with rain and we took shelter in a doorway. Jeff stood out on the pavement, pulling against me at the end of his lead. The wind flattened his thin hair to his side.

'This is *poxy*,' Alex said.

'What is?' I asked.

We heard a key in the lock behind us. 'Excuse me, I'm sure,' a woman said, coming out of the house. We moved away from the step while she locked the door behind her. 'There's such a thing as private property,' she said.

'Such a thing as a crabby old bat,' Alex said.

The woman dropped the key into her purse. 'There's usually a policeman just around this corner!'

As soon as she was out of sight Alex moved back into the doorway.

'Maybe she'll bring a copper,' I said.

He drew himself into his jacket so that his neck disappeared, then twisted his mouth and got down from the step. We walked around the corner and stood in the shelter of a wall.

'He's let me down again, Jeff,' Alex said.

'You can't blame him, it's other people. He's foreign and they take advantage.'

'That last lot was rubbish and people don't like it. *Look*!'

He pulled up his pullover and his shirt to show the side of his belly.

'What's that?' I said.

'A bruise, isn't it?'

'Well, there's *these*,' I said.

I held one out to him. He took it and looked at it between his finger and thumb. 'These are new,' he said, halfway between eagerness and suspicion. He tested it with the tip of his tongue and screwed up his face. 'This stuff's poison!'

'They're just strong, that's all.'

'Are they from the hospital?'

'You don't need to know.'

'I can't sell these, anyway.'

'Just try it. These are *special*.'

He shook his head and started pushing at me with a yellow look in his eye. We struggled against the wall. I had the dog lead in one hand and the paper bag in the other. The dog started to growl and snap. It jumped up against our legs.

Alex stood back, short of breath. The colour came and went in his face.

'Hey, I can't mess around. I need some for tonight.'

I held up the bag. 'There's fifty?'

'Let me count!'

I snatched it back. 'No, there's fifty!'

He sneered and pulled a note out of his back pocket. I took it and smoothed it out. It had been torn across and then repaired with Sellotape turning stiff and yellow.

'That Wally's a get!' he said.

'He's okay.'

I walked back through the town. It was about four already with the traffic getting busy. As we crossed to the station the dog sat down in the middle of the road and started to croon, flattening his ears and lifting his muzzle. His mouth was delicate and pursed. Cars blew their horns and swerved to avoid us. The dog's noise started in his belly somewhere and then passed through his rib-cage to come out of the jaws like a

189

musical note. I pulled at his lead but he wouldn't budge, as if he were glued to the tarmac.

A van stopped and the driver got out. 'What the hell's this?' he asked.

'The dog's sick!'

'Sick, is it?' He slipped his fat fingers under the dog's collar and tugged hard. Jeff still wouldn't move but I could see the leather cutting into his throat. The tone of the noise he made changed. The van-driver squatted down and looked into the dog's face.

'This animal's *blind*!' he said.

'No it isn't!'

He stared at me with his hands on his hips. More drivers were blowing their horns behind him. 'Why, anyone can see it is!'

The dog meanwhile was now standing quiet on all fours and sniffing at his own smell on the road. The loop of the lead was slack in my hand.

We walked the rest of the way home. Jeff kept bumping into things. The circles which had once been barely visible and then only at certain lights and angles had thickened now and closed so that they covered the whole of his eyes.

My mother was at home, sitting by herself in the kitchen. 'You know you have to go into hospital?' she asked.

'I know! I know that! There's something the matter with the dog, Mam!'

'I keep telling you but you won't take it in.'

'I mean his eyes.'

'I'm talking about *you*, Leonard, not just a dumb animal.'

My aunt came back from the shops. She unpacked the things in almost silence. After our silent tea she decided to take the dog to the vet.

'I'll go,' I said.

'It's better me. I might have to pay him something.'

'I've got some money.'

She laughed. 'Whoever heard of a child having money?'

She clipped the lead on to the dog's collar. The dog sighed and whined, confused but still eager to be taken out. I followed them into the hall.

190

'Your mother's *sad*,' my aunt said. 'Because she lost her job.'

'Why?'

'There's no why about it, Leonard: they sack people whenever they want in those places. They've done it to the Poles already . . . So if she starts talking funny to you, you just have to take no notice.'

'What do you mean funny?'

She smiled and nudged me. The dog was pulling her towards the front door. 'Well, not funny exactly. You can't really call it funny.'

After she'd gone I sat in the living room and my mother sat in the kitchen. After about half an hour she called to me.

'Leonard, they searched my locker, you know.'

'Why did they do that?'

'They had me in the office. They asked all sorts of questions.'

'What sorts of questions?'

'Questions about pills. Wanting to know about these *pill* things.' She turned away from me and then back. She said, 'Leonard, I never hear you *sing* nowadays.'

'I can't sing, Mam. I never could sing.'

She laughed. 'Oh, anyone can sing, Leonard. And it would do my heart good if you were to sing for me.'

'Only I *can't* sing,' I said.

My mother cleared her throat. I waited, reading a book. After about another hour my aunt came back without the dog.

'Where's the dog?'

She sat down without taking off her coat. 'Well, you know those white things it had, in its eyes? Well, that was because of a worm.'

I got up from the table. I could hear my mother being quiet in the kitchen. 'How could a *worm* cause it?'

'Not exactly a worm,' my aunt said. 'Something like a worm but smaller.'

She unclipped the top of her bag and took out the dog's lead and its collar. They still smelt of the dog.

Nineteen

Mrs Rinse did not get better. My mother coughed as she sat in the kitchen, a dry noise. Aunt Irene turned from the rent-books to stare into the open doorway. Walking to the pet-shop, I saw a dog like my dog that died. There'd been an accident near the war memorial and metal barriers closed off the pavement.

I bought two large boxes of the grey pills, a hundred to each. 'You're thinking in bulk now,' Mr Webster said with a wink.

He wiped the corner of his eye carefully with a knuckle. A black spot had gathered between his grey trimmed moustache and his nose. I looked towards the back of the shop and saw the monkey as it leapt from one side of its enclosure to the other. It crashed against the wire mesh and then flung itself towards its dead tree and ran down towards the floor fist-after-fist.

'Some of them are for a friend,' I said.

He stared at me for a second, breathing down his nose, his eyes careful and doggish. 'Then does he have worms as well?'

Trudy laughed behind her till. She dropped the boxes into a paper bag and then rang up the sale. It came to over three pounds.

I paid with a five-pound note. 'There's such a thing as an abuse of medicines,' Mr Webster said quietly. He stared at me and then nodded towards the window with its stickers and display of cacti. 'And here's a relative of yours.'

I went outside. Aunt Irene was standing on the pavement holding the arm of a man. 'This man needs to catch a train,' she told me. 'He's blind.'

The blind man smiled at us. He was tall and square-faced, with short dark hair neatly combed to the side. He wore a light raincoat and held his stick upright and close to his body so that the end of it did not quite touch the ground.

'I was looking at the monkey,' I said.

She looked anxious. 'Monkeys are a lot of trouble, Leonard. They should leave them in Africa.'

'Yes,' I said.

'Later this week your mother has to go to Leeds after a job. It's only an interview first of all and so she'll be back soon.'

'She's *ill*,' I said.

My aunt nodded sympathetically. 'Only life must go on, Leonard.'

'What kind of job is it?'

She smiled and looked up at the blind man. 'Oh, you can't be particular with jobs. You have to take them as they come.'

'Is the job in Leeds?'

'No, just the interview: we won't build up our hopes.'

The Poles left the next day. I saw Oscar standing with his wicker suitcase in the bus terminus. Next to it was a tartan holdall with a rip in its side repaired with black insulating tape. I knew that must be Wally's luggage. At first Oscar frowned and pretended not to see me, but then when I went closer he beckoned me over. He took out his tobacco tin and rolled two thin cigarettes. He lit them both between his lips and passed one to me.

'In Poland everyone smokes, Leonard. Even babies in their cribs. It's a cold place and it heats the air through the lungs. At the beginning you feel a little sick, but you should persevere.'

'Where's Wally?' I asked.

He sighed and lowered his eyes. 'He's having his hair cut.'

I looked at the sign above the stop. I knew it was the place where people waited for the long-distance coaches.

'So where are you going?'

He held the cigarette in the middle of his mouth and pulled a face around it. I knew then that I shouldn't have asked. We stood silently looking up the aisle. Buses came and went, juddering on their fat tyres, and more people joined the back of the queue. After about ten minutes Wally arrived with a newspaper and a packet of biscuits. He wore the thick leather jacket he'd bought for the bike and his hair was very short at the back and sides, combed across the top of his head in shiny furrows.

He opened the packet of biscuits and offered me one but the cigarette had spoiled my appetite. He laughed and bit into it himself. His hair smelt of Brylcreem and his exposed ears were small and round, bluish at their tips.

Oscar and I smoked while Wally ate the biscuits. When the bus came it had *Doncaster* on the front. 'Only our first stop,' Oscar said quickly. He turned to his friend. 'Have you any quids left?'

Wally frowned.

'Yes, *quids*!' Oscar said in a louder voice. Then he began to speak quickly in Polish. I watched Wally, who stared at the trembling side of the bus. Oscar held his hand out to his friend with the palm flat. Wally went through the zippered pockets of his jacket one by one and finally pulled out a roll of notes held tight by a rubber band. He stripped the band into a twisting worm and let it drop to the pavement. Carefully he peeled away a couple of notes and held them out to me.

'And more!' Oscar said.

Wally separated another few notes and held them out with his barbered head lowered. I took them and stuffed them into my pocket.

Then Oscar put his hand on the other man's shoulder and whispered secretively to him in Polish, although no one there would have been able to understand. People were squeezing past us now to board the coach. Wally handed me more of the money. The roll had uncurled and he separated the notes with his flattened thumb.

'Leonard, this is for your mother,' Oscar said.

Wally lifted his face and smiled. I could see from his crooked teeth that he was suffering.

My mother was working in the back garden with the wooden-handled shears. She opened and closed the stiff blades with effort and chopped at the tough clumps of grass. The slopes of the roofs were shiny with fine rain. After a while the shears became clogged with damp ends of grass and she had to stop and free them. She saw me standing in the yard and I walked towards her on the herringbone path. The money in my fist soaked up the dampness of the air. My mother closed the blades of the shears and held them upright before her. She had greased the swivel with lard.

'There's some money,' I said.

'From *him*?'

'The other as well,' I said.

I held it towards her but she turned to the side. She bent over the lawn again, one leg set before the other. She wore shiny rubber galoshes to save her shoes.

'Are they gone then . . . Already?'

I didn't answer. She laughed and started to cut again, working away from me along a long edge of the lawn. The chop of the shears threw ends of grass into the air.

'There's quite a lot,' I told her. I spread the notes out in my hand but she wouldn't look.

'Just burn it!'

'You can't burn money!'

'Just chuck it on the fire!'

I pushed the money into my pocket and went through the back door into the kitchen. The clack of the shears followed me. Aunt Irene was sitting at the living-room table. The fire was damped with ashes to last through the day. Its slippery warmth oozed into the room.

'The Poles have gone,' I told her.

She took her hand from her mouth. 'Yes, Leonard: I'm not insensible.'

I went upstairs with the money. I counted it sitting on my bed and then slipped it flat under the edge of the carpet. There was nearly enough now. I turned to the wall and looked at the features of the moon. I read out the names for luck.

'Lost the dog?'

I didn't answer.

'And the Poles as well!'

'They've gone.'

'Then who's this from? This *stuff*!'

'I can't tell you that.'

He massaged his belly. 'They give you the gut-ache!'

'You should take them with water.'

He laughed. He'd bought a pair of shoes with high polished

heels. He walked awkwardly, splashing through mud, rounding his elderly shoulders.

When I got back to the house I saw a copper standing in the hall. He had his back to me. He held his helmet behind him with his black gloves laid inside, talking to my Aunt Irene, who stood close with my mother slightly behind. Then another copper stepped out from the Poles' room carrying an empty bottle. This one was in plain clothes: a white raincoat, collar and tie. He stared at me as I came up the hall.

'This is the lad,' my aunt told him.

'Yes I can see, missis.' He held up the bottle. 'Now, have you any idea what this is?'

'*Miss*,' my aunt corrected.

The uniformed copper pointed to my mother. 'Missis here is missis.'

The other one turned to me. 'And this is the man of the house?'

'Leonard is *ill*,' my aunt said. 'He's to go into hospital quite soon.'

'I'm sorry to hear that,' the plain-clothes copper said. He showed her the empty bottle again. 'Only there's half a dozen of these under the bed and they all smell of drink.'

I noticed that the bottle was not quite empty but had a slip of clear liquor in the bottom.

'Well, there's nothing wrong with a fellah taking a drink,' my aunt said. 'Especially not a single fellah. Especially not two single fellahs sharing together.'

The copper put the bottle down upright between his feet in their brown shoes. 'That depends on how it was obtained, you see . . . You know we've got authority for the whole house,' he added.

'And what does that mean?'

He glanced at the uniformed man. 'That means, love, we could go through every room if we wanted.'

Aunt Irene turned to my mother but she shook her head as though she could not speak. She hung back, near to the padlocked door of the cellar.

'This is a lodging house,' my aunt said. 'Those are private dwellings and they have their own keys.'

The copper smiled. 'That means you have to be careful then, love. Do you ask for references?'

'Only I'm not your love,' my aunt said. 'Far from it.' She reached out to tap me on the shoulder. 'You go upstairs now, Leonard!'

Up in my room I hid the worming tablets in the inside pocket of my disused school blazer and then pushed the money deeper under the carpet. Then I tried to flatten the bulge with my foot. There was always more of it – grubby, torn, ink-stained notes which gathered under my bed like shameful litter. After a while I'd stopped counting; it seemed like too much labour to separate that greasy wad. Now I thought: money has its uses.

When I heard the coppers leave I went downstairs again.

'They look at you as if you're shite!' my aunt said. 'The one in uniform was more respectful but the other was a cheeky young get!'

My mother touched her throat with her fingertips. She started to massage it as if she had a pain there. 'They've got me upset now, Irene. I feel all fluttery inside.'

Aunt Irene looked at her from the corner of her eye. 'Now, Eileen, you musn't let it affect your interview!'

She packed her case. She folded her clothes inside and tucked away toilet items.

'Just a small case,' she said. 'It's what you call an overnight bag.'

I watched as she snapped it shut and locked it with a tiny key. 'Only for an interview?'

'It's in *catering*, Leonard, and they can be very particular. I could be handling money and all sorts. But I might not get it and so we mustn't build our hopes.'

'No, the way things are there'll be hundreds have applied,' my aunt said.

'There'll be thousands in my position,' my mother said. 'More than you could count!'

She walked towards the railway station. She passed the closed pub and crossed the road in front of the dairy. She turned and waved me back. I waited out of sight until I knew

197

she would have disappeared and then walked around the streets for a while. A man with a theodolite stood on the wasteground among the parked lorries. He directed another man with a striped pole. When I went back to the house Aunt Irene was sitting at the table in her best clothes, her white kid gloves beside her. She had put out the fire.

'Now we must go as well, Leonard.'

I saw that some of my clothes were airing on the line. 'But where to?'

'You mustn't ask me that till later. You can change your clothes now because I'd like you to be smart.'

She went into the kitchen. I put on the warmed clothes. The sweater was new and soft wool but with a tight crew neck.

'Put your collar outside, Leonard!'

She had powdered her face and the scent of the powder came before her. She was dressed in a suit of knobbly tweed with a short rainproof cape. There was a rabbit's-foot brooch in her lapel, its silver mounting set off by small red stones.

'This was our mother's,' she said, touching it. 'These are what you call garnets.'

'It's nice.'

'Whatever happens in life, you must never neglect your appearance, Leonard. Everything depends on it. People are lazy and they see no further. If people see you with dirty shoes or a grubby collar then you fall right down in their estimation.'

'Yes,' I said.

'So put your coat on. And your scarf.'

Her shoes made a sharp sound, as if she gave a special emphasis to each step. She carried her small tartan bag with a cloth closing the top.

'Put your arm in mine. We're not going far and after that we can come straight back. I've packed a flask and some sandwiches – the tea will be stewed but we must make do.'

A single-decker bus waited beside the stop where I had last seen the Poles. It was new-looking with a white top and yellow sides.

'Eileen will be on her train now, God-speed to her,' Aunt Irene said.

198

The motor of the bus was already running. The folding doors opened and we took a double seat near the back. When the conductor came my aunt asked for a place I'd never heard of.

'You'll have to change,' he said.

She frowned. 'Will you tell us when then? It's years since I've been that way.'

The bus left town by the long avenue which passed the cemeteries.

'Do you remember the old fellah?' she asked.

'Of course I do.'

'There's no of course about it, Leonard. People are soon forgotten. Your gran's buried in there, you know. Not this part but the next.'

'I know.'

She laughed and shook her head. 'It's hard to tell you anything!' She gripped her bag with the flask inside, keeping it upright on her lap. 'I could just as well be your mother, you know. Though that wasn't what was intended.'

I pretended that I hadn't heard.

'Let me know when you'd like a cup of tea,' Aunt Irene said.

I looked out of the window. We'd reached the edges of the town, where the houses had big front gardens behind high wooden fences. My aunt unwrapped the egg sandwiches and handed one to me. The bread was pale and limp, greasy with melted butter. When I took one a slice of hard-boiled egg slipped out on to my trouser-leg. I picked it off and pushed it back between the two halves of bread.

'You're almost out in the country here,' Aunt Irene said. 'Is this the sort of place you'd like to live when you're older?'

'Where are we going?' I asked.

She lifted her hand to show that I should be quiet. A few minutes later we were among the fields. There was a big red-brick house ahead, but when the coach reached it I saw that it was two buildings separated by a cobbled yard. In the middle of the yard a long-bodied pig scratched its side against an iron frame.

'You see, I fell, Leonard,' Aunt Irene said.

'*Fell*?'

She chuckled. 'It's just one of the daft things people say. It's an expression.'

The fields on either side of the road were filled with churned-up mud. Derelict-looking buildings stood among low clumps of trees. We ate our sandwiches. Our teas shivered and spilled over the rims of the cups. The bus stopped a few times to let people on but no one seemed to get off, although the cabin was always less than half full. We turned off the road and went through the narrow streets of a village.

'That's a memorial,' Aunt Irene said as if she was recalling things. She stretched across me to point. 'For people who died in the war. They put flowers on Armistice Day when there's two minutes' silence. *In memory*. That's the Ouse,' she said when we went over a bridge. I half stood in my seat but couldn't see the water. The conductor called to us from the front of the bus.

'We have to change now, Leonard.'

We sat on a bench near the stop. A river came into the middle of the village in a ditch behind fences. I could hear the water.

'Is it still the Ouse?'

Aunt Irene uncorked the vacuum-flask. 'No, it's another river. More what you'd call a stream.' She stared at a woman who smiled at us from across the road. 'People are inquisitive in the country. They've nothing to occupy their minds. If anyone asks you questions you must tell them to mind their business. Then if they persist tell them you've come to visit your father.'

A cattle lorry went by slowly. The cattle poked their noses out through holes in the wooden sides and I heard the sucking sound of their breath. 'It's a shame to keep things confined,' Aunt Irene said. 'Life's full of cruelty when you look at it.'

The next bus was shorter and squarer with a wooden rack on the top for luggage. Its sides were splashed with mud. There was no conductor and the driver collected the money before we started. My aunt said the name again. 'Frodham, please.'

'*Frodham?*' the driver asked with a different way of speaking.

My aunt nudged me. 'That's the quaint way they talk, Leonard.'

At first the bus followed the side of the river so that I could sometimes see the shine of water behind trees. Then it climbed a hill and the engine started to rattle and shudder. There was the grassy slope of the hill on one side of us and white sky and flat countryside on the other. Dark square rocks pushed out of the ground. My ears popped and then I belched because of the sweet stewed tea.

'Bless you, Leonard!'

The bus turned away from the hill and descended in tight bends into a narrow line of trees which became higher and darker. The small lights lit up along the cabin. The taste of the tea was still at the back of my throat. The bus stopped and I looked through our window at the top of a bush. Every twig and leaf of the bush was dusted with a thin white powder which caught the light in shining points. The bus-driver turned and winked at us.

'Here you are,' he said. 'Little Lapland.'

Aunt Irene stood in the aisle buttoning her jacket. I was still looking out of the window and she tugged at my arm. 'Here we are, Leonard.'

'You can lead a horse to water,' the driver said as we stepped down on to the verge. He grinned at us and then back along the length of the bus. The remaining passengers laughed as the folding doors closed.

My aunt looked sad and angry. 'People are sly in these country places. They have to pass comments.'

The bus left in a white cloud. The road and the grasses to the side of it were frosted and shiny with the powder which blew about in the air as we started to walk. Although it was white in itself it floated against the white of the sky as a dark film. Already I could see specks of it on the shoulders of my aunt's jacket.

'You get used to it when you work here,' she told me. 'And they give you special clothing and a mask.'

We followed a tall wire fence with white bushes behind. Each stand of wire had a thin capping of dust. When I plucked at the links the powder flew up in a cloud.

'That fellah is watching us, Leonard.'

There were open wire gates and a barrier for lorries. A man

in a peaked cap sat in a booth behind wired glass. My aunt put her mouth to a sort of grille. I saw the head of an alsatian dog which the man stroked as he spoke through his telephone. He opened the door of the cabin to point.

'He wasn't very civil,' Aunt Irene said as we walked on. 'He was rather *brusque*.'

We followed a tarmac road between plots of grass and mud. The mud had mixed with the white powder to make a chalky grey colour. A rumble like the turning over of a big motor came from low long buildings with sides and roofs of corrugated grey.

'That's where they work, Leonard. To make *asbestos*: it's saved thousands of lives in the world. An asbestos house will never burn!'

The long windows of the buildings were blank and white. A pair of double doors was open at the front. White powder billowed out although it looked dark inside. A couple of lorries were parked facing us and a man stepped out from behind them and came towards us. He was average-sized and wore a white overall and a mask and goggles. He stripped off the mask as he came nearer and then removed the goggles. Without them his face looked dark-patched and clownish. He waved and my aunt waved back.

'Wave to him, Leonard!'

'Why?'

'You don't want to seem stand-offish.'

The man took off his white cap. The top of his head was bare and shiny, as if the skin had been waxed. He seemed to carry his own atmosphere of floating whiteness, the breeze blowing clouds of it from his shoulders and the folds of his clothes.

'That's never Leonard,' he said when he came close.

'It's no one else, Jeff,' Aunt Irene said.

She turned away as if this didn't concern her now, as if she wished to let things take their course. The man wiped his hands on the front of his overalls. His palms came up dark against the white backs. The hair behind his ears was white and I could see the dust on his eyebrows and the tips of his eyelashes. My aunt walked a few yards and looked back towards the gate.

He laughed as if he felt uncomfortable. He made a circle with his arm. 'Well, this is where I work, Leonard.'

I looked at the dusty buildings and grass. A forklift truck was working at the back of one of the lorries, loading a pallet-ful of white panels. I coughed and put my hand to my mouth. 'It tickles your throat!'

He winked at me. 'That's why we wear a mask.'

'Is this where you live?' I asked.

He smiled and beckoned with his finger. 'You follow me.'

We walked towards the corner of the building where the lor-ries were parked. The white powder covered the ground nearly as far as you could see, but then there was the dark side of a hill which looked almost black by contrast, then the line of an-other behind that. My father cleared his throat and spat at the white ground. His spit made a dark circle with a speck of white inside. A gust blew and the dust started to clear from his face. I could see the dark lines on it extending and meeting one an-other, knitting together.

He pointed. 'You see that far hill?'

'Yes.'

'Well, what you can't see is that there's another hill on the far side of it. And between the one you can see and the one you can't, that's where I live.'

We looked around at the buildings and the grounds. My aunt still kept her distance. The guard had left his cabin and was standing outside with his dog. The alsatian pulled against its leash and barked out white clouds. Another door opened in the building behind us and the turning rumble of machinery became louder.

'You can think it's snow sometimes,' Jeff said. 'You can pre-tend that it's Christmas all year.'

'It's more like the moon.'

He laughed. 'My imagination doesn't stretch that far.'

'You weren't long!'

'He doesn't say much.'

'That's the way he's always been. You have to draw him out if you want a conversation.'

There was a bench near the bus stop. We brushed powder from the seat and sat down.

'Was the dog named after him?' I asked.

She nodded, smiling. 'That was Eileen's idea. She's funny sometimes. She's got her own ways of turning the tables.'

We waited for the bus for about an hour. We finished the sandwiches and brushed dust from each other's clothes. Aunt Irene looked at her face in the mirror of her compact. 'I've such a big nose,' she said.

'It's not.'

She clicked shut the case. 'He couldn't make up his mind, you see. Or he wouldn't. Then in the end he decided that one of us was as good as the other.'

'But then who's my mother?' I asked. 'Only one of you must be.'

I saw the bus coming from a long way off, in the sunshine at the other end of the avenue of white trees. My aunt folded the paper the sandwiches had been in.

'Only it isn't as easy as that, Leonard! Mebbe you could think of it as being that we both are. If you think of it that we're both the half of it.'

Twenty

My mother came back ill and stayed in bed. I listened to her through the wall between the rooms. I moved the cup northwards from the Ocean of Storms. The peaks and craters clustered near the lunar poles, foreshortened and collecting shadows. She called out. I moved the cup again along the spine of the Apennines. She sighed as the rim of the cup touched the crater Tycho with its spokes of powdery light. Then she cleared her throat and groaned. I could not take the cup from the paper. My ear was held by negative electricity to the end of an everlasting siphon. She said something quietly in the dark.

Aunt Irene carried in a basin covered by a cloth. The cloth steamed where it was stretched and smelt of eucalyptus. Later she took in a mug of soup and closed the door.

I listened to her coaxing. 'You should eat the soup at least: it's oxtail.'

'I'll never eat again,' my mother promised.

Aunt Irene spoke to me on the middle landing, lowering her voice so that I could hardly hear. 'She's in torment with her bowels, Leonard! The bowels are a woman's weak spot.'

I thought about Mrs Goffrey's cream-coloured telephone. 'Shall I call for the doctor?'

She shook her head. 'Doctors are no use with this, Leonard: it's *internal*.'

She sat in the bed eating drinking soup with pieces of bread, sipping from the side of the spoon. Outside Aunt Irene vacuumed the stairs in her pale blue housecoat. She turned off the Hoover with her heel.

'She feels better now, but she's still ill. The train was late and she was waiting for hours on the platform. Standing there with her cases.'

'Why didn't she wait in the waiting room?'

'Maybe it was closed, Leonard. Or maybe it was too smoky. There were men inside smoking and cursing. *Drink*, you see. A woman on her own, she decided to wait outside where the air was clearer, but that was her mistake! She took a chill standing on the platform and it struck at her bowels.'

The bedroom had a sweetish smell like burnt milk. She sat up against her pillows with the curtains closed and the light on close to the bed. Her lips had creases through them and her eyes were darker and smaller. She pushed out her hand and caught my arm above the elbow. The cold of her fingers went through my sleeve.

'He's *different* to me,' she said. 'In these last few days.'

Aunt Irene held a mug of tea with the handle facing outwards. 'These youngsters change all the time, Eileen. And there's nothing you can do to stop it.'

Mrs Rinse started to move her things downstairs into the old fellah's room. My aunt shelled peas in the kitchen. She put her head to one side as if she was listening. 'She's awake now . . . Take her some tea.'

The whistling kettle blew from the stove. I carried the cup slipping against its saucer up the stairs. The gravity in the house was becoming unpredictable. When I reached the landing I saw Mrs Rinse holding a big fold of gold-coloured eiderdown before her, her small hands clasped around its front. The worn rings shone on her fingers. She did not speak as I squeezed past her but ran down the rest of the stairs quietly and with surprising swiftness.

'Open the curtains,' my mother ordered. 'No, keep them closed.'

She sipped the tea.

'I've a taste in my mouth that poisons everything!' she said. 'It's something like cabbage.'

She listened to the movements on the stairs. The footsteps backwards and forwards accelerated into a mouse-like ripple.

'Where's her bad chest now?' she asked. She let her hand fall. Her forehead turned shiny in a second. 'Tell Irene to come *quick*!'

I ran downstairs holding the empty cup. The old fellah's door was open with the light on inside against the dark afternoon. My aunt was in the kitchen, rinsing a sponge under the hot tap. She took down a small enamel bowl. 'You go out now, Leonard. For a walk.' She took the cup from me and stood it in the sink.

I thought about the platforms of the world joined to one another by the thread of the rails. A continuous cold wind passed over each of them. I went to the wasteground to watch the men at the fire. A police car was parked opposite with two coppers inside eating fish suppers. In the evening Mrs Rinse fell down the bottom flight of stairs and lay on her back in the hall. Her legs were uncovered and a net of thick blue veins covered both her thighs.

'Poor Muriel,' my aunt wailed.

'Muriel?'

'Why, that's her name!'

The commotion brought my mother out of bed. She looked down from the bend in the stairs. Mrs Rinse's eyes were closed and her face was white and blotchy. Aunt Irene knelt down and put an ear to her chest. She listened for a second and then stood up again. 'I can't hear a heart but she's still breathing . . . You should run for an ambulance, Leonard!'

I ran out into the street. A fat liver-coloured dog with a studded collar was standing outside Mrs Goffrey's main door so that I had to step over it to reach the bell. I rang until she answered. She opened the door by about three inches to show just her face.

'Can I use the phone?' I asked.

'I'm afraid it isn't convenient, Leonard. Is it an emergency?'

'It's Mrs Rinse.'

'I'm sorry to hear that but there's a public phone-box nearby!' She nodded at the dog. 'Is that your animal?'

'No,' I said.

'Then can you please shoo him away?'

She smiled and closed her door quietly and dropped the latch.

The phone-box was on the opposite corner of the street.

There was a woman inside leaning so that her bottom pressed against the glass. She turned her back to me more squarely as I waited outside the door. A man on a moped went by. When she dropped another coin into the slot I remembered that I didn't have change. I walked back to Mrs Goffrey's. The dog was still standing outside. This time she opened the door wider. She was wearing a canary-coloured dressing gown.

'I've no change for the phone.'

She nodded. 'I see your friend is still here.'

'He isn't my dog, Mrs Goffrey.'

She closed her eyes. 'Wait here a second.'

She left the door open and went back into the house. Her feet were bare with a dirty plaster on the back of one heel. When she came back she said, 'Hold out your hands.'

She opened her fist over them. There was about five shillings in loose change so that it was too much to hold. Some of it spilled on to the pavement and rolled away. The dog trotted further down the street. Mrs Goffrey closed her door when I bent down to pick up the money.

'You shouldn't wish for too much,' my mother said. 'You have to hold yourself in check. Only it was in her grasp and she wanted to make certain. When the ambulance-men picked her up she was just like jelly: her flesh had given up the ghost. Wilf is on overtime. They've sent someone to his work and he'll go straight to the hospital. This last straw will break his heart.'

I counted pills into a clear plastic bag and then folded the top and slipped it into the inside pocket of my coat. I went downstairs. The noise of the Hoover came from the middle room. The door was half open and the padlock hung from its staple. My aunt had taken the curtains down from the windows. You could see nothing of the dark yard, only something like another, dimmer room hinging at an angle from the first. The glass rattled in the wind funnelling along the back garden.

'I'll throw these out,' my aunt said. 'These old pictures of black people. What use are they?'

'I'm going for a walk,' I said.

She stared at me for a second. 'Always for a walk! You must miss that dog.'

I crossed the street to the wasteground. There was a crowd standing close-shouldered along the pavement, staring at something with their backs to me. There was a rattle of chatter and the squad car was there again, or it had never left. Its revolving lamp lit up the blank wall of the typewriter factory and then moved off into darkness. The crowd seemed cheered and excited by something I couldn't see. I looked for a space, stretching to see over their shoulders. I heard a smooth purr of ball-bearings and turned around. Alex stopped with a squeak of new brakes.

'They're clearing the dossers!'

'What for?'

He laughed. 'What d'you mean what for?'

'They'll have nowhere to go,' I said.

'They can leave town then. They can emigrate!' He sat upright on the saddle with his arms folded. I couldn't stop looking at the bike, it was so new and shiny. 'They're going to build something here,' he said.

He started to ring the bike's bell and push at the legs of the crowd with his front wheel. A woman turned on us. 'No need to ladder my bloody stockings! Cheeky little sod!'

We gave up and tried nearer the corner. The crowd thinned out there and we were able to squeeze into a space between a woman with a push-chair and a fat man with a terrier dog. A black police van was parked backing on to the bombsite. The back of the van had its doors open and I could see a bench on either side of the lit inside. A pair of coppers in long raincoats were sitting talking at the end of one of the benches.

'It's the paddy-wagon,' Alex said.

The fat man laughed and belched. He was drinking from a bottle of beer. The dog started to yap and he choked it off by yanking on its lead, almost pulling it into the air. There were no police I could see in the squad car now but it still had its headlights on, aimed into the middle of the wasteground. The piles of brick and rubble had a lunar look in the one-sided light. Then Alex nudged me as another pair of coppers came into sight dragging one of the dossers towards the van. When the man was within reach the pair inside bent down to take hold of his arms and pull him inside. The dosser struggled but not very much. The people on the pavement started to cheer as the coppers pulled him up into the van.

'They're going to build a car park,' Alec said with excitement.

'It's already a car park.'

'This'll be *multi-storey*!' He nodded at the police van. 'They were at your house then!'

'Looking for the Poles,' I said. It gave me a feeling of distinction.

He nodded, tucking his chin into his chest. 'They'll find them for certain. The Poles are foreigners and everywhere they go they'll stand out.'

I started to laugh. It seemed funny and strange that Wally and Oscar could be fugitives. Alex gave me a sideways look. It was quiet on the wasteground for a while, just the headlamps making brightness and sharp shadows on the piles of bricks. I passed the time by looking at the bike. It had a racing frame and complicated gears. When I laid my finger on the dropped handlebars the chrome gave a sting of cold like electricity.

'Where did you nick this?'

He lifted his chin. 'I don't nick things now – I just *pay* for them.'

He coughed and passed me four pound-notes under cover of his sleeve. I folded the money tight and slipped it into the pocket of my coat.

He watched me. 'What do you want it for? You never go anywhere!'

'I'm saving up,' I told him.

He sneered. 'Yeah, for a fortnight in Moscow.'

'No, further than that.'

Now the coppers were forcing another man towards the van. He was struggling and one of them was holding his wrists together behind his back. When the man saw the coppers waiting in the van he kicked back with his heel and managed to get one arm free. He twisted around, lashing out with it. I saw that it wasn't a man but the woman.

'It's that old brass,' Alex said.

'She just looks old.'

'She's *ancient*! She uses shit for make-up!'

The people watching from the pavement began to cheer, mocking the coppers as they struggled with the woman. They were holding her now by the sleeves of her coat. She tried to tear away but her heels skidded on the mud. She slipped to the ground on her side. One of the coppers in the van was standing in the open doorway, arms spanning the sides, watching with the light behind him.

'I know that one – he's a right get!' Alex said.

The woman lay in the mud with the coppers still hanging on to her sleeves. They tried to drag her upright, pulling with both hands at her clothes as if they did not want to touch her skin. The crowd jeered and the coppers in the van started to yell advice. The woman twisted on the ground and managed to free herself from the coat. She fell on to her hands and knees and then tried to get up but the copper with the torch caught her suddenly with his arm around her throat, forcing back her head. I saw her struggling, gasping face in the lights from the squad car.

Behind the cages of fidgeting mice and hamsters, the woolly monkey leapt without noise from wall to wall, from its dead tree to the wire ceiling, to the floor and then back again to a wall. It did not rest for a second so that it was a moving shape of darkness in the cage.

'Is it ill?'

Webster shook his head. 'It's had its injections. Only it can't *reconcile* itself.'

We watched, standing together. The monkey timed its jumps so that it seemed barely to touch the outlines of its space, flicking itself from barrier to barrier without force or noise, its precise fingers gripping the mesh exactly, its tail counterbalancing the spidery weight of its body and limbs. I thought that if the cage was removed it would still make the same shapes in the shit-smelling air.

'So why don't you just let it go?' I asked.

He laughed. 'It isn't as simple as that! They can bite or spread disease. People forget that they're wild animals.'

211

He shook his head and went to the counter. Trudy yawned and showed the pink inside of her mouth. She put down her magazine and without being asked she reached for a box of tablets. I went to the front of the shop to look at the potted plants.

'Will it flower?' my mother asked.

'I don't know.'

'Still, the leaves are nice. Like marble. This type of plant isn't hardy, though: you shouldn't spend your money on them.'

She reached down behind the bed and took something from the floor.

'I've bought you these. Do you like them?'

She held up a pair of pyjamas, still folded and pinned inside their cellophane wrapping. The cloth had a stiff and shiny look and the stripes were bright and hard. I knew my aunt must have chosen them for her.

I stood the plant near the window. 'When are you getting up?'

'When is a matter of time, Leonard.'

I carried an empty soup bowl downstairs. Aunt Irene was in the kitchen scrubbing new potatoes.

'I have something to tell you,' she said. 'And it's an awful thing: Mrs Rinse is dying.'

'With her lungs?' I asked.

'Those are only the start of it. When those men picked her up her body flopped about as if it was not properly held together. It was awful to see and upset me. Wilf is taking time off work to be with her. If you see him you must say hello but not ask any questions.'

'What about the Poles' room now?' I asked.

'I've locked it up again. You mustn't go anywhere near that place or the police will see your fingerprints. Those men were both criminals as it turned out. What with all the lodgers leaving us we soon won't be able to afford the place and then where will we live? We shall walk the streets, I expect. This is between you and me. You mustn't worry your mother with it when she's already persecuted.'

Mr Dorman came again. He sat on the couch with his pigskin

case between his feet. The electric fire on its stripy snake of flex was trained on the air between us.

'It feels cold in here even with that fire,' Aunt Irene said. 'Shall I turn on the extra bar?'

He stretched his small hand towards her. 'There's no need, thanks. It's quite a pleasant day outside.'

'The air in the house lags behind the weather,' Aunt Irene said. 'Leonard's mother is unfortunately ill. She has a bad chill and is off work.'

Mr Dorman opened his case and lifted a thin cardboard folder on to his lap. He unscrewed the top of his fountain pen and then screwed it tight again so that the thread squeaked. 'May I see her for only a minute?'

My aunt shook her head. 'Not even for that long. You see, she's *bed-ridden.*'

After she had left the room Mr Dorman lit a cigarette and read slowly through my exercise books, turning the pages with his stained thumb. When he had finished he made a pile of them on the couch beside him.

'There are a few signs of a lackadaisical attitude creeping in, Leonard. Always remember that O-levels are the key to A-levels and A-levels are the key to the future! Many well-known people were forced to overcome disadvantages. For example, the young Winston Churchill had a serious stutter which he overcame by reading from Homer aloud – in the original Greek as he was a keen Greek scholar from quite an early age. Homer was the author of many famous books including the *Iliad.* Do you know of Homer, Leonard?'

'No,' I said.

'And that former stutterer became our greatest war leader whose speeches played an important part in defeating the Nazis. Afterwards they were issued as a series of gramophone records.'

'A Greek stayed here,' I said. 'From Cyprus.'

Mr Dorman slipped a finger between his collar and his throat. 'We need to distinguish between the ancient Greeks and the modern.'

'There's something feminine about a man who wears rings.'

213

'It's only a signet ring.'

'On his white hands like putty before it sets . . . He asks for Eileen but I'll allow no man near her again. Because she's already suffered too much!'

She poured more tea. I carried it upstairs. I tripped on the worn stair carpet and spilled some into the saucer. My mother sat up against her pillows, smoking and reading the *Daily Mirror*. She swallowed some of the tea and then finished her cigarette and stubbed it into the glass ashtray. 'Irene makes tea like water,' she said. 'Parsimony is a vice with her.'

I heard a force in her tone. 'Are you feeling better then?'

'The fact is that I'm past caring. She had to give them that room, you see, and *undermine* me. And look what it led to . . . And now I learn that her tongue has been flapping! On some things you shouldn't follow her, Leonard. You should listen but take no notice. She had a disappointment early on, you see, and it's plagued her over the years. She's brooded on it and it's turned her mind.'

'Mr Dorman was here. We talked about Winston Churchill.'

I went down again with the cup and two empty plates.

'She's feeling better,' I said.

'Did she say that?'

'It's what I thought.'

She nodded. 'I'm glad that you're using your eyes, Leonard, because Eileen and me, your mother and I if you prefer it, won't talk from now on. She's sworn a silence towards me and I had to do the same. Or mebbe I did it first, it doesn't matter. So until we are both in our graves we'll never open our lips to talk together and even then.'

She rinsed the table with a dishcloth and hot water. The smell of bleach lifted. 'But how will you manage the house?' I asked.

She looked at me cleverly. 'Mebbe it's time to give up this big place! Or mebbe it'll be taken from us. But that's what I'm saying, Leonard. That's what I hoped you'd understand. If we have anything to do with one another at all, she and I, then it'll be only through a third party!'

Twenty-One

Ralph sat in darkness except for the glow of the fish-tanks and the narrow shine of his anglepoise lamp. He wore his special spectacles with the clip-on magnifying lenses and his floating magnified eyes had the colour of mussel shells. Sour vapours of modelling adhesive rose in the updraught of the lamp. The V2 with its elegant double taper stood against a lattice gantry on a base of glaring sand while white-coated scientists kept their safe distance behind a wall of fire-brick. I went closer and stared down into the tent of light, seeing something disturbing and inexplicable.

'It's got USAF markings!'

He looked pleased with himself. 'Every detail is historically accurate, Leonard. You see, despite the bolshie propaganda the Yanks were the first into space!'

'What?'

He nodded. 'Yes, using one of their own missiles and a modified V2 as booster. That was at White Sands rocket base. In 1947. *Ten* years before the Sputniks. They reached a height of two hundred miles. That's above the furthest limits of the atmosphere!'

He sat back as if he had conclusively proved something. I turned away from the bright table towards the dimness of the rest of the room. I could hear my heart above the throb of the air-pump, beating strongly and purposefully not from fear but to strengthen me for combat.

'But it wasn't a *real* space journey, Ralph. There was no pay-load and the rocket fell back to Earth – it never even reached escape-velocity! You have to defeat gravity or it's no good!'

I had raised my voice and it seemed to hang in the air with the bitter odours of glue and fish-food. I listened for a second to its echo. Ralph bent over his work again and applied a pin-head of adhesive carefully to the base of one of the scale figures, squeezing the small tube between his finger and thumb. His injured leg was stretched out to one side and I could see that he was excited or agitated because of the trembling of his false foot, a rotating movement which swung it in a short repeating arc on the spindle of the ankle.

'The Yanks were always years behind,' I said, unable to stay quiet. 'They tried twice after Sputnik but one rocket failed and the other blew up on the launching pad. And by then the Russians had already sent up Sputnik 2!'

I turned around. My anger was mirrored in the fish tanks by a thrill of movement, as if the flesh were fleeing from approaching danger.

Ralph sighed to himself. 'Sputnik 2!'

'The one with the space dog,' I told him. 'Laika! The first living thing to leave the Earth!'

He took off his glasses and unclipped the special lenses. He snapped them into their dust-tight case.

'A *dog*! They sent it up knowing that it would die. Man's best friend! You see, they've no respect for life, animal or human!'

He began to stand up, pushing against the edge of the table and using his maimed leg as a kind of lever.

'Like the thousands that have died in their labour camps. They sacrifice everything to the state, you see. That's their be-all and end-all. What you call the philosophy of the ant-heap!'

I had to answer him. I stood with my back against the fish tanks. Their heavy warmth gave me courage.

'No, Ralph: it's the future.'

I waited. I thought I saw him flinch. His face was half turned from me and he spun around quickly, lifting his hand. Was he signalling to me or attacking? His artificial foot slid sideways over the carpet, leaving him off-balance. He reached for the corner of the table for support, tilting back his head, his teeth clenched against the backwash of light from the ceiling. I looked up also and saw cobwebs and their lengthened shadows.

'Oh!' he said. Then he fell, toppling sideways as if he were rotating on a swivel, dragging the chair with him. The back of his head cracked against the angle between the skirting and the floor, in the bare corner where the carpet did not reach. With a thrum like a plucked cable the whole room shifted about one inch to the left.

'Ralph!'

The water slopped heavily in the fish tanks, threatening to spill over the sides. The fish were swept forwards and backwards. There was something comical about their helpless movements. The table lay over Ralph's legs and the model rocket had broken into separate sections, its base and fins still sticking to their upturned desert, the rest scattered about the floor. I could not remember crossing the room but I was at the open door now and my mother calling from downstairs. I was frightened by the calamity and wished to fold myself into some small, defendable space.

'Leonard!' she shouted. '*Leonard?*'

I looked back. Ralph's eyes were closed but his feet kicked against the fallen table.

'*Ralph . . . ?*'

I saw a movement on the floor near one of his helpless hands, a flickering alteration of the light. One of the small silver fish had spilled from its water and lay arching and twitching on the rug. Aunt Irene's voice came from the hall, different in its alarm from my mother's, fearful and already expecting the worst. I went to the stairs and leaned over. I could see both their faces in the telescoped space. 'It's Ralph!' I called. 'He's fallen!'

My mother heard me and turned away. Her hair was loose and the landing light caught her parting like a long smile. Aunt Irene began to climb towards me slowly from downstairs. She wore the thick plastic gloves she sometimes used for housework. Her pink hand gripped and released the rail.

She reached the landing and passed me in silence. 'He slipped,' I explained. 'We were only talking!'

'*Help me,*' my aunt said. 'Help me to pick him up!'

'Only his pride. Only his pride will be hurt,' my mother said.

'He's got a lump on his head,' I said. 'And a graze on his elbow.'

'Did she take him into that room?' She jerked her chin at the ceiling. She meant his illustrated bedroom.

'We carried him to the couch. Then I found his specs for him. They were under the sideboard.'

'She's *besotted* with him, you see. A woman has always to sacrifice herself.'

'Besotted!' I did not really believe it. It sounded like some state of harmful dampness.

Gagarin lay on the inclined couch. Only inches separated the skin of his spacesuit from the inner wall of the capsule, as if it had been built around him. He spoke into the tiny microphone. Distorted by wind and the flat echoes of open spaces his voice was broadcast from loudspeakers mounted on the chaotic scaffolding of the launch gantry.

'Hello, "Earth". I am "cosmonaut". I have tested the communication systems. The tumblers on the control panel are in the assigned initial positions. The navigating globe is at the point of division. My heart beats normally and I am fine. I have put on the gloves, closed the helmet. I am ready now for the start.'

'He's feverish,' Aunt Irene said. 'Feel his brow.'
    'There's no need for me to feel it.'
    'He won't say that he's ill.'
    'Because what's the use to say it?'
    'Because of pride then?'
    'Then there's nothing wrong with pride.'
    'Only,' my aunt started.
    'Excuse me? What *only* is that?'

I woke on the night of the new moon. Over the ridge of the roofs mud-coloured cloud was lit on its underbelly by the lights of the town. A wooden municipal caravan with shuttered windows and a stove flue occupied the site of the new car park. A man sat smoking on its steps, his knees drawn close to his belly. I saw the spark of his cigarette as he inhaled.

The waters were under the house again! I felt the tug of the spring tide. I dressed without turning on the light, picking up clothes from their dark shapes on the floor, pulling on my pants, slipping a sweater over the jacket of my pyjamas, pushing bare feet into the chill of my shoes. I took the candle from its place and then the matches. I stopped on the landing to listen. The breaths of the sisters sounded through their door.

I felt my way into darkness with my hand on the banister, treading on the edges of the steps so as to make no noise. I struck a match when I reached the hall and held it to the candle. The flame leaned against the black stub of wick, squeezing out slow liquid, generating parallel wisps of smoke at its tip. The smell of the wax was startling. The edges of things had a fine shiver. I dredged for the wad of my handkerchief and unpicked its folds, uncovering the notched silver key. The lock opened after a silent, awkward struggle.

The water was deep enough to cover the third or fourth step. The iron handrail ran down and deflected into murk. A sweet-sour smell of salt and rot lifted and the flame of the candle brightened as if it were feeding on trapped gases. I went down two steps, and then another, until I was below the suspended joists of the ground floor and a foot or so above the water.

I stopped and watched, angling the candle so that the melted wax did not burn my fingers. The water had a slow rise and slippage, a shy movement damped by the Earth's mass. I knew it was the edge of the estuary brought there by the moon. I sat down on one of the steps and stood the candle in its wax between my feet.

I don't know how long I waited. I didn't hear the rattle of the bike until it hiccuped itself to silence. A big shape showed in the water, submerged and bulging, turning with a shine to it and then dull, smoky-coloured like the back of a cat, generating slow patterns and then sloughing their etched outlines so that they floated like oil-films. At last it dredged a disc of light from the dirty belly of the water, spinning it along the curve of its side.

I climbed the steps again, into the hall. A bright circle grew behind the frosted panels of the front door, too bright for my eyes so that I had to squint against it. The short black key was already turned sideways in the lock. I tugged at the handle and opened the door on the bike's dazzling headlight.

Moths bombarded the lamp, clustering against its lens. The rider was bareheaded except for his clumsy rubber goggles. He raised his hand to me and then turned the front wheel so that the light was no longer in my eyes. When I'd blinked away its red ghost I saw him sitting back against the saddle, supporting the machine with one heel braced against the kerb. It was not the glossy-tanked BSA but something similar to the skinny foreign machine on which they'd ferried their belongings to the house. He reached backwards to the rack above the rear wheel and lifted his white helmet by its strap. He held it out to me, grinning.

'Wally?'

I stepped out of the door and looked up at the front windows of the house. They were dark, the curtains closed and blind.

'You've come back for some things?'

He shrugged. I went down the steps. My shoes squealed slightly and left angled tracks of damp. I looked at the bike again. I could see now that it was identical to the one which had burnt so fiercely outside the house, the same or a twin.

'You've fixed it?'

He held out the helmet again. I took it and lowered its snug weight over my head. It fitted closely, deadening sound, but I still heard the cough of noise as he kick-started the engine. He stopped down the throttle so that the racket changed to a shaking rattle and then nodded to himself, as if pleased with the quality of the noise. He signalled with a jerk of his chin that I should mount behind.

The sky was made of overlapping scales of different shadings. There was the thinnest of moons, on its side, rolling along the edge of a cloud like a mad thing, a piece of broken glass skimming along a pavement.

The Pole leaned lower and opened the throttle to climb the hill. The buzz of the motor located itself in my belly. I looked forward over his shoulder at the dark column of the road flanked by its lights, its surface marbled with reflections. It was empty at first but then a lorry came quickly towards us. I shut my eyes against its smeared lamps and felt the bike slope into its suction. A horn blared and died.

Near the old cemetery five or six buses were parked in a

row, their windows blanked by condensation and the blinds drawn on the drivers' cabs. He slowed as we passed them and pointed a thumb towards the barrier of bushes and half-grown trees guarding the burial ground. A car went past with its wipers scooping out dark fans. I lifted the vizor and felt fine rain on my face.

We went at a walking pace, keeping a meandering path close to the kerb. He stripped off his goggles and squinted towards the wall of trees as if searching for an entrance, trailing his heel as he hesitated. I touched his arm and pointed at the iron gate leaning open at an angle. The crooked opening seemed larger this time, as if the ironwork had been forced backwards. He turned the bike towards it and we made an S-bend through the gap and into the path behind with its slippery clay. He ducked his head and shouted a warning. The end of a branch scraped against my helmet.

I crouched lower. Mud thrown by the wheels struck my hands and face and my shoes were already crusted by it. Wally avoided a fallen stump by guiding the bike through the thicket at the edge of the path. The dark overlaps of the bushes shone with wet and between them I could see sometimes in the headlight the pale shine of a monument. The track soon turned into a muddy slide between trees so that we had to guide the bike with our feet. After a few more yards the wheels were caught almost up to their axles. Wally shrugged and turned off the engine. The rain was still falling in the headlights, angled drops with the slowness of snow.

I dismounted. My feet sank instantly into the soft mud. The Pole dragged at the bike's handlebars and scooped the stand into position with his toe. I took off the helmet and looked around. Smells of vegetable damp and sour clay mixed with the fumes of the bike. Wally stood with his hands on his hips, watching his machine carefully as it slowly tilted. For a second it looked as if it might topple but then it stayed at a sharp angle, its wheels bound in the clay. He patted the narrow seat and seemed thoughtful. Then he wiped the rain from his eyes and took a small shiny torch out of his pocket. Its beam made a misty circle in the rain.

'Where are we going?'

It was impossible that he would answer. He pointed ahead. He made a scooping motion with his arm and set off impatiently, holding on to the trunks of the young trees. Almost at once he slipped and fell on to his knees, gaping a silent laugh as he picked himself up. I struggled a pace behind, the mud over my ankles.

We seemed to be climbing now, along a gully between trees, slipping backwards every third or fourth step, catching at low branches to pull ourselves along. A section of bark came away in my hand like damp paper. We stopped to catch our breaths. The night ahead of us was lightened by smears of silver with a dark mass beneath – something flat and heavy, weighed down by darkness but caught here and there with sparks of light as if its whole surface were electrified and in motion.

I was bewildered for a second. I did not know if I looked down on ground or sky. Then I realised that it was the wide spread of the river at its estuary and that we stood on the side of a hill, the sky before us and the ground falling steeply. But I was still confused. Had we already climbed so high? The Pole did not seem impressed by the view but shone the torch around him, as if searching for something he'd mislaid at some time past. The narrow beam seemed to fade after a while and he turned it off. We were anyway out from under the trees now so that there was more light from the sky. He made a gruff noise somewhere between chest and throat and pointed. I saw the thin curve of the moon a second before it was covered by a cloud. After a half-minute it emerged again from the other side. It seemed brighter than before, as if the air were clearer here. Its brilliant arc cupped the dark portion of the disc which was now faintly luminous.

Wally spread his arms and looked back at me, tilting his head. I nodded. I knew the ghost shine cupped by the arc of the moon was the reflected light of the Earth. He set off again and we walked together down the hillside of low, leaning grasses. Carved stones lay among them, not the angels and obelisks nearer the road but modest crosses and tablets set against the slope of the ground, half hidden by the tufts. The Pole wandered among them, stooping now and again to peer at their carvings. Once or twice he stopped to look more carefully, squatting among the grasses to gaze at an inscription, giving it a rationed shine of the torch.

'What are you looking for, Wally?'

He gave no sign that he had heard. The rain had stopped or was holding off and when the moon vanished again we made our way by the electrical flashes from the estuary. When we reached nearly level ground the sky seemed to jump suddenly closer. A dark freighter was passing across the water with lights before and aft.

We stopped. He shook his head but without especial concern. Maybe he'd decided by now that we'd lost our way. He crouched to examine another of the leaning stones, using the last strength of the torch. The town was visible below us now as blocks of darkness between the grey web of its roads. It seemed out of perspective with the rise of water behind it, as if we were looking at it from a still greater height. The night seemed to have stretched thinner and I wondered if the day was already starting.

Wally clicked his tongue in annoyance. He lifted his shoulders and gave a mime of laughter. I stared down at the town. There were strands of light along the roads and I could see the grey domes of civic buildings with the flat darkness of a park set like a lake between them. I recognised the lit glass roofs of the railway station grouped close to the vibrating edge of the river. Behind them, a few city blocks away, the big rectangle of the new hospital stood like a domino set on its side, its columns of stairs glowing and a few lights visible among its wards. I realised that the town had changed and its squares and avenues had somehow been rearranged. I thought of all that this would require – the laying of new roads and drains, the re-routing of the railway, the demolition of neighbourhoods – and knew that years must have passed. I had a feeling of looking at things after my own life had gone by. My mouth held the powdery taste of non-existence.

Wally clapped his palms together. He stamped the grass flat to show the sloping stone. He pointed the torch. A moth flew at us. I saw a small tablet, bleached white, pitted in bands as if the stone were of different consistencies and had weathered unevenly. It had already lost its corners and squared edges. There were carved letters in Cyrillic and then Roman script and then a disc of the Earth showing Europe and Asia. Wally placed a hand on my shoulder. I squatted on one knee in the soaked grasses.

Major Yuri Alexeyevich Gagarin, I read, *Cosmonaut, Hero-Pilot of the Soviet Union. 1934 to 1968.*

'Why, it's not yet!'

Wally sniffed as if he were starting a cold. I touched the disc of the Earth. It was sunk slightly below the surface. Its continents were worn so that the details of their coastlines had been lost. A raised band sloped across them and then continued in a loop cut through the surrounding stone. It returned and then disappeared behind the disc: Gagarin's single, tilted orbit.

Twenty-Two

'They're staying in a caravan. On the cliffs near Scarborough.'

Pale anaesthetic light came in through the tall windows. My mother looked down the ward towards the TV and its empty armchairs. She crossed her legs the other way.

'Don't ask me how I know, Leonard. Because I listen to people and use my mind.'

She closed her eyes. When she opened them again a woman had come with a tea-urn mounted on a jangling trolley.

'Another cup, dear?'

'Another? So when was the first?'

The woman sighed and turned the tap. The tea came out as a black stream. Milk from the enamel jug turned it mahogany. My mother sipped from it once and then left it out of harm's way on the bedside cabinet.

'They've made a mistake with Scarborough: it's too posh and they'll only stand out there,' she said.

Nearer to the TV a fat woman in a blue coat was sitting on one of the narrow stacking chairs. She was facing away from us. Her back and bottom pushed out from the chair at either side. A white bottle with a clear tube looping down from its neck hung from a tall stand near her shoulder. The small-flowered curtains were half drawn around the bed.

My mother stared at her. 'It's that fat Derek,' she said. 'In with his eye.'

She stayed thoughtful for a minute.

'That Muriel died, you know. The funeral is next week. It was more the shock that killed her than just the fall.' She made a movement of her mouth between pity and scorn. 'That room's bad luck now. The old fellah started it, like you'd prime a pump.'

'What about Wilf?' I asked.

'Oh, he's what you call bereaved. He's given up the french-polishing now and says he'll be moving. He says a cousin of his owns a chicken-farm.'

Twice a week after the visiting hour the porter rolled a set of scales along the ward on squeaking metal castors. The nurse closed the curtains around the bed. Dr Munro smiled with his pale teeth as he fiddled painfully with the milled screws at the base of the scales. He shut one eye and squinted at a bubble floating in green liquid behind a disc of glass.

'Must we always have this?' he asked the nurse. 'This procedure?'

The nurse stood by the machine watching him. The porter looked at the nurse from behind and then withdrew behind the curtains, whisking them back to cover the gap he had left.

'I'm coming to the view that this floor is less than level,' Dr Munro said. 'Which is a serious fault in a modern building.'

The nurse ducked her chin. I got out of the bed and stood in my pyjamas on the wrinkled rubber mat. Dr Munro slipped chromed weights up and down until the arm was balanced and then called out the reading. The nurse made a note and then rested her clipboard against the books on the top of my locker. She smiled at me.

'I've never known a boy to read so much: it makes me afraid for his eyes!'

Dr Munro glanced at the spines of my library books. He twitched his mouth to one side and then took the chart and wrote his signature across the bottom of the sheet.

'A parcel came for you,' Aunt Irene said. 'It was too big to go through the door and I had to collect it from the post office. You go to a place round the back, like a yard. You have to stand and wait with the rain blowing in and then I nearly collapsed with the size of it. It was from a place in Glasgow . . .' She laughed. 'I'll never know how I managed to carry it! The rain was like ice in your face and the wind kept catching it and taking me off my feet. I couldn't stop shaking when I reached home – you know how it is when the cold gets inside you.'

'It's a kit,' I told her. 'Some of the parts are delicate.'

'Fragile, it said.'

She drank her tea slowly, frowning as she held the cup to her face. Since I had been in the hospital both of the women looked smaller, as if their mutual silence had reduced them by about a third. I had thought their not talking would last for just a few days.

'You could ask Ralph to assemble it,' I said.

'Ralph's still poorly. That fall woke the nerve-endings in his leg and now it feels as if it's still there. The part that's missing, I mean.'

'He enjoys making things. It'll take his mind off.'

She shook her head and smiled. 'Poor Ralph. His hands tremble now.'

The lights of the ward were turned off leaving the private shine of a few reading lamps. The nurse read at the long desk with its several vases of flowers. She did not lift her head when I got out of bed and put on my slippers. For a second the floor floated from under my feet and then it found itself again. At the end of the ward five or six armchairs were pulled in a defensive group around the TV. I could see the backs of heads against the shine of the tube. The news. Soon cocoa or milk would be served and it would be darkness proper except for the strict tent of light at the nurses' table.

Derek was listening to the radio through headphones, one eye open, the other covered by a lid of plaster. When I stopped by the foot of his bed he shut his good eye and pressed the lids together tightly so that only the dark line of the lashes remained. A full bottle of Lucozade still in its cellophane wrapper stood on his cabinet beside the water-jug. I waited, looking sometimes at the TV and sometimes at him. I took the stone from my dressing-gown pocket. When he could no longer ignore me he took off his headphones and squinted in my direction, his head leaning sideways. The headphones hissed before he turned down their volume. The unbandaged part of his face was white with the freckles standing out like ink marks.

'What's that?'

'Something I found.'

227

I held it between finger and thumb to show him its absent centre. He looked at it but only sideways and then shrugged against his pillows. The patient in the next bed made a whinnying noise and we both turned towards him. He was sleeping with his face under the covers so that only his grey hair was visible. Each of his breaths chased the next but did not quite catch so that there was an interval of silence which made you listen.

I moved one of the stacking chairs so that I could sit down. 'Would you like it?' I asked.

'*What?*'

'This. Would you like to keep it?'

He shrugged. I drew the chair closer still, until my knees just touched the bed.

'I'm in for an operation,' Derek said. 'They're going to try to straighten my eye.'

I put the stone on the glass top of the bedside cabinet, next to the Lucozade. I looked at it lying on its side with the smooth hole and the fine dark lines running through it like a grain. For a second I was tempted to take it back.

'Don't you want this?' I asked.

He sniffed and put his headphones back on. I could only see the bandaged side of his face. The trolley with the drinks was being brought through the double doors of the ward. The woman opened the heavy doors and then fixed them back, pushing home their rubber wedges with the toe of her shoe. She then dragged the chiming trolley between them. The muscles of her back strained against her pale grey coat.

His mother came with the little girl. She sat with her back to me again. The girl fidgeted. Derek kept his headphones on most of the time. The ward was warm and stuffy during the day. When the bell went Mrs Dolbey roused herself and walked out pulling the girl after her. Before she reached the door the girl began to cry and scream in a tantrum. Mrs Dolbey began to struggle with her, gripping both her wrists and almost pulling her from her feet. A nurse went towards them smiling and smoothly clicking her heels. Mrs Dolbey met my look and stared at me. Her eyes were ringed with dark

228

make-up and as the nurse calmed the little girl they separated themselves from the fat freckled face and flew towards me like wasps.

My mother came with a change of library books. 'Norris has gone! He's left us his hi-fi in lieu of rent.'

'Will you sell it?'

'Maybe not. We can't have a fellah on the ocean and us selling his effects. And the way things are we'll be ruined anyway . . .'

'Is he sailing straight away?'

'He caught the train to Southampton. He has to kit himself out for a sailor's life.'

She laughed to herself. Instead of thinking of Norris I pictured the house with nearly everyone gone, only the matched silence of the sisters and Ralph working on the telescope in his attic room.

'He's still messing with that thing of yours,' Aunt Irene said. 'He says now there's something missing.'

My stomach fell and bounced back.

'Something that's important,' she said.

I thought of the various parts. Each of them was vital. 'Is it the eyepiece?'

'No, I don't think so.'

'A mirror then?'

She thought for a second. 'Maybe that's it.'

'There should be two of them! The large mirror collects the light and brings it to a focus while the small deflects it towards the eyepiece.'

'Then it must be the smaller one from what I gather.'

I felt tears pressing behind my eyes. 'Has he looked through all the packing?'

She nodded. 'You know how careful and meticulous he is.'

'Then he'll have to send off for it! To the manufacturers!'

'It would break his heart not to finish anything . . .' She smiled. 'He had some news for me yesterday. Someone saw those two rogues in Bridlington, working at an amusement arcade. The tall one sits all day in a glass booth and gives out change and the other walks around with a big bunch of keys. They are *plausible*, you see, and someone's taken pity.'

'My mother says they're both in Scarborough.'

'She has a trusting heart, Leonard: that would be just to throw her off the scent.'

The doctor measured my arms and legs with a pair of callipers, first cross-wise and then front to back. He measured each limb at three points, while the nurse noted the results. Along the ward the TV was blank and an old man sat in Derek's bed.

'That boy,' I said. 'Who was in the bed over there...'

Dr Munro looked at the nurse and then back at my leg. 'I think he's gone for surgery,' the nurse said.

'What surgery?'

She laughed as if I'd asked a stupid question. 'Why, something to make him well!'

The doctor held the callipers. The opposed arms were a pin-point of ice at each side of my calf. He cleared his throat. 'When *you* leave here you might take a holiday, Leonard!'

'Where?' I asked.

He laughed as if I'd made him awkward.

'Well, anywhere is a holiday!' the nurse said.

Ralph worked by the light of his special lamp. He assembled the tubes and bearings and aligned the mirrors. The counter-weighted mounting allowed movement through 180 degrees in any plane. The clockwork drive with its special gearing would follow the smooth paths of the stars. My mother talked with Dr Munro near the double doors of the ward. The lights were on and the tall windows were a smear of darkness.

'You'd expect common sense from a doctor!' she said when she sat down.

I turned a page of my book.

'If you aren't going to talk,' she said.

'It's *interesting*.'

'And I'm not?' She pointed at the plastic tube. 'What's that?'

'It's only extra vitamins.'

The tube ended in a valve taped tightly into the crook of my elbow. Every half-minute or so a bubble began its journey up to the clear glass bottle. It was not uncomfortable except that the joint of my elbow felt stiff and breakable and I could no longer move it freely when I turned a page.

'I was thinking about Ralph,' I said.

'It's useless to spend thought on some people: there's no profit in them. The Poles have moved to Hornsea now. One of them works in a restaurant and the other hires out rowboats.'

'That wasn't what Aunt Irene said.'

'She's at best mistaken.'

'Are you still not talking?'

'I'll speak just one word to that woman before I die.'

'What's that?' I asked.

She moved her lips awkwardly as if she already had it in her mouth. 'It's only a word between me and her. To another person it would be nothing.'

'That mirror arrived. It's so small you can just see a part of your face in it. I thought the box was a piece of wedding-cake: it was just that size.'

'You didn't touch it, did you? You can easily mark the surface.'

'I wouldn't lay a finger. Ralph has it now: he's taken charge, you see.'

My aunt's olive-green coat was drying in the warmth of the ward. I could smell the evaporating rain.

'That cheeky kid with the bike called at the door yesterday. He was asking for Jeff. Why, no Jeffs live here now, I said. He pulled a comical face then and did a sort of dance on the front step. I had to laugh! You see, he's the kind of lad who can't stop moving. He'd brought that bike of his up to the door as if he meant to push it inside. Is he a pal of yours?'

'Not really a pal.'

She looked at me sideways as if I'd disappointed her. 'You shouldn't deny your friends, Leonard!'

My bed was moved after lights out. I looked up from my pillow to see the shiny ceilings of the corridors. The wheels of the bed squealed and rumbled and the bottle of saline caught the passing lights. We passed through several sets of double doors.

231

At a corner where the corridors met the long fluorescent lights changed to bright globes suspended in grilles of iron. We went down in a shuddering lift and then crossed an aerial walkway with rain blowing in through the open sides. The sharp air was unfamiliar to me and for the first time in weeks I heard the hiss of traffic passing through the wet. I wanted to question the nurse but my mouth only ate the words.

'If you feel strange,' she said, 'it's because we've given you an injection.'

My new home was smaller, a ward with only four beds. Two of the others were unoccupied, but in the corner opposite I could see a dry hank of hair on the pillow. What I had thought was the sound of some kind of ventilator was the other person's breath. The nurse flicked at a switch and then I saw only a long reddish light which stood like a guard at the window.

I couldn't sleep for a while. The breaths of my room-mate seemed to involve the whole atmosphere of the room, as if it were being emptied to a tight vacuum and then refilled. I tried to break the cycle by listening to the stray sounds of the outside and fixed on the faint drone of a bike.

'Look who is here! Look who I have found!'

A woman came in with Aunt Irene. She had light brown hair with a fringe.

'Don't tell me you won't speak, Leonard.'

Her belly came before her. She sat on the hospital chair with her knees apart, brown shoes planted wide to take the weight.

My aunt smiled between us. 'Don't be ignorant, Leonard. You shouldn't turn your face on old acquaintance.'

The woman laughed. She tugged at the joints of her fingers. 'He doesn't know me now, Irene!'

'I'm sure he does,' my aunt said. 'Why, it's *Susan*!'

A taste came into my mouth like orange-peel. I could not help but stare at the bulge behind her sky-blue sweater.

'He'd pass me in the street nowadays,' Susan said. She looked down and blushed. 'I've just let my natural hair grow out, you see.'

She came forward to kiss me, leaning awkwardly across the

bed. I pecked her on the cheek, which wasn't as scented and powdery as before.

'Susan's what you call it, having a baby,' Aunt Irene announced.

Susan laughed and put her hands on either side of her belly. 'I've *changed* you see, Leonard. I'm not just a girl now.'

'Not a lass any longer,' my aunt said. 'You have to give up to gain.'

She looked about the ward. The man in the other bed was still lying with only his hair showing like a tangle of string. During the daytime his breath withdrew and was regular and quiet. She stared at his shape in the bed and pulled her chair closer.

'Doesn't he get any visitors?' she asked in a whisper.

'He's always asleep.'

'There must be someone to look after him: even a dog has its keeper . . .' She sighed and tugged her glance from him. 'Ralph says he's nearly finished with that instrument of yours. It stands in the middle of his room under the loft window. He doesn't talk much nowadays but you can see that he's pleased with it.'

'A fellah needs an interest,' Susan said. 'They're like kids in that.' She searched in her bag and held out to me a photograph of a ship taken from the air. It had four smoking funnels and left a trail of disturbed whiteness in the blue-brown sea.

'I had this from Norris. It's the latest *Queen*, you know. He says that he's fortunate to sail on her.'

My aunt nodded. 'He's got a job in the kitchens and so he travels for free. She's the most beautiful ship ever built and luxurious to every degree.'

'I'm glad that he's content,' Susan said. 'Now that our water is under the bridge.'

She moved in the chair to ease herself. I looked at the date of the card. I could not believe that I had been here for so long. My aunt pointed to the postmark. 'It's posted on board, you see. They have their own post office and then they pass the letters to a ship going the other way.'

'Ships in the night,' Susan said. 'That's life all over.'

My aunt nodded and twisted her big hands. 'He was very

upset that he had to go at short notice and didn't have time to visit you. He wrote a sort of will before he left and he's given you all his records. He knows you don't care much for music but he hoped you'd take the time to listen and get the hang of it.' She started to look thoughtful. 'I think he's better off in America, a fellah like him.'

'He isn't made for this world,' Susan said. She put her hand against her belly.

My aunt stared at it. 'Why don't you show him?' she asked with a spark of mischief.

Susan looked away, smiling. 'Why, show him what, Aunt Irene?'

Aunt Irene laughed. 'Why, what you have got!'

She looked uncomfortable for a second, as if she might refuse. 'What if somebody comes?'

'No one comes in here,' my aunt said. 'Or only medical people.'

Susan nodded towards the man opposite. 'And what about him?'

'You can see he'll never wake,' my aunt said.

Susan made her eyes round. Then she plucked at the hem of her sweater and began to roll it upwards in soft folds, unveiling herself.

'Would you believe this is me, Leonard?'

'Not only you,' my aunt said.

I stared at Susan's belly. It was swollen so smooth and tight that its smoothness reflected the light of the window. Her belly-button had been pushed by the pressure within into a little dome of translucent flesh.

'I can't believe that I'll be the same again,' Susan said.

My aunt laughed. 'Why, of course you won't!'

'But will I ever lose this belly?'

'Many a nice-looking lass has a belly,' my aunt said. 'There should be a fashion for it.'

When I slept I dreamed about the QE2. The captain, the old fellah, was on its wide white bridge. He called through a tube-thing for the engineer to stop the engines and then the ship cruised massively through the water, curling back the waves, slowing. I woke and it took me a minute to find the source of the silence. I called and a nurse came holding a vase of cut flowers.

'He isn't breathing!'

I pointed to the bed in the corner. She stood the glass vase on his cabinet. 'Who isn't?' Then she laughed and pulled back the curl of covers. '*Mr Nobody!*'

I watched her bare arms as she dragged the blankets and dented pillows on to the floor beside the bed. There was slanting light from the windows and fine currents of dust were turning in it. The yellow of the daffodils lit up the shady part of the room like a lamp.

'What's happened to him?'

She winked at me. 'Well, if he's not here then he must have been moved!'

She took the flowers again and walked from the room, giving me a passing smile. I stared at the empty bed. In a few minutes she was back again with a bundle of clean bedding and a black plastic sack. She began to clear the cabinet, pulling out the small drawer and upending it into the bag, opening the door and pulling out woollens and a plaid dressing gown, slippers.

The next time they came within minutes of one another and sat at opposite sides of the bed. I did not know if this was a mistake or had been silently planned. My aunt took fruit from her bag and arranged it in the bowl. She hesitated and then removed a pear which was on the turn and dropped it into the waste-bin. My mother produced a box of dates and laid them on the side of the bed close to my hand.

'The Yanks are all over space!' Aunt Irene said. 'Only they have foreign names . . .'

'Because they *are* foreigners,' my mother told me.

My aunt gave no sign that she had heard the interruption. 'Ralph says that it's only the start. He reckons they'll be on the moon next! He's agitated about it, you can tell: he listens to the reports on his radio.'

My mother stripped the cellophane from the box of dates, pressed it into a ball and threw it into the bin. For the next hour or so I could hear the small crackles as it uncurled. She opened the box and took out the wooden fork.

'Do you know what he calls it, Leonard?'

'No,' I said.

She jerked her head to one side. 'He calls it *scientific destiny*, but what's the use when millions are starving? The piccaninnies have swollen bellies but it's only air inside! It breaks my heart to watch it on the telly. He sits in that room of his like an evil spider with no thought for human suffering.'

'He's finished your telescope as makes no difference,' my aunt continued. 'He's waiting for a clear night to test it. What he calls the optics. He says the moon will be as close as your hand.'

I ate one of the dates. 'Put the stones in this saucer,' my mother said. 'You have one and you want another. It's like everything else, you see. Greed. Insatiable appetite. People are never satisfied with only enough.'

Aunt Irene pressed her thumb into a pear and left a crescent bruise. 'Those pears are as ripe as anything, so you mustn't let them spoil. Ralph says that when you're better you'll be able to look through it at whatever you like. The stars. The planets. And then the three of us will go away together...'

I was surprised. 'With you and Ralph?' I asked.

My aunt laughed. 'You, me and your mother, of course.'

I turned to my mother, who had the thoughtful look of someone listening to a conversation in another room. 'But you don't talk to one another!'

My mother took a stone from her mouth and swallowed the soft meat of the date. 'That doesn't mean we won't need a holiday.'

Twenty-Three

The other beds were still empty in the evening. My mother sat on one of the stacking chairs in an angle of the walls, waiting with a magazine on her lap. She looked up at me when I opened my eyes.

'There isn't a clock in here, Leonard.'

'It must be seven,' I said, guessing. It was the short space of time between the daylight fading and the lamps of the hospital coming on.

She let the magazine fall with a soft flop and came closer, dragging the chair behind her. Its rubber feet made a juddering noise against the floor.

'Has Irene gone?' I asked.

She twitched her lips. 'We're like the couple in a weather-house.'

She sat close to me, her legs against the edge of the bed. She had changed her clothes since the morning and now she wore a biscuit-coloured suit and black shoes with diamanté bows. I saw the box of dates with its empty plastic stem in the folds of the bedclothes.

'She's been saying things,' my mother said. 'Now that we don't speak, you see. Now that we don't speak I only have to listen! I've had some practice at that . . .'

'About my dad?' I asked.

She leaned forward to touch my leg through the covers. 'You have no dad as far as I can see: I finished long ago with that kettle of fish. It's only *her* who's bringing him back! She can never stop from interfering! She's breathed life into him and he'll soon come knocking.'

She sat with her face lowered for about five minutes. The door was ajar on the clatter of the long corridors. It was now nearly dark and I waited for the stutter of the fluorescent tube.

'*Here,*' she said. She lifted her head. A tiny parcel wrapped in silky blue paper lay on her open palm.

'I had this from the Poles. An ambulanceman stopped me in the street and gave me it. The postmark says Flamborough but you can take that with a pinch of salt. The Poles will never settle now, you see. They'll always be from place to place. They're married in a way and a lot of people don't like that.'

I was surprised. 'But how can a man marry a man?'

'Well, Leonard, every marriage is different . . .' She smiled down at the package. 'I think we're meant to share it but I'll just have a taste.'

The front of the parcel was just big enough to accommodate the stamp and the address. She broke the seal with her thumbnail and stripped away the festive wrappings. There was a glossy cardboard box and inside that a dark slab of cake.

'I'm fond of currants but can't eat sultanas, Leonard. You'll find that it's usually one or the other with people.'

When she passed me the piece of cake it broke apart in my hand. 'It's *dry.*'

'That's only because it's been a while in the post. Bread goes stale but a cake *matures*. You'll have to eat it, Leonard, or you'll send them bad luck!'

I chewed and swallowed a corner. When my saliva had wetted the dry crumbliness I was surprised by the dark richness of the flavour. Its warming passage towards my stomach reminded me of the Poles' moonshine liquor.

My mother took a pinch of crumbs from my palm. 'Just enough for a mouse . . .' She swallowed and pulled a face. 'We need sherry for a toast but we'll have to make do with tea.'

She smacked her lips. We waited together for the approach of the trolley.

I listened to the bike. The air had a mixed grain of bright and dark. The note of the motor changed constantly as if the rider were weaving skilfully between obstacles. I heard the catch of the gears and the frustration of the rubber as the wheels spun on a turn. The shapes of light on the ceiling checked themselves and then reversed so that they were streaming into my side of the room. I caught the flash of the headlight for a second and knew that I must have seen its reflection in one of the windows opposite. I pushed myself half out of the bed. The bike's noise racketed through the courtyard below, fracturing on the angles of the walls, bouncing into the distance to bound back, meeting with itself in a spiralling din until he cut the engine. He pulled it on to the stand and dismounted. His steel-clegged boots made a precise noise on the gravel.

I sat up in the bed. There was something warm on my forearm. I felt with the tip of my finger and found a thin track of blood. The plastic hose had broken from its small valve in the crook of my elbow and now hung loosely down from its bottle. A drop of fluid fell from the bare end. My arm was bleeding slowly from the catheter. I found the plastic screw and turned it until I felt it tighten.

The bedclothes slipped from me. I kicked out my feet. My heart beat quickly as I crossed to the window, a noise filling the space of silence left by the bike. I could see the wing opposite, a lit window, a stairwell, a stone plaque lit by an updraught of light. *1927*. The glass was beaded with water carrying pinpoints of brightness. I put my cheek to its coldness and levered my stare down into the yard, as close to the building as I could. The bike was leaning solitary, a bar of reflection along the narrow tank, its handlebars angled to jaunt the wheel.

I went back to the bed and sat on its edge. The bedclothes had fallen to the floor in a dark bundle, the grey blankets out. A door opened outside in the corridor, two sets of heels, women's voices: 'He offered me a cigarette and so I pointed to the sign.'

'You can see your face in that suit of his!'

'He just laughed. Kind of *laughed*, like. It's hard to describe . . . You know, *that* kind of laugh . . .'

I waited and then went to the door. My feet did not quite connect, barely brushed the floor. Through the wired glass I could see the corridor with its hanging overhead lights. I angled my head to look in both directions. They were empty and identical. I tried the handle. It was stiff at first but then I turned it the other way and the catch released without a sound. I stepped through and let the door close behind me. The corridor ended in a blank wall to its left and to the right in a junction with another corridor. Water moved in a silver-painted pipe which followed the angle of the ceiling. I began to walk. The soles of my feet sucked against the rubberised surface of the floor. One of the side doors was open with a light on behind and I stepped by quickly without looking inside.

The next corridor was broader but darker. A current of cooler air passed along it as if it were open somewhere to the outside. The lights swung slightly on their chains, the movement passing along over my head down the long perspective. Some of the globes were not working, or missing altogether, exposing the fittings which had held the lamps. There was a sense of distant commotion and clatter which did not quite reach me as sound.

A man stood before me in a grubby blue jacket, a cigarette between his fingers, the thumb hooked over the handle of a striped mug. He had a bristly, night-man's face. He stared at me and then down the corridor as if looking for help.

'Where you going, sunshine?'

'Toilet,' I said.

'*Toilet*?' He scratched at a fold of his neck and looked at my feet. He stared along the corridor again and lifted his chin as if he were about to call out. I started to walk in the opposite direction. I'd expected him to follow me but he kept his ground, as if moored to the doorway behind him. He beckoned me. '*Hey*!' Tea slopped from the rim of his mug.

I thought that I was on the third or fourth floor but I could not see a window, only the glazed tops of doors and the occasional darkened hatch. I turned a corner. There was the coiled snake of a fire-hose on its red reel. I pushed sideways through a set of double doors, towards light and a scratch of music. I saw with relief the polished rail of a staircase. The music was sliding strings. It stopped.

'*More from Ted and the orchestra in just a moment!*'

A man leaned back against a tall radiator holding a woman tight against him. He wore a dark uniform. The woman had on a blue overall, pushed to one side by the man's arm. One of his hands pinched the woman's waist while the other was out of sight down the back of her skirt. There was a window above them, a tiny pane set high up in the wall like an awkwardly placed inspection panel. The woman made a noise and tilted back her head. I saw the curl of the moon, thin and shy in the window.

'It's your imagination,' he said.

She pushed at him and stepped back. 'No, there is someone!'

The man took his cap from the shelf of the radiator and put it on, the shiny peak first, pushing back his hair. He stepped towards me, frowning. The music came again, *cha-cha*. I wondered if he could see me in the dark. I stepped backwards until my back touched the railing.

I ran down the stairs, careening myself across the landings. My hand squealed against the polished curve of the banisters. Their stone chilled my feet, drawing aches from my bones. After three or four flights I stopped for breath and saw the dimmed space of a ward, like a ship in darkness. The doors were hooked back and a nurse sat at her lit table, frowning. She wrote something, scratching with her pen. A moth flew into the hot cone of the lampshade and she sighed and touched her cheek.

She was writing a letter, filling the blue page of the pad with her small handwriting. The ward was filled with sleeping men, their heads turned this way and that with sometimes a hand extended on the covers. Electrical cables looped slackly from the walls to end in boxes with glowing operating lights. I listened to the whispers of breath. The nurse turned her paper and stared at it, thoughtful.

I went through another set of doors, quietly, catching them with my foot to prevent them slamming. Behind was a narrow room, a kind of entry, lined with shelves carrying white folds of linen, a washbasin of glossy steel with a mirror above, the white upright of my face. The room beyond was much larger, its edges dim but with a bright tent of clear plastic at its centre, suspended by ropes and pulleys from the high ceiling. The tent was open at its front, the edges of the opening caught back to show the space inside filled with white light, painful at first to look at. The plastic drapes ended above the polished floor so that I could see feet below, many of them, planted with their shadows. I went closer, into the larger room. The drapes bulged with movement. I slitted my eyes to peer through the opening. Figures in masks and grey surgical dress clustered around something in their centre, a quiet threading of talk between them. Just above their heads a rubber diaphragm expanded and deflated.

'Point three . . .' A woman's voice blurred by a mask. 'Point two.'

One of the men half turned. He wore a mask and heavy-framed spectacles. He tugged down the mask. 'Not happy with point two.'

'Down to four now!'

He snapped back his mask. 'Bring it closer then!' A coil of white cable was drawn across the space over the bed and pulled tight. Between the hips of two of the medics I saw the waxy sole of a foot.

'The left,' he said. 'Quick now!'

The foot kicked twice as I watched it. The diaphragm inflated and then was sucked flat into a twitching disc. The doctor bent over his patient, his shoulders tense and high. There was a hum like a tiny drill.

'Thank you!'

A movement like a visual sigh passed through his assistants. He stood up. The bladder refilled and then half emptied. It caught its slow rhythm again, and in the same second my arm started to itch violently. I looked down and saw the clear plastic body of the catheter-valve filled with red blood.

'You may as well give it to me!'

He'd stepped back from the bed and seemed to look directly towards me where I stood just outside the curtains. His lenses flashed and I thought for a second that he must have seen me.

'A pity,' he said. 'We could not save it.'

He held a shiny steel bowl with high, inward-curving sides balanced on the palm of his hand. He pulled his mask down fully. His lips were quivering and he wet them with his tongue. A gold ring with a smooth red stone shone on his little finger. One of his helpers reached out, gripping something in a fold of damp surgical wadding. The doctor looked aside as if the sight had made him thoughtful and then gave a nod of assent. I saw a glassy gleam, something round, off-white, veined with darkness. It struck the bottom of the basin with a rolling clatter.

*

A window was open to the outside. Rain sloped through a red wash of light. I leaned out for a second to fill my lungs. An alarm-bell rang somewhere. The mesh of a fire escape extended downwards and I could see the white roof of an ambulance. I walked on. There was darkness for a second as the lights flickered. Then they came on again in series, their impulse overtaking me. The stutter of light made me turn and at the very end of the corridor I saw the dog.

I did not know it at first or I wasn't certain. It came swiftly towards me, its shape not distinct against the shimmer of the floor, animal-like only in its size and motion. Then as it came closer I saw the thin spike of its tail.

I stood still. 'Jeff,' I called. 'Jeff!'

It lifted its muzzle. Its eyes were silver like hammered lead. I caught a sunken glow from them and then its look turned quite dark, as if it saw me and then did not.

'Jeff?'

The clitter of its paws did not slow but it changed its path a fraction to avoid the spot on which I stood. Its head looked pondering and heavy as it passed by, the snout greyer than I recalled, the nose crusted like something burnt. Its long back was still matted and scabby and I smelt something like singed hair. Then it was gone, climbing the shines of the corridor, giving me the blind stare of its arsehole as it trotted away.

Then came a guard in cap and uniform, a heavy man, half running, a nurse following behind him, the narrow space filling with people moving in a hasty crush like the beginning of a race.

There was a notice-board opposite and I pretended to be studying the lists and timetables. The guard went by, wheezing, pulling the cap from his head and wiping his face with his sleeve. The rest of them followed with a hot rush of talk, jarring me but too excited to notice, pushing me close against the wall.

I turned to watch their jostling backs. They rounded a corner, colliding with one another, laughing. I listened to the fading hubbub and then started to walk in that direction. There was something festive about them which made me want to follow. When I turned into the next corridor they were already out of sight, leaving only a disturbance in the air, a scent of haste and excitement.

Suddenly I was in a panic that I would lose them altogether and started to run. I came to a crossroads. A woman with powerful bare arms pushed a churning machine around a corner and directly in front of me. I managed to avoid it but then caught myself in its black loop of cable so that I almost fell.

She put her hand over her mouth and stared at me.

'Where did they go? This way?' I pointed into the distance.

She shook her head and pushed a button to turn off the motor. The machine had left a shiny trail of wet. I freed my ankles. There was an office, the lights on behind frosted-glass. A man with a pink party-hat fixed to the top of his security-guard's cap suddenly pushed his head through an open hatch and pointed with the burning stub of a cigarette.

'You'll miss it!' he told me. 'You'll have to run!'

He pulled himself back inside. I followed his signal across a hall lit by a tank of tropical fish standing in an alcove. A nozzle bled bubbles into its corner. There was a door ahead with a round window showing darkness. I could still hear the watchman's radio, a slow voice with gaps of silence. I pushed against the panel and the door opened inwards onto heavy felt which then slipped aside to show snow-white brightness.

The rocket was standing with the letters up its side:

C
C
C
P

The staff of the hospital sat in sloping rows of seats, the smoky beams of the projector slanting over their heads. There was a plume of boiling oxygen along the fuselage, then the figure of the cosmonaut as seen under murky water. I stood with my hand on the back row of seats. The commentary was in Russian. Words in Cyrillic flashed across the image. The cosmonaut waited, CCCP above the visor of the helmet. The focus slipped and the operator fiddled with the lens. There was a projector with the screen of a TV behind, fizzing with blue light, then a single tall loudspeaker. The words which sounded urgently in the air came from its torn cloth cover.

Eight hundred thousand pounds of thrust. The darker edge of the fuselage against white snow. The steam of boiling oxygen, the enormous C. Close-up to broken grainy lines of the pilot. *Pilot-hero of the Soviet Union.* He moves his head in a swinging blur. The slow commentary, like lists of ingredients and telephone numbers.

'Oh, let him fly!' a man calls out.

The picture slips again to hisses and whistles. The beam of the projector shudders as the operator struggles to focus. When it comes right the C is lifting smoothly and another comes into sight and slips up towards the top of the screen: C C.

Nervy smoke shifts in clouds in the long paths of light. Half the screen is a lifting band:

C
C
C
P

Then comes a shuddering cluster of nozzles and the total white flash of ionised gases. The speaker begins again in fear and emotion: trembling words I don't understand. The camera tilts after the accelerating rocket, tracking through the air the white-hot cloud-dispersing flash.

A shrill whistle and then a mounting roar. The ship lifted slowly. The noise contained a multitude of new pitches and shades that no composer has ever put down in music or any instrument or human voice can as yet reproduce. The rocket's huge engines were fashioning the music of the future which I imagine is much more exciting and beautiful then the greatest productions of the past.

*

'He's gone.'

I was in the crush in the doorway.

'But will they get him back?'

A bottle was passing in the tiled hall. A man in a green suit tipped it back, leaning against the aquarium. The coloured scraps of fish rocked. Water slipped down the glass front.

'*Hey*!' The guard leaned pointing from his hatchway.

'It's humanity's greatest hour!' the drinker told him.

'That's no excuse for loose behaviour!'

People were climbing the first curve of the stairs. Their voices made a seashell noise in the twists of marble. I was carried along, pushed. The steps were chilly smooth stone. I tucked myself behind a pair of white-coated doctors and began to climb, holding on to the rail. My mismatched feet were uncertain and I slipped at the turn. A hand steadied my arm. I glanced up and saw the tightening spiral of the stairwell. A black wheel of electric lamps hung from the apex of the dome.

She looked down into my face and laughed. 'Nearly!'

'Almost,' I said.

She touched my cheek and then showed me the tips of her fingers with a white coating of skin-flakes as if she had wiped away dead cells. I knew that I was shivering.

'Walking about like that!' She held my arm again. People were pushing past, hurrying upwards. 'If you want to see you'll have to wear this!'

She slipped off her black cloak with its red lining. She was bare-armed underneath.

'And what about your slippers?' she asked with mock sternness.

'I don't know.'

'You don't know! And how old are you?'

'I'm fifteen,' I said.

She sucked in her breath and pulled the cloak about my shoulders, fastening its tasselled cord around my throat. The lining was smooth and body-warmed. She smiled and lifted her face to the twists of the stairs.

'Do you know him?' she asked. 'The man in the sky?'

'Yes, I met him once. He waved his cap.'

She stared at me, nodded solemnly. Then a man in a scruffy

porter's uniform began to overtake us and she turned to him with her face gone humorous and teasing. I wondered then if she believed me at all.

'He's tall for his age but *thin*!' she said.

The porter laughed and a wink passed between them. 'Oh, he'll soon fill out!'

The three of us climbed together. I looked over the polished balustrade and saw more people following. Most seemed to be porters or medical staff but I saw a few patients in dressing gowns and one man with his head bandaged supported by a doctor and a nurse. It seemed that the whole able-bodied population of the hospital was climbing with us. After a couple more turns we came to a place where an angel stood, looking up from its scroll as if it were reading aloud or thinking deeply on what it had read. Its long robe had a silvery shine to it but its face was dark and a skull lay at its feet with grasses growing through the empty holes of eyes. Underneath, the names were set in columns. I touched them and felt the letters raised in the glass.

'The memorial,' my nurse said. 'For the staff who were killed in the last war.'

'And the one before that!' the porter said.

The nurse smiled at me with her white, rounded teeth. 'You're *shy*,' she said. 'What's your name?'

'Leonard,' I told her. 'And I'm not shy.'

She looked at me sideways, holding my arm. 'I think you are, Leonard!'

We went on. We passed the hanging electrolier with its flame-shaped lamps. The staircase ended in a platform under the dome. I sensed the dark night sky behind the curving segments of glass. We joined the broad queue before an open pair of red emergency doors.

'It's a crush,' the nurse said. She looked at me teasingly and then gripped my shoulders with her strong, short-fingered hands. 'Patients first!' she shouted. 'Youth before wisdom!'

She pushed me before her. I wondered if she was a little drunk. A part of the crowd gave way before her high, laughing voice. We climbed a pair of shallow steps and then stepped up on to a flat space flanked by the roofs and tall chimneys of the old wing. There was smooth tar under my feet with frozen bubbles embedded and a black shine on its surface. People were standing in groups, excited and laughing, gesturing with the lit ends of cigarettes. Bottles of wine and beer were circulating. When I looked above the heads of the crowd a few stars began to shiver into sight.

'The World and his Wife,' the nurse said. She sighed and rubbed her bare arms, looking about, impatient suddenly. She waved to a friend. 'Well, excuse me for a second, Master Leonard . . .'

I watched her go and then went forward wrapped in her warm cloak. I pushed between the chattering groups. The sky opened out to the front where the flat roof looked out over the dark tops of trees. The crowd thickened along the parapet and I spotted Dr Munro in a dark, smart suit, standing with one foot on the low wall and talking rapidly and excitedly to a group of younger doctors, gesturing with his small hands. I pulled up the hood of the cloak to keep my anonymity. I could see the southward spread of the sky above its margin of trees. Small clouds like trails of steam were sailing through the spaces between the stars, powered by a wind which we could not feel. As I watched their undersides began to lighten with silver. One by one the groups fell silent. We waited.

The women sat in wicker armchairs placed close together but at an angle, so that their eyes need not meet. Sighing, hand over hand, Ralph pulled at the cord which worked the window pulley. The ratchet squeaked and resisted before the seal of old paint was broken. Then the window tilted out to let in cold, slatey air. Ralph put his narrow head on one side and listened to the hiss of night noises as if the unheard sounds always present in the room had been released.

'Will he be there yet?' Aunt Irene asked.

He shook his head. 'It's a long way, you see!'

He checked his watch and paced the room. An hour. The women waited in their squeaking chairs, careful that their glances would not intercept, smoking their last allowed cigarettes. He turned on the radio. Hilversum. Tashkent. The World Service. Nothing new on the news. He had turned out all but the mythical light of the fish tanks. Both bars of the electric fire glowed in brown shadow. He tugged at the window cord but the ratchet would not engage another tooth. The nerves of his crippled leg burned like fireflies. The telescope stood on its swivel stand under the skylight, tracking slowly the drift of the stars, the mechanism of its drive ticking. The mirrors were exactly aligned, the smaller at 45 degrees to the plane of the larger.

'Leonard would be in his element!' my aunt said.

'Our Leonard,' said my mother.

Ralph saw a line of light at the edge of the window. 'Whoever's he is,' he said impatiently.

'They say the moon will move from its orbit,' my aunt said. 'To make floods and earthquakes.'

My mother made a rattle in her throat. 'They're against progress. They want the high to remain and the rest to stay below. Science, you see, will move mountains.'

Ralph stood at the telescope, swearing as it shook under his hand. He put his eye to the lens and turned the screw which focused the eyepiece. Tattered light was blowing through space. A quarter of a million miles. He guided the body until the rays were caught by its open end.

'There's something now!'

The women moved in their wicker chairs, their glances never meeting. He focused on the sun-reflecting arc.

The sky looked very dark and the Earth was bluish. The sunlit side was visible and one could easily make out the shores of continents, islands and great rivers, large areas of water and the folds of the land. Over Russia I could see the big squares of collective-farm fields and it was possible to distinguish what was ploughed land and what was meadow. During the flight I saw for the first time, with my own eyes, the spherical shape of the Earth.